AXE

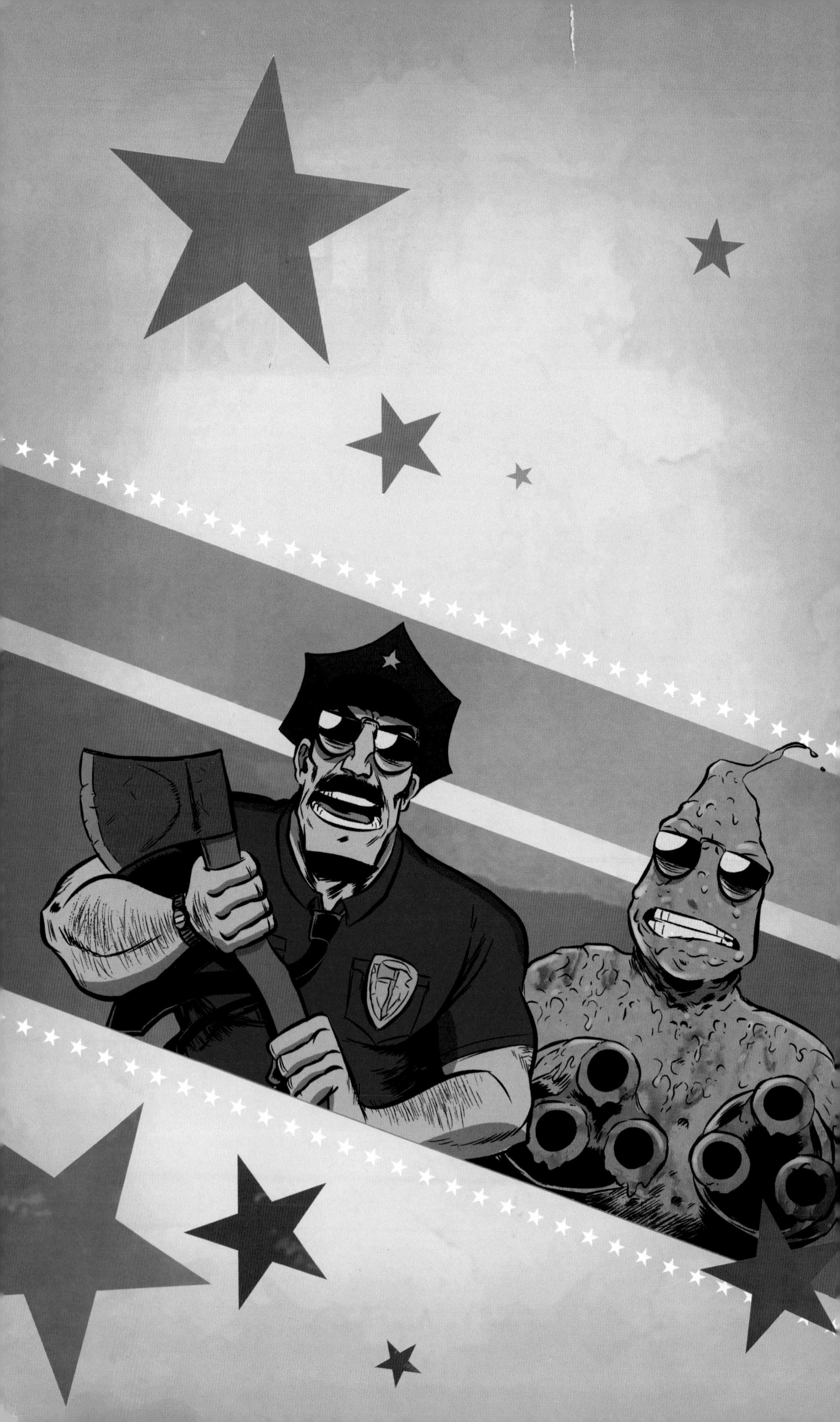

AXE COP
PRESIDENT OF THE WORLD

WRITTEN BY ★ **MALACHAI NICOLLE** (AGE 8)
DRAWN BY ★ **ETHAN NICOLLE** (AGE 32)
COLORED BY ★ **DIRK ERIK SCHULZ** (AGE 29)
COVER BY ★ **LEE MOYER**

INTRODUCTION BY ★ **ZACK CARLSON**

DARK HORSE BOOKS

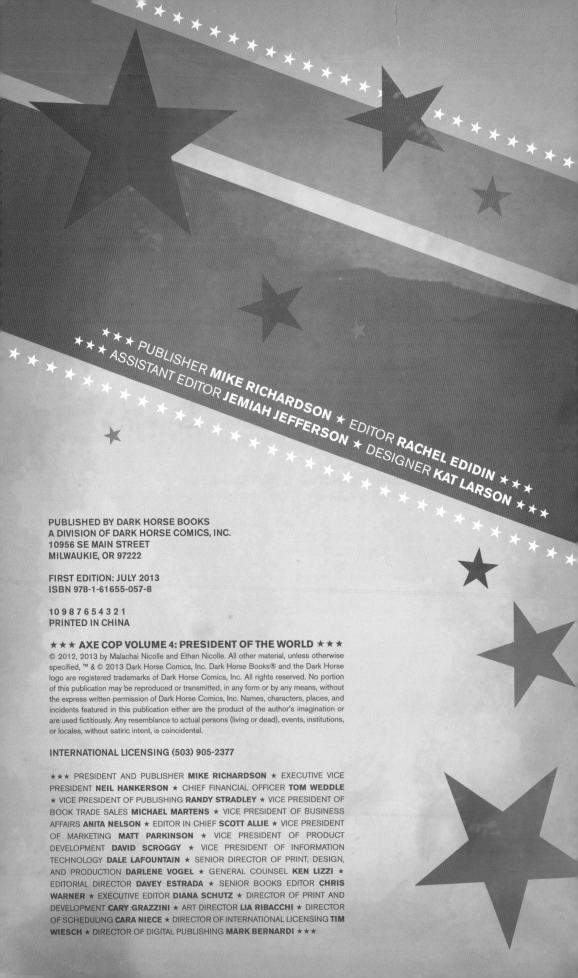

★★★ PUBLISHER **MIKE RICHARDSON** ★ EDITOR **RACHEL EDIDIN** ★★★
★★★ ASSISTANT EDITOR **JEMIAH JEFFERSON** ★ DESIGNER **KAT LARSON** ★★★

PUBLISHED BY DARK HORSE BOOKS
A DIVISION OF DARK HORSE COMICS, INC.
10956 SE MAIN STREET
MILWAUKIE, OR 97222

FIRST EDITION: JULY 2013
ISBN 978-1-61655-057-8

10 9 8 7 6 5 4 3 2 1
PRINTED IN CHINA

★★★ **AXE COP VOLUME 4: PRESIDENT OF THE WORLD** ★★★

INTERNATIONAL LICENSING (503) 905-2377

★★★ PRESIDENT AND PUBLISHER **MIKE RICHARDSON** ★ EXECUTIVE VICE PRESIDENT **NEIL HANKERSON** ★ CHIEF FINANCIAL OFFICER **TOM WEDDLE** ★ VICE PRESIDENT OF PUBLISHING **RANDY STRADLEY** ★ VICE PRESIDENT OF BOOK TRADE SALES **MICHAEL MARTENS** ★ VICE PRESIDENT OF BUSINESS AFFAIRS **ANITA NELSON** ★ EDITOR IN CHIEF **SCOTT ALLIE** ★ VICE PRESIDENT OF MARKETING **MATT PARKINSON** ★ VICE PRESIDENT OF PRODUCT DEVELOPMENT **DAVID SCROGGY** ★ VICE PRESIDENT OF INFORMATION TECHNOLOGY **DALE LAFOUNTAIN** ★ SENIOR DIRECTOR OF PRINT, DESIGN, AND PRODUCTION **DARLENE VOGEL** ★ GENERAL COUNSEL **KEN LIZZI** ★ EDITORIAL DIRECTOR **DAVEY ESTRADA** ★ SENIOR BOOKS EDITOR **CHRIS WARNER** ★ EXECUTIVE EDITOR **DIANA SCHUTZ** ★ DIRECTOR OF PRINT AND DEVELOPMENT **CARY GRAZZINI** ★ ART DIRECTOR **LIA RIBACCHI** ★ DIRECTOR OF SCHEDULING **CARA NIECE** ★ DIRECTOR OF INTERNATIONAL LICENSING **TIM WIESCH** ★ DIRECTOR OF DIGITAL PUBLISHING **MARK BERNARDI** ★★★

INTRODUCTION

Adulthood is the enemy.

We grownups are locked in an agonizing hell of auto repair, backaches, and divorces. Worse yet, when the overpowering limpness of reality becomes too much, we senselessly clamor for only the most mundane distractions. For many postadolescents, today's high point will be watching a kitten video on their laptop. We blew it.

Somewhere along the line, cell phones and electronic cigarettes took the place of slingshots and action figures. We voluntarily traded in fantasy for tragedy, and allowed our imaginations to shrink to the size of a corn nut. It's a sad truth that we willfully ignore on our slow shuffle down the escalator to the afterlife.

But as bad as things are—and they really are—we still have *heroes*. Blinding beacons of honor and power that rise above our species' failures and remind us that there's more to this no-good existence than pocket-sized gizmos and expensive wines. Pure-hearted crusaders like Ralph Wrinkles, Vampire Wolfer (RIP) and Junior Cobbb, the giant space gorilla with robotic gun fists. And, of course, Axe Cop.

Leading these soldiers in the war against maturity are the Nicolle brothers, both of whom have managed to dodge the adult world in different ways.

Fearless commander Malachai is a tireless tactical genius, constantly devising methods to rescue the human race from lethal boredom. His deceptively wee skull contains every item in the universe: a bursting storehouse of weaponry, aliens, candy bars, talking reptiles, and paranormal supervillains.

His intrepid co-honcho Ethan is older, but has somehow remained equally skilled in the deadly art of entertainment. Ethan translates Malachai's boundless ideas into images that can be comprehended by intellectually limited creatures (i.e., us). Countless impossibilities flow freely from his pen. Chee-rexes, uni-babies, and mermaids with mean faces are just the shrapnel of his explosive talents.

These two battle-hardened men and their myriad creations have the thankless duty of elevating our world above its miseries. Manufacturing pure, unfiltered fun is a difficult job, and it takes a third grader and his thirty-two-year-old brother to do it.

All they ask in return is that we throw down the shackles of sophistication and take up the Crayola-scrawled banner of childishness. It's easier than you might think, and the only way you're going to enjoy the final 80 percent of your lifetime on this crummy, fallen planet.

So take a breath, grab an axe, crack open your joyless brain, and let the sea ghosts and doody soldiers slide in. And the next time someone tells you to "grow up" . . .

CHOP HIS HEAD OFF.

Zack Carlson
February 2013

Zack Carlson has been involved with the production of films including Best Worst Movie, The American Scream, Destroy All Movies, *and* Kid-Thing, *and is the current programmer at the Alamo Drafthouse Cinema.*

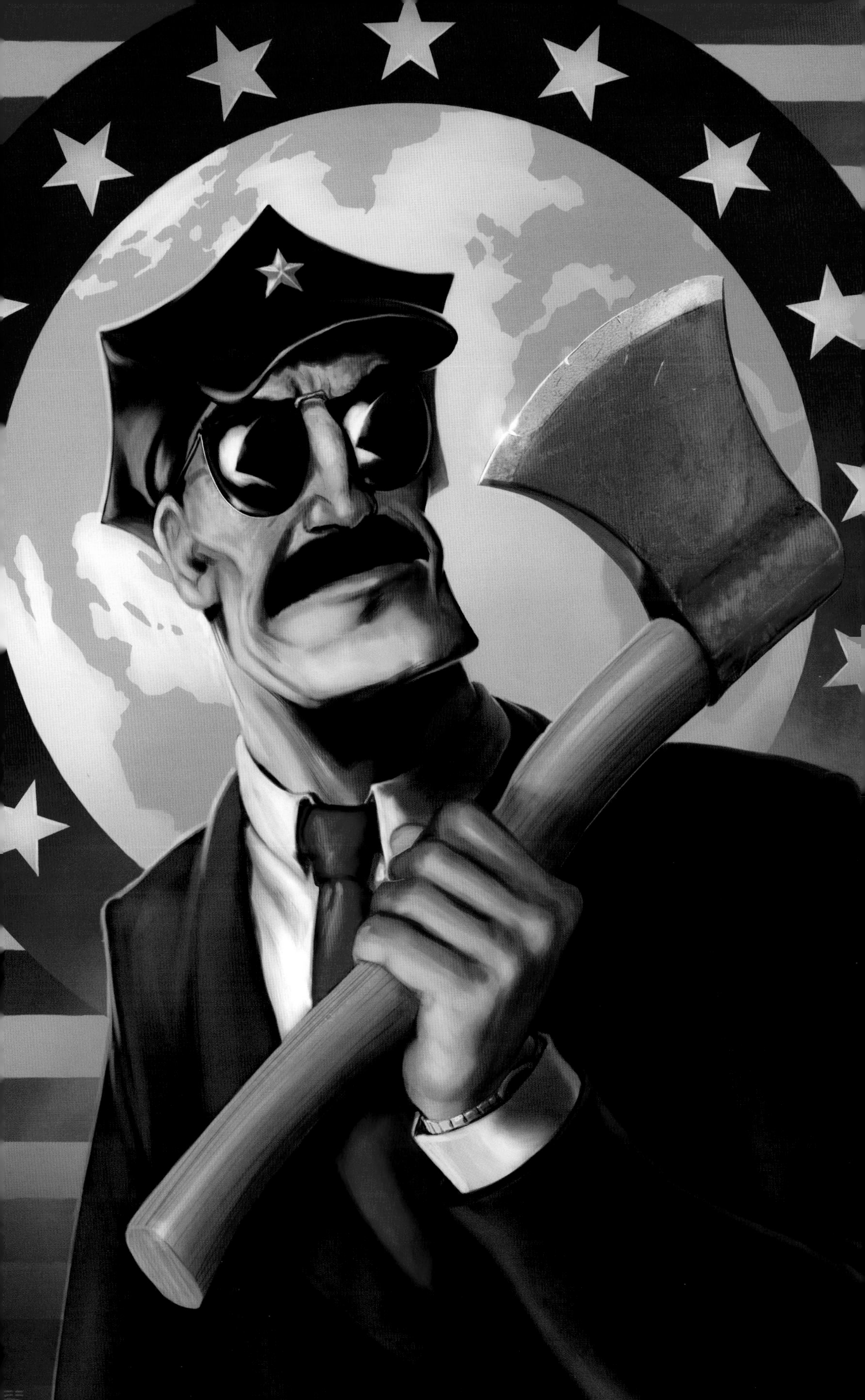

PENCILED BY **ETHAN NICOLLE** ★ PAINTED BY **LEE MOYER**

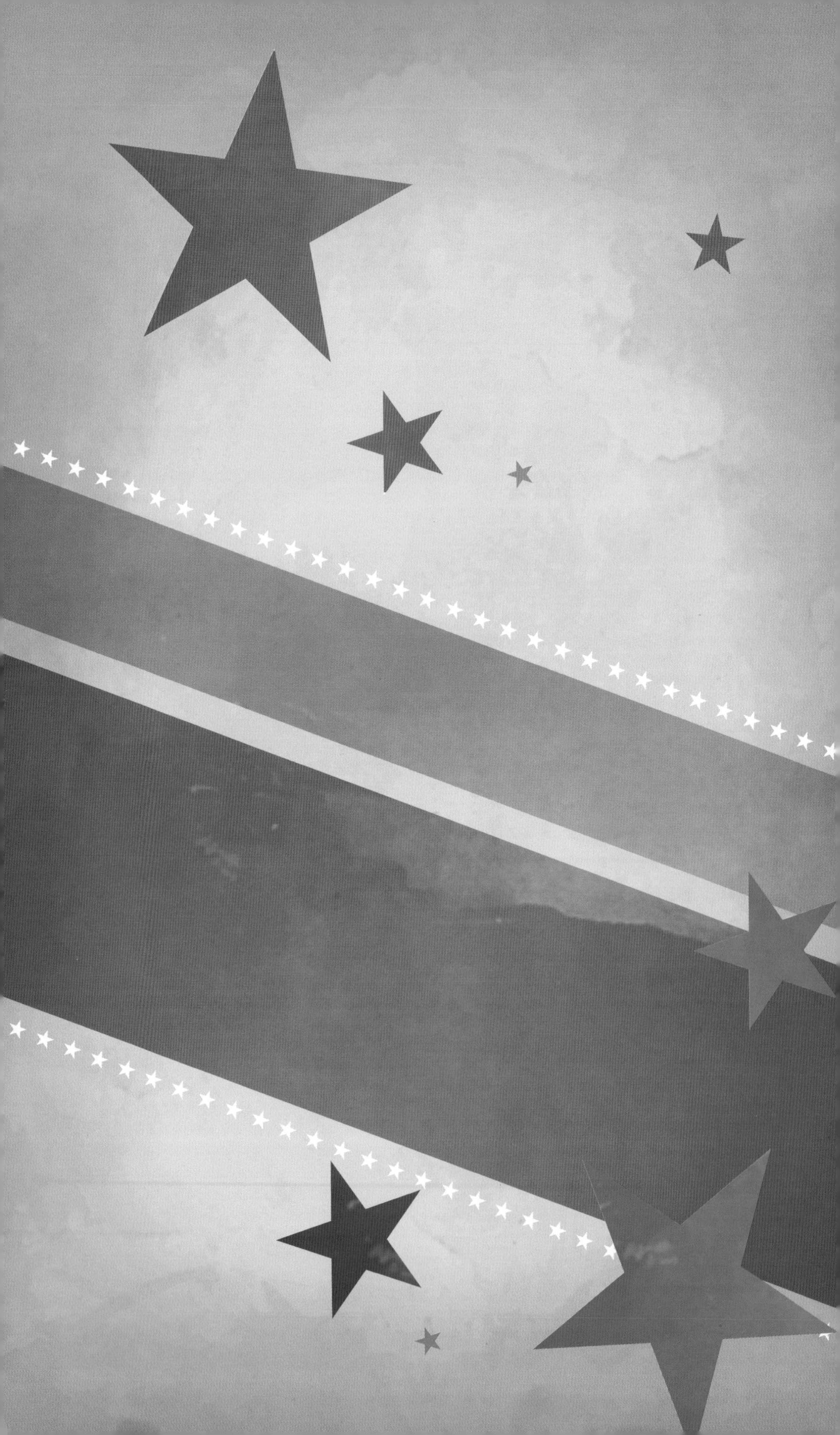

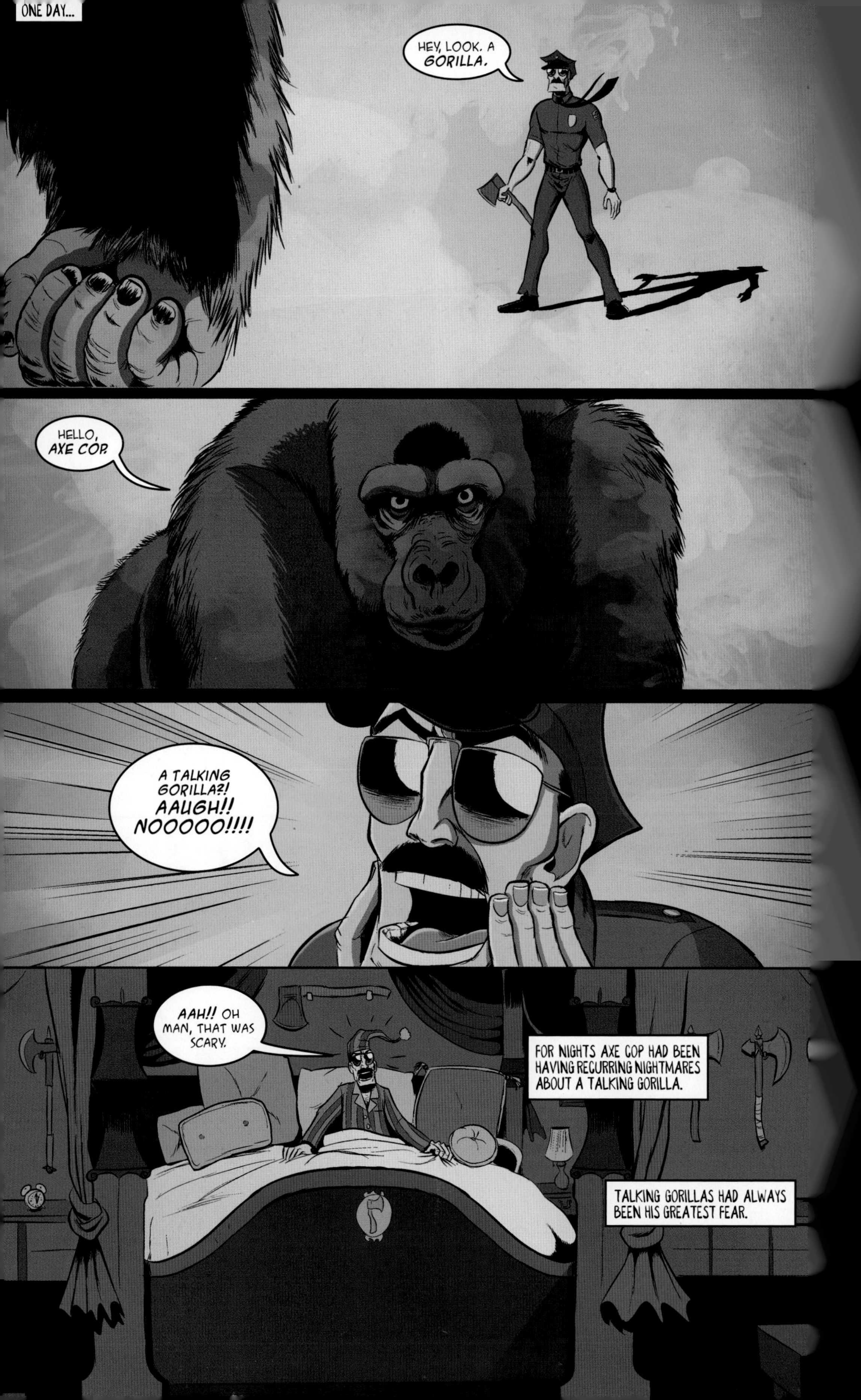
ONE DAY...
HEY, LOOK. A GORILLA.
HELLO, AXE COP.
A TALKING GORILLA?! AAUGH!! NOOOOO!!!!
AAH!! OH MAN, THAT WAS SCARY.
FOR NIGHTS AXE COP HAD BEEN HAVING RECURRING NIGHTMARES ABOUT A TALKING GORILLA.
TALKING GORILLAS HAD ALWAYS BEEN HIS GREATEST FEAR.

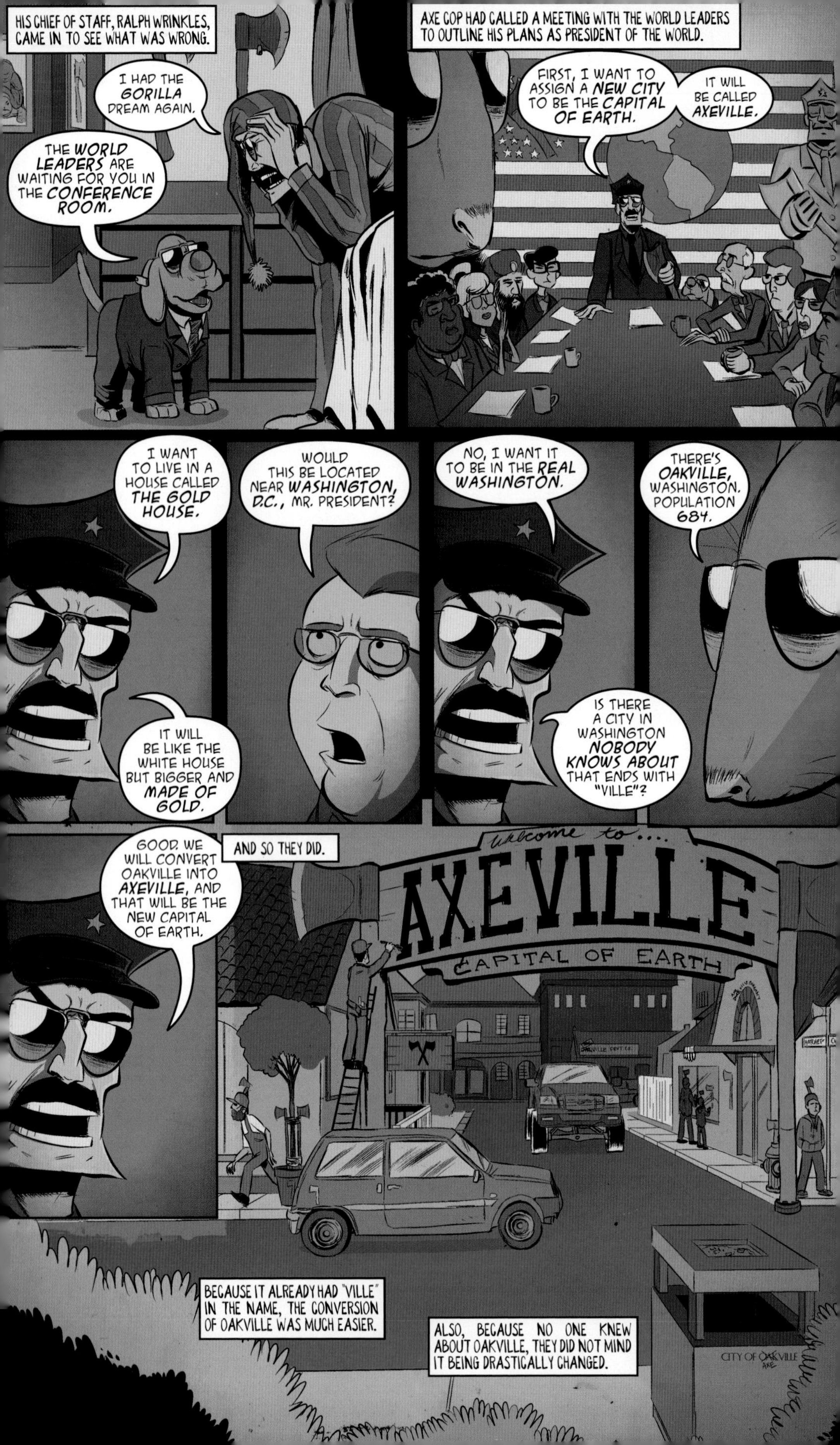
HIS CHIEF OF STAFF, RALPH WRINKLES, CAME IN TO SEE WHAT WAS WRONG.
I HAD THE GORILLA DREAM AGAIN.
THE WORLD LEADERS ARE WAITING FOR YOU IN THE CONFERENCE ROOM.
AXE COP HAD CALLED A MEETING WITH THE WORLD LEADERS TO OUTLINE HIS PLANS AS PRESIDENT OF THE WORLD.
FIRST, I WANT TO ASSIGN A NEW CITY TO BE THE CAPITAL OF EARTH.
IT WILL BE CALLED AXEVILLE.
I WANT TO LIVE IN A HOUSE CALLED THE GOLD HOUSE.
IT WILL BE LIKE THE WHITE HOUSE BUT BIGGER AND MADE OF GOLD.
WOULD THIS BE LOCATED NEAR WASHINGTON, D.C., MR. PRESIDENT?
NO, I WANT IT TO BE IN THE REAL WASHINGTON.
IS THERE A CITY IN WASHINGTON NOBODY KNOWS ABOUT THAT ENDS WITH "VILLE"?
THERE'S OAKVILLE, WASHINGTON, POPULATION 684.
GOOD. WE WILL CONVERT OAKVILLE INTO AXEVILLE, AND THAT WILL BE THE NEW CAPITAL OF EARTH.
AND SO THEY DID.
Welcome to....
AXEVILLE
CAPITAL OF EARTH
BECAUSE IT ALREADY HAD "VILLE" IN THE NAME, THE CONVERSION OF OAKVILLE WAS MUCH EASIER.
ALSO, BECAUSE NO ONE KNEW ABOUT OAKVILLE, THEY DID NOT MIND IT BEING DRASTICALLY CHANGED.
CITY OF OAKVILLE AXE

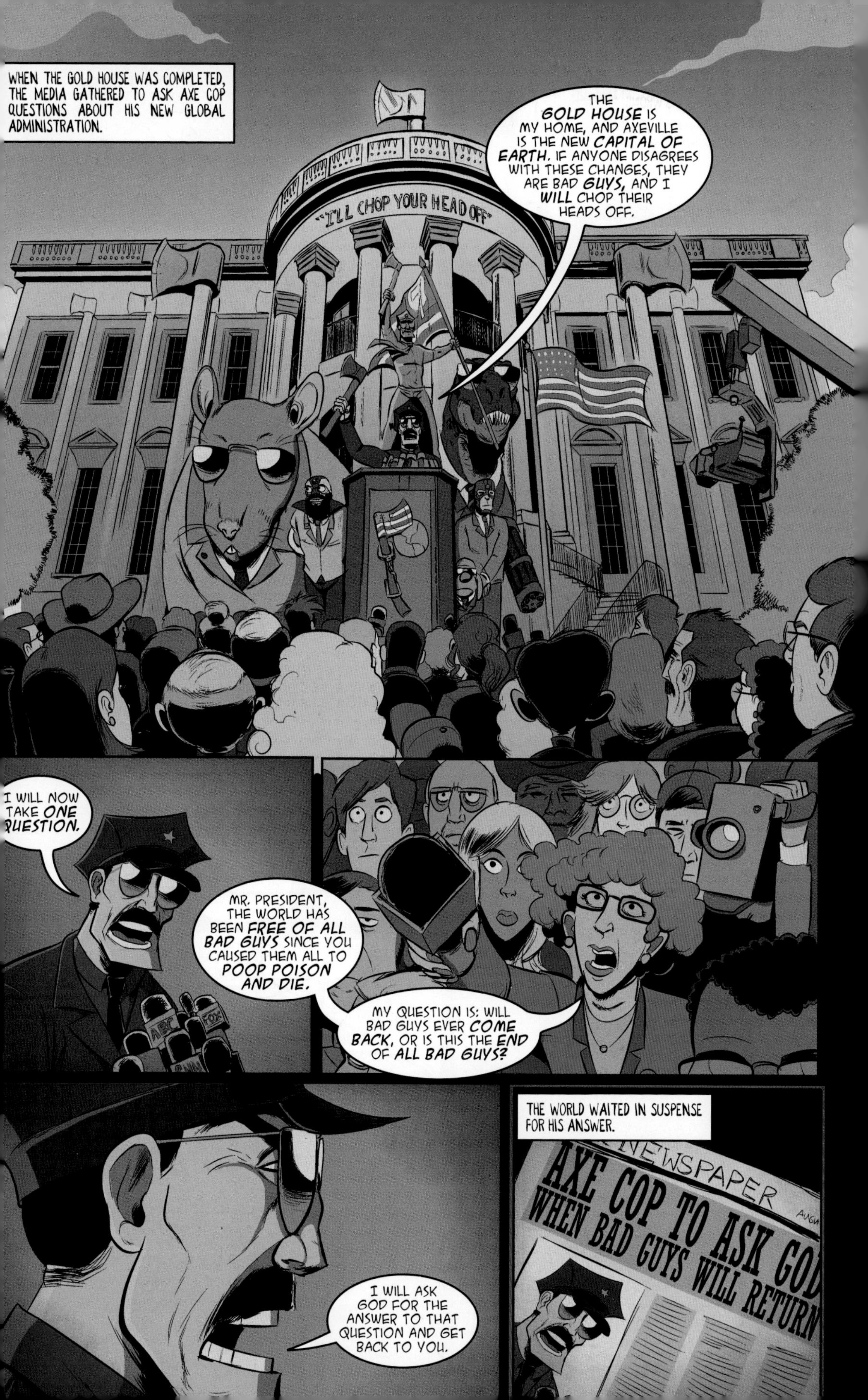
WHEN THE GOLD HOUSE WAS COMPLETED, THE MEDIA GATHERED TO ASK AXE COP QUESTIONS ABOUT HIS NEW GLOBAL ADMINISTRATION.
THE GOLD HOUSE IS MY HOME, AND AXEVILLE IS THE NEW CAPITAL OF EARTH. IF ANYONE DISAGREES WITH THESE CHANGES, THEY ARE BAD GUYS, AND I WILL CHOP THEIR HEADS OFF.
"I'LL CHOP YOUR HEAD OFF"
I WILL NOW TAKE ONE QUESTION.
ABC
FOX
CNN
MR. PRESIDENT, THE WORLD HAS BEEN FREE OF ALL BAD GUYS SINCE YOU CAUSED THEM ALL TO POOP POISON AND DIE.
MY QUESTION IS: WILL BAD GUYS EVER COME BACK, OR IS THIS THE END OF ALL BAD GUYS?
I WILL ASK GOD FOR THE ANSWER TO THAT QUESTION AND GET BACK TO YOU.
THE WORLD WAITED IN SUSPENSE FOR HIS ANSWER.
NEWSPAPER
AXE COP TO ASK GOD
WHEN BAD GUYS WILL RETURN

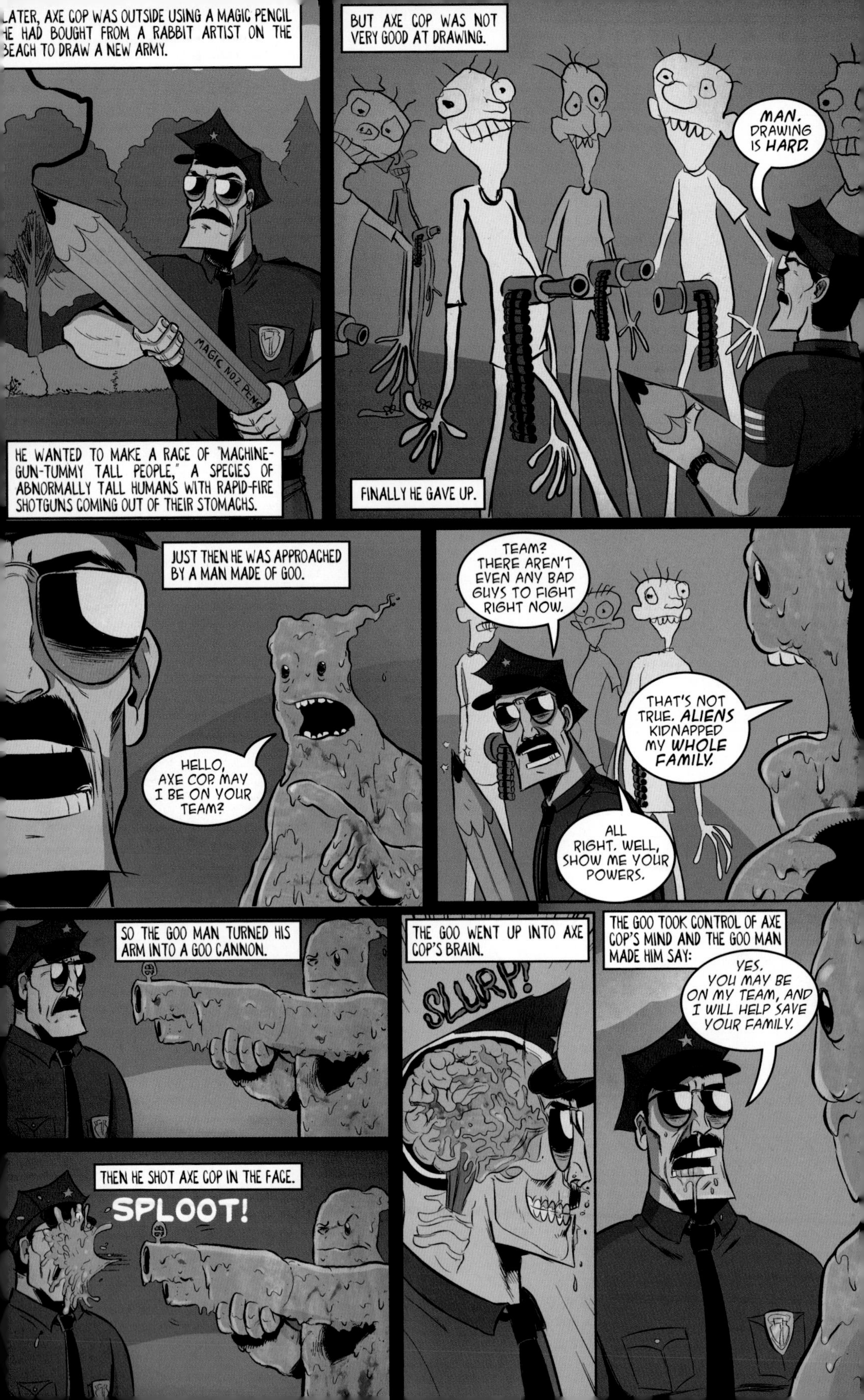

LATER, AXE COP WAS OUTSIDE USING A MAGIC PENCIL HE HAD BOUGHT FROM A RABBIT ARTIST ON THE BEACH TO DRAW A NEW ARMY.
MAGIC NO.2 PENC
HE WANTED TO MAKE A RACE OF "MACHINE-GUN-TUMMY TALL PEOPLE," A SPECIES OF ABNORMALLY TALL HUMANS WITH RAPID-FIRE SHOTGUNS COMING OUT OF THEIR STOMACHS.
BUT AXE COP WAS NOT VERY GOOD AT DRAWING.
MAN. DRAWING IS HARD.
FINALLY HE GAVE UP.
JUST THEN HE WAS APPROACHED BY A MAN MADE OF GOO.
HELLO, AXE COP. MAY I BE ON YOUR TEAM?
TEAM? THERE AREN'T EVEN ANY BAD GUYS TO FIGHT RIGHT NOW.
THAT'S NOT TRUE. ALIENS KIDNAPPED MY WHOLE FAMILY.
ALL RIGHT. WELL, SHOW ME YOUR POWERS.
SO THE GOO MAN TURNED HIS ARM INTO A GOO CANNON.
THEN HE SHOT AXE COP IN THE FACE.
SPLOOT!
THE GOO WENT UP INTO AXE COP'S BRAIN.
SLURP!
THE GOO TOOK CONTROL OF AXE COP'S MIND AND THE GOO MAN MADE HIM SAY:
YES. YOU MAY BE ON MY TEAM, AND I WILL HELP SAVE YOUR FAMILY.

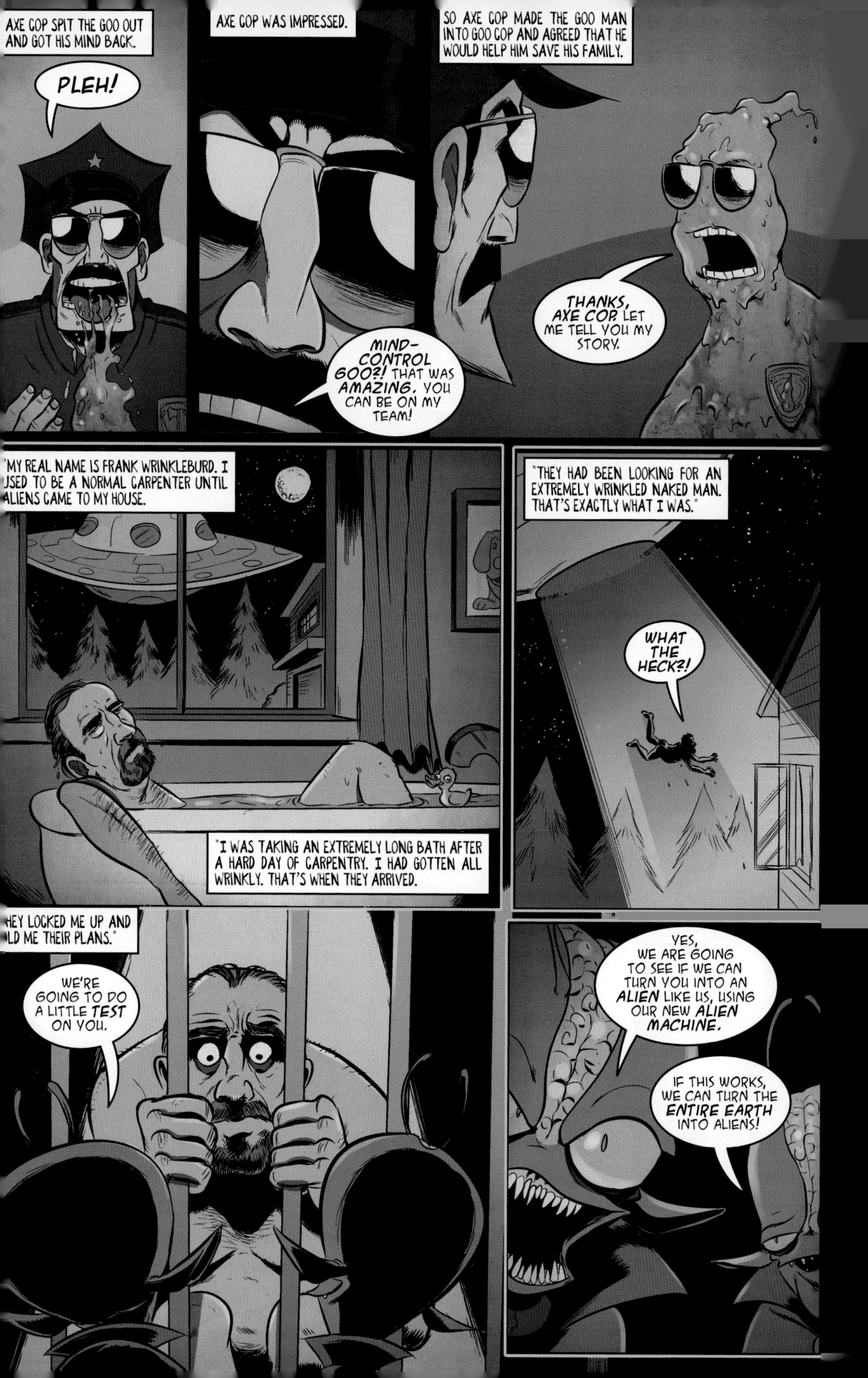
AXE COP SPIT THE GOO OUT AND GOT HIS MIND BACK.
PLEH!
AXE COP WAS IMPRESSED.
MIND-CONTROL GOO?! THAT WAS AMAZING. YOU CAN BE ON MY TEAM!
SO AXE COP MADE THE GOO MAN INTO GOO COP AND AGREED THAT HE WOULD HELP HIM SAVE HIS FAMILY.
THANKS, AXE COP. LET ME TELL YOU MY STORY.
"MY REAL NAME IS FRANK WRINKLEBURD. I USED TO BE A NORMAL CARPENTER UNTIL ALIENS CAME TO MY HOUSE.
"I WAS TAKING AN EXTREMELY LONG BATH AFTER A HARD DAY OF CARPENTRY. I HAD GOTTEN ALL WRINKLY. THAT'S WHEN THEY ARRIVED.
"THEY HAD BEEN LOOKING FOR AN EXTREMELY WRINKLED NAKED MAN. THAT'S EXACTLY WHAT I WAS."
WHAT THE HECK?!
HEY LOCKED ME UP AND LD ME THEIR PLANS."
WE'RE GOING TO DO A LITTLE TEST ON YOU.
YES, WE ARE GOING TO SEE IF WE CAN TURN YOU INTO AN ALIEN LIKE US, USING OUR NEW ALIEN MACHINE.
IF THIS WORKS, WE CAN TURN THE ENTIRE EARTH INTO ALIENS!

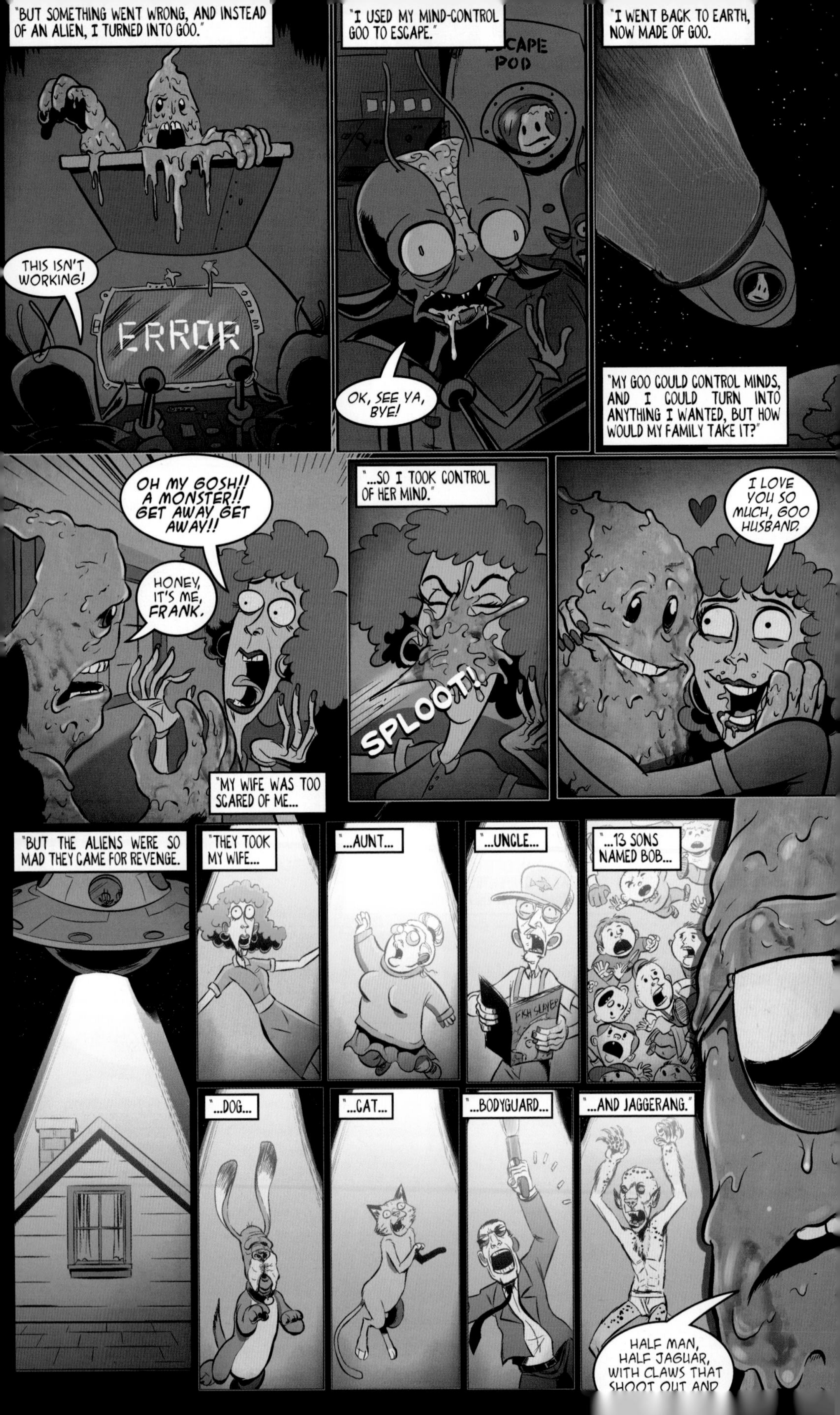
"BUT SOMETHING WENT WRONG, AND INSTEAD OF AN ALIEN, I TURNED INTO GOO."
THIS ISN'T WORKING!
ERROR
"I USED MY MIND-CONTROL GOO TO ESCAPE."
ESCAPE POD
OK, SEE YA, BYE!
"I WENT BACK TO EARTH, NOW MADE OF GOO.
"MY GOO COULD CONTROL MINDS, AND I COULD TURN INTO ANYTHING I WANTED, BUT HOW WOULD MY FAMILY TAKE IT?"
OH MY GOSH!! A MONSTER!! GET AWAY GET AWAY!!
HONEY, IT'S ME, FRANK.
"MY WIFE WAS TOO SCARED OF ME...
"...SO I TOOK CONTROL OF HER MIND."
SPLOOT!
I LOVE YOU SO MUCH, GOO HUSBAND.
"BUT THE ALIENS WERE SO MAD THEY CAME FOR REVENGE.
"THEY TOOK MY WIFE...
"...AUNT...
"...UNCLE...
FISH SLAYER
"...13 SONS NAMED BOB...
"...DOG...
"...CAT...
"...BODYGUARD...
"...AND JAGGERANG."
HALF MAN, HALF JAGUAR, WITH CLAWS THAT SHOOT OUT AND

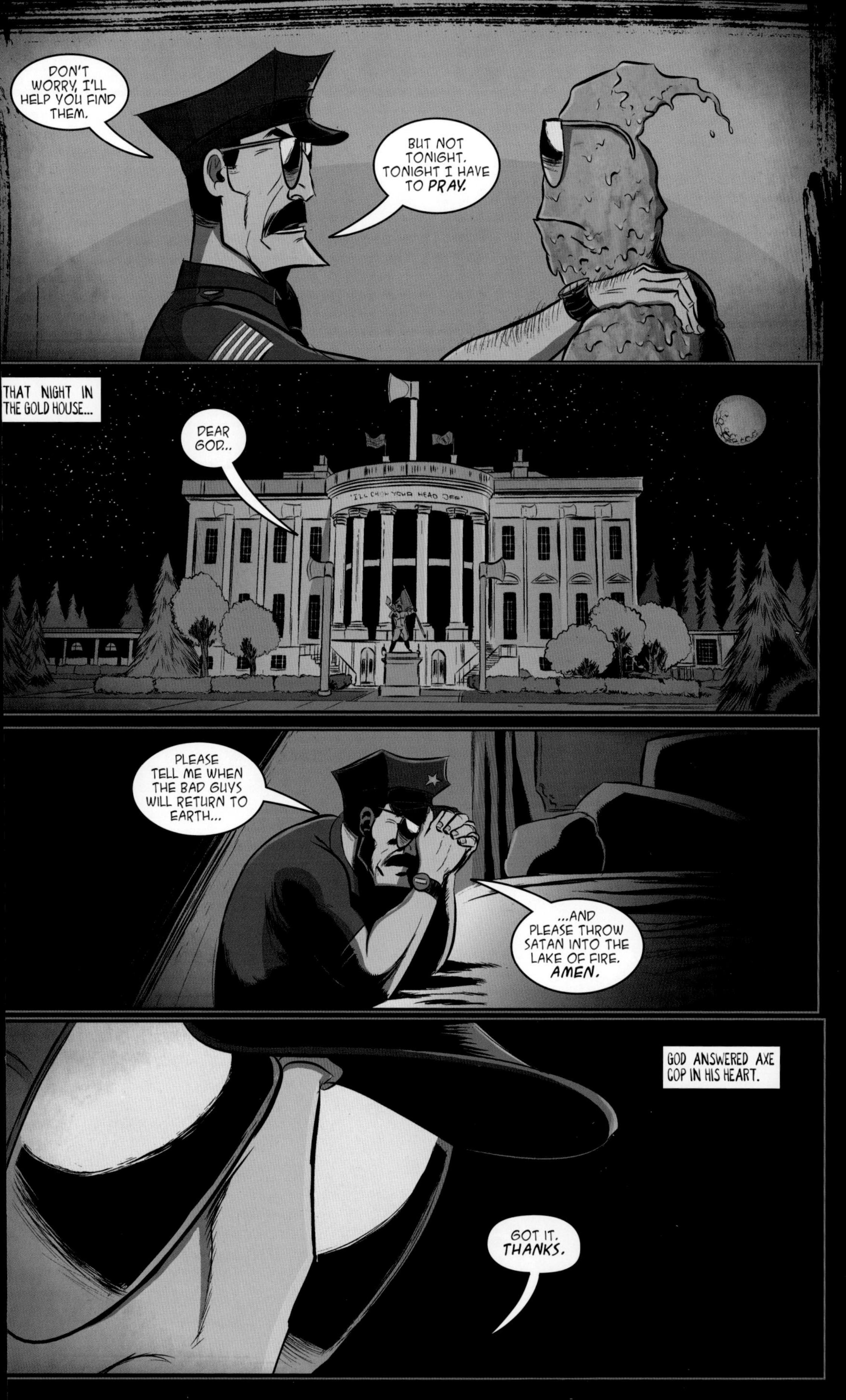
DON'T WORRY, I'LL HELP YOU FIND THEM.
BUT NOT TONIGHT. TONIGHT I HAVE TO PRAY.
THAT NIGHT IN THE GOLD HOUSE...
DEAR GOD...
"I'LL CHOP YOUR HEAD OFF"
PLEASE TELL ME WHEN THE BAD GUYS WILL RETURN TO EARTH...
...AND PLEASE THROW SATAN INTO THE LAKE OF FIRE. AMEN.
GOD ANSWERED AXE COP IN HIS HEART.
GOT IT. THANKS.

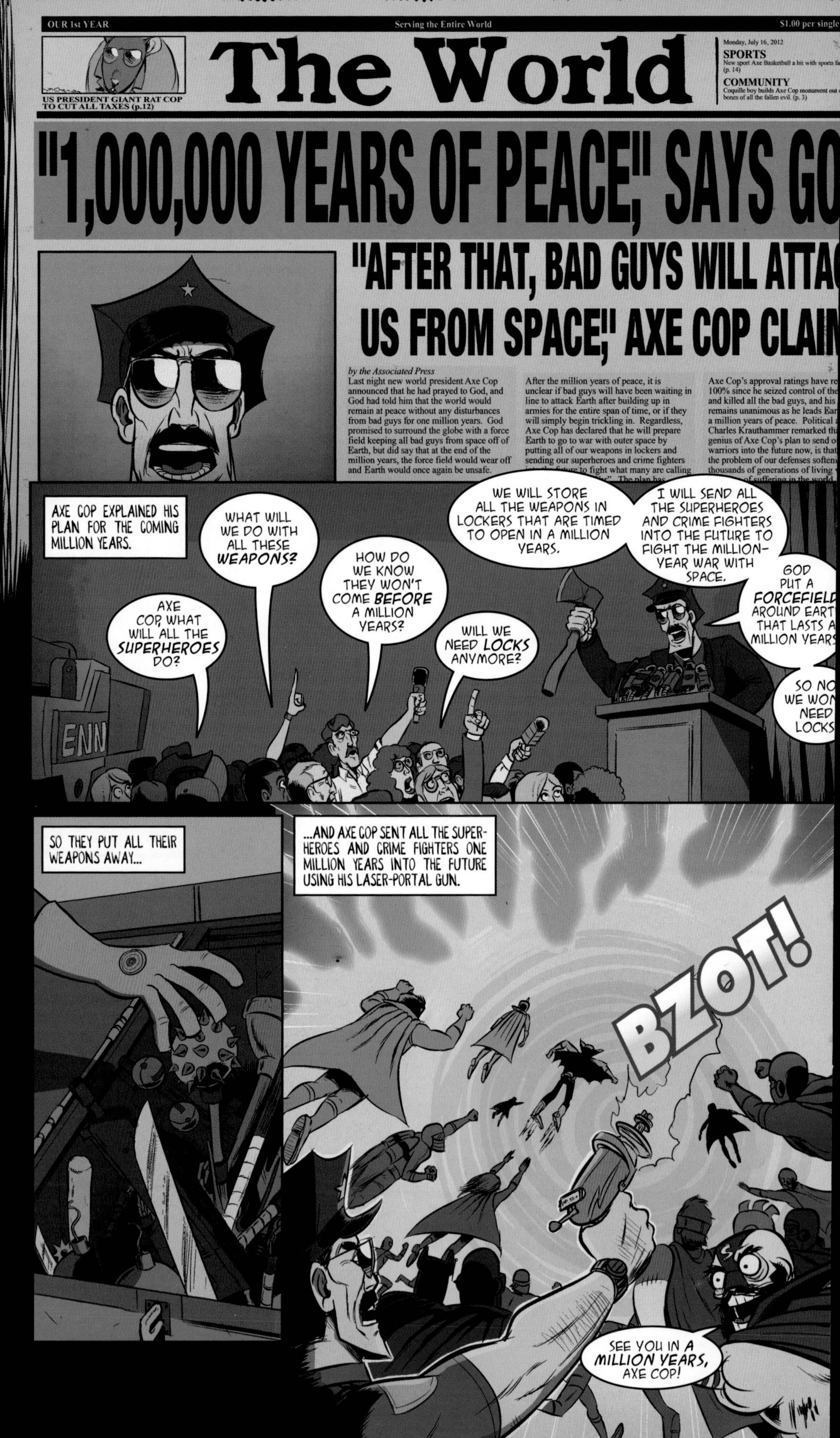

OUR 1st YEAR
Serving the Entire World
$1.00 per single
The World
US PRESIDENT GIANT RAT COP TO CUT ALL TAXES (p.12)
Monday, July 16, 2012
SPORTS
New sport Axe Basketball a hit with sports fa
(p. 14)
COMMUNITY
Coquille boy builds Axe Cop monument out
bones of all the fallen evil. (p. 3)
"1,000,000 YEARS OF PEACE," SAYS GO
"AFTER THAT, BAD GUYS WILL ATTA
US FROM SPACE," AXE COP CLAI
by the Associated Press
Last night new world president Axe Cop announced that he had prayed to God, and God had told him that the world would remain at peace without any disturbances from bad guys for one million years. God promised to surround the globe with a force field keeping all bad guys from space off of Earth, but did say that at the end of the million years, the force field would wear off and Earth would once again be unsafe.
After the million years of peace, it is unclear if bad guys will have been waiting in line to attack Earth after building up in armies for the entire span of time, or if they will simply begin trickling in. Regardless, Axe Cop has declared that he will prepare Earth to go to war with outer space by putting all of our weapons in lockers and sending our superheroes and crime fighters
Axe Cop's approval ratings have re
100% since he seized control of the
and killed all the bad guys, and his
remains unanimous as he leads Ear
a million years of peace. Political
Charles Krauthammer remarked th
genius of Axe Cop's plan to send o
warriors into the future now, is tha
the problem of our defenses soften
thousands of generations of living
AXE COP EXPLAINED HIS PLAN FOR THE COMING MILLION YEARS.
AXE COP, WHAT WILL ALL THE SUPERHEROES DO?
WHAT WILL WE DO WITH ALL THESE WEAPONS?
HOW DO WE KNOW THEY WON'T COME BEFORE A MILLION YEARS?
WILL WE NEED LOCKS ANYMORE?
WE WILL STORE ALL THE WEAPONS IN LOCKERS THAT ARE TIMED TO OPEN IN A MILLION YEARS.
I WILL SEND ALL THE SUPERHEROES AND CRIME FIGHTERS INTO THE FUTURE TO FIGHT THE MILLION-YEAR WAR WITH SPACE.
GOD PUT A FORCEFIELD AROUND EART THAT LASTS A MILLION YEARS
SO NO WE WON NEED LOCKS
ENN
SO THEY PUT ALL THEIR WEAPONS AWAY...
...AND AXE COP SENT ALL THE SUPERHEROES AND CRIME FIGHTERS ONE MILLION YEARS INTO THE FUTURE USING HIS LASER-PORTAL GUN.
BZOT!
SEE YOU IN A MILLION YEARS, AXE COP!

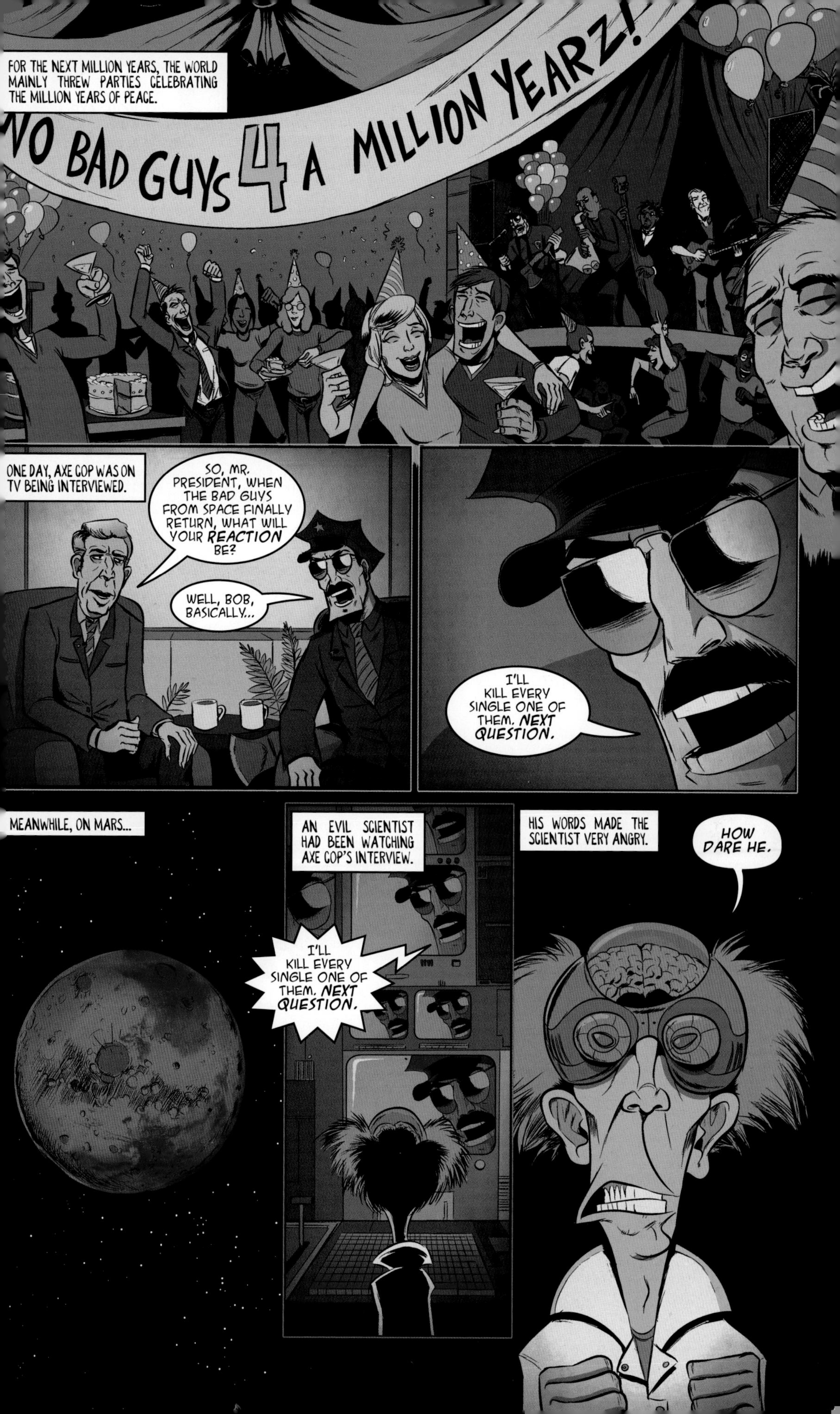
FOR THE NEXT MILLION YEARS, THE WORLD MAINLY THREW PARTIES CELEBRATING THE MILLION YEARS OF PEACE.
NO BAD GUYS 4 A MILLION YEARZ!
ONE DAY, AXE COP WAS ON TV BEING INTERVIEWED.
SO, MR. PRESIDENT, WHEN THE BAD GUYS FROM SPACE FINALLY RETURN, WHAT WILL YOUR REACTION BE?
WELL, BOB, BASICALLY...
I'LL KILL EVERY SINGLE ONE OF THEM. NEXT QUESTION.
MEANWHILE, ON MARS...
AN EVIL SCIENTIST HAD BEEN WATCHING AXE COP'S INTERVIEW.
I'LL KILL EVERY SINGLE ONE OF THEM. NEXT QUESTION.
HIS WORDS MADE THE SCIENTIST VERY ANGRY.
HOW DARE HE.

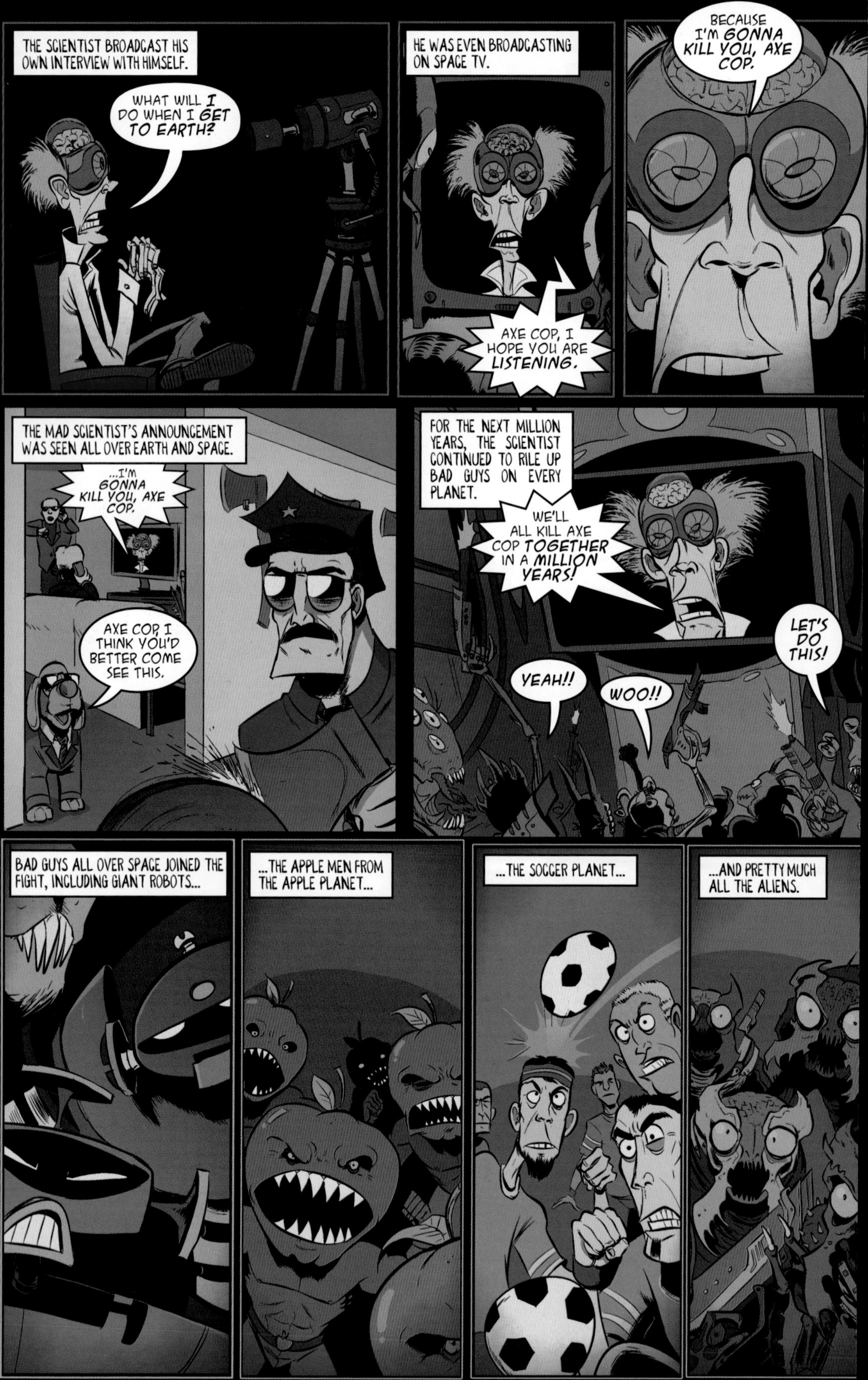
THE SCIENTIST BROADCAST HIS OWN INTERVIEW WITH HIMSELF.
WHAT WILL I DO WHEN I GET TO EARTH?
HE WAS EVEN BROADCASTING ON SPACE TV.
AXE COP, I HOPE YOU ARE LISTENING.
BECAUSE I'M GONNA KILL YOU, AXE COP.
THE MAD SCIENTIST'S ANNOUNCEMENT WAS SEEN ALL OVER EARTH AND SPACE.
...I'M GONNA KILL YOU, AXE COP.
AXE COP, I THINK YOU'D BETTER COME SEE THIS.
FOR THE NEXT MILLION YEARS, THE SCIENTIST CONTINUED TO RILE UP BAD GUYS ON EVERY PLANET.
WE'LL ALL KILL AXE COP TOGETHER IN A MILLION YEARS!
YEAH!!
WOO!!
LET'S DO THIS!
BAD GUYS ALL OVER SPACE JOINED THE FIGHT, INCLUDING GIANT ROBOTS...
...THE APPLE MEN FROM THE APPLE PLANET...
...THE SOCCER PLANET...
...AND PRETTY MUCH ALL THE ALIENS.

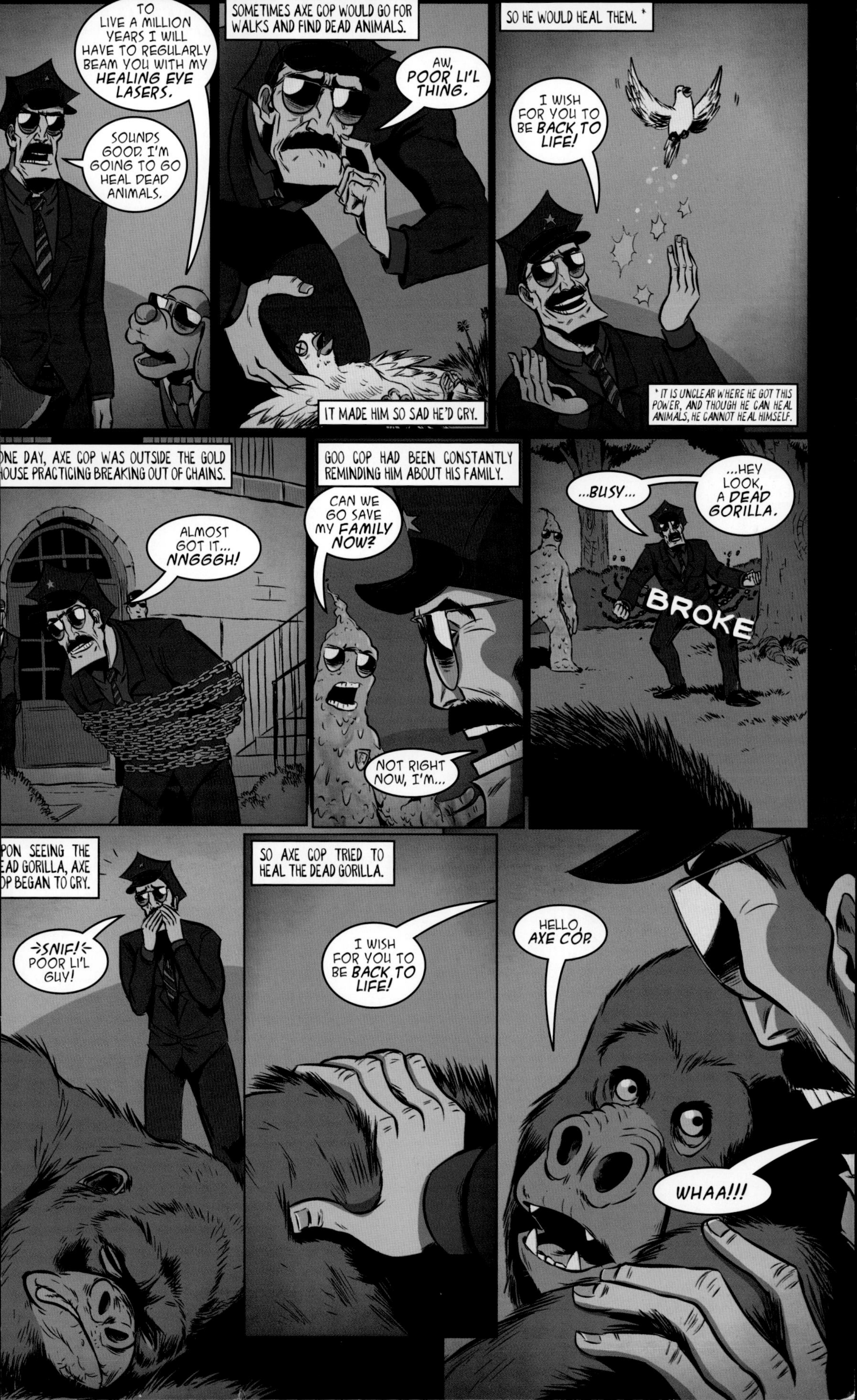
TO LIVE A MILLION YEARS I WILL HAVE TO REGULARLY BEAM YOU WITH MY HEALING EYE LASERS.
SOUNDS GOOD. I'M GOING TO GO HEAL DEAD ANIMALS.
SOMETIMES AXE COP WOULD GO FOR WALKS AND FIND DEAD ANIMALS.
AW, POOR LI'L THING.
IT MADE HIM SO SAD HE'D CRY.
SO HE WOULD HEAL THEM. *
I WISH FOR YOU TO BE BACK TO LIFE!
* IT IS UNCLEAR WHERE HE GOT THIS POWER, AND THOUGH HE CAN HEAL ANIMALS, HE CANNOT HEAL HIMSELF.
ONE DAY, AXE COP WAS OUTSIDE THE GOLD HOUSE PRACTICING BREAKING OUT OF CHAINS.
ALMOST GOT IT... NNGGGH!
GOO COP HAD BEEN CONSTANTLY REMINDING HIM ABOUT HIS FAMILY.
CAN WE GO SAVE MY FAMILY NOW?
NOT RIGHT NOW, I'M...
...BUSY...
...HEY LOOK, A DEAD GORILLA.
BROKE
PON SEEING THE EAD GORILLA, AXE OP BEGAN TO CRY.
SNIF! POOR LI'L GUY!
SO AXE COP TRIED TO HEAL THE DEAD GORILLA.
I WISH FOR YOU TO BE BACK TO LIFE!
HELLO, AXE COP.
WHAA!!!

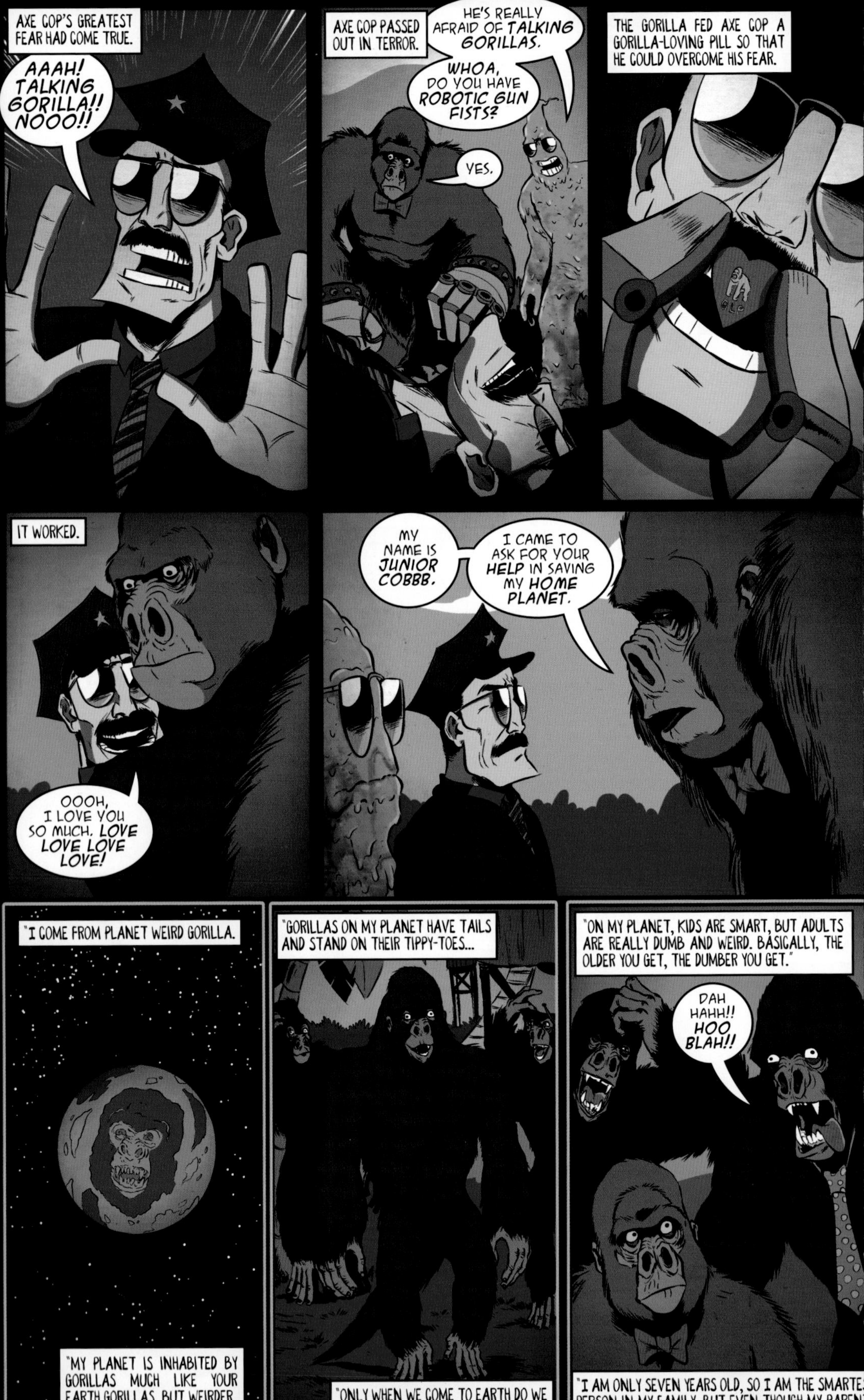
AXE COP'S GREATEST FEAR HAD COME TRUE.
AAAH! TALKING GORILLA!! NOOO!!
AXE COP PASSED OUT IN TERROR.
HE'S REALLY AFRAID OF TALKING GORILLAS.
WHOA, DO YOU HAVE ROBOTIC GUN FISTS?
YES.
THE GORILLA FED AXE COP A GORILLA-LOVING PILL SO THAT HE COULD OVERCOME HIS FEAR.
IT WORKED.
OOOH, I LOVE YOU SO MUCH. LOVE LOVE LOVE LOVE!
MY NAME IS JUNIOR COBBB.
I CAME TO ASK FOR YOUR HELP IN SAVING MY HOME PLANET.
"I COME FROM PLANET WEIRD GORILLA.
"MY PLANET IS INHABITED BY GORILLAS MUCH LIKE YOUR EARTH GORILLAS, BUT WEIRDER.
"GORILLAS ON MY PLANET HAVE TAILS AND STAND ON THEIR TIPPY-TOES...
"ONLY WHEN WE COME TO EARTH DO WE HUNCH AND WALK USING OUR FISTS.
"ON MY PLANET, KIDS ARE SMART, BUT ADULTS ARE REALLY DUMB AND WEIRD. BASICALLY, THE OLDER YOU GET, THE DUMBER YOU GET."
DAH HAHH!! HOO BLAH!!
"I AM ONLY SEVEN YEARS OLD, SO I AM THE SMARTES PERSON IN MY FAMILY. BUT EVEN THOUGH MY PARENT ARE SUPER DUMB AND WEIRD, I STILL LOVE THEM.

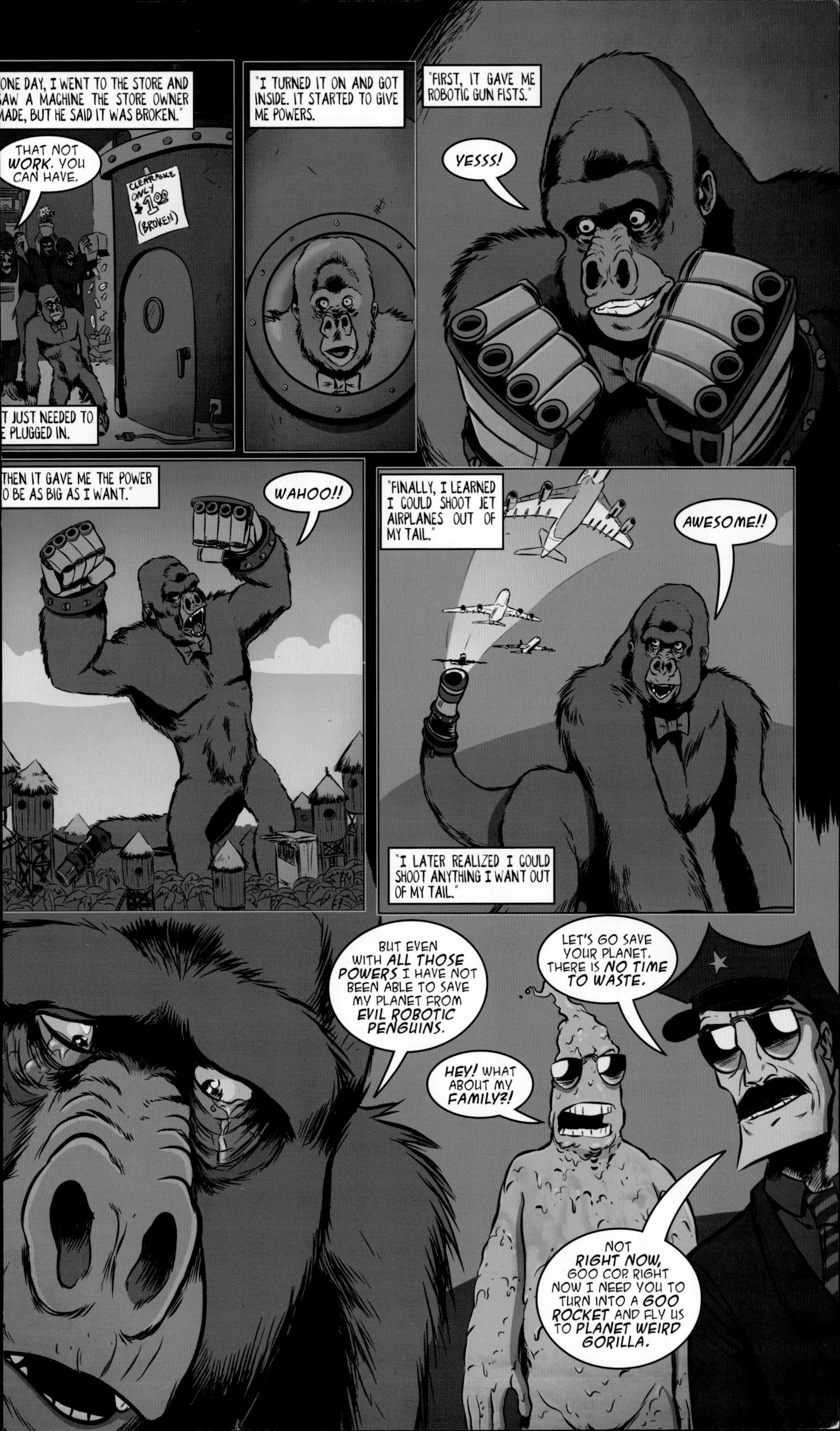
ONE DAY, I WENT TO THE STORE AND SAW A MACHINE THE STORE OWNER MADE, BUT HE SAID IT WAS BROKEN."
THAT NOT WORK. YOU CAN HAVE.
CLEARANCE ONLY $1.00 (BROKEN)
IT JUST NEEDED TO BE PLUGGED IN.
"I TURNED IT ON AND GOT INSIDE. IT STARTED TO GIVE ME POWERS.
"FIRST, IT GAVE ME ROBOTIC GUN FISTS."
YESSS!
THEN IT GAVE ME THE POWER TO BE AS BIG AS I WANT."
WAHOO!!
"FINALLY, I LEARNED I COULD SHOOT JET AIRPLANES OUT OF MY TAIL."
AWESOME!!
"I LATER REALIZED I COULD SHOOT ANYTHING I WANT OUT OF MY TAIL."
BUT EVEN WITH ALL THOSE POWERS I HAVE NOT BEEN ABLE TO SAVE MY PLANET FROM EVIL ROBOTIC PENGUINS.
LET'S GO SAVE YOUR PLANET. THERE IS NO TIME TO WASTE.
HEY! WHAT ABOUT MY FAMILY?!
NOT RIGHT NOW, GOO COP. RIGHT NOW I NEED YOU TO TURN INTO A GOO ROCKET AND FLY US TO PLANET WEIRD GORILLA.

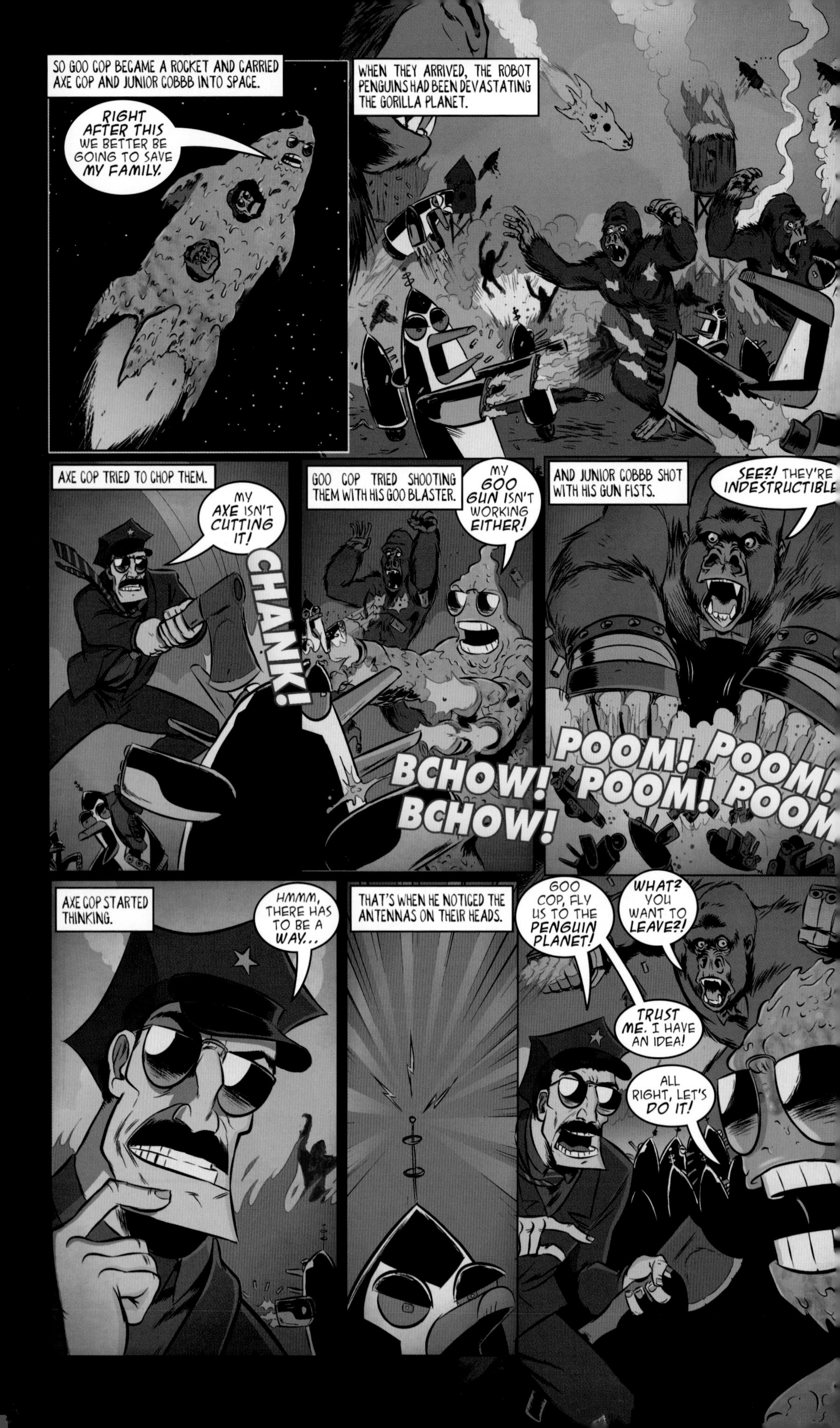

SO GOO COP BECAME A ROCKET AND CARRIED AXE COP AND JUNIOR COBBB INTO SPACE.
RIGHT AFTER THIS WE BETTER BE GOING TO SAVE MY FAMILY.
WHEN THEY ARRIVED, THE ROBOT PENGUINS HAD BEEN DEVASTATING THE GORILLA PLANET.
AXE COP TRIED TO CHOP THEM.
MY AXE ISN'T CUTTING IT!
CHANK!
GOO COP TRIED SHOOTING THEM WITH HIS GOO BLASTER.
MY GOO GUN ISN'T WORKING EITHER!
BCHOW! BCHOW!
AND JUNIOR COBBB SHOT WITH HIS GUN FISTS.
SEE?! THEY'RE INDESTRUCTIBLE
POOM! POOM! POOM! POOM
AXE COP STARTED THINKING.
HMMM, THERE HAS TO BE A WAY...
THAT'S WHEN HE NOTICED THE ANTENNAS ON THEIR HEADS.
GOO COP, FLY US TO THE PENGUIN PLANET!
WHAT? YOU WANT TO LEAVE?!
TRUST ME. I HAVE AN IDEA!
ALL RIGHT, LET'S DO IT!

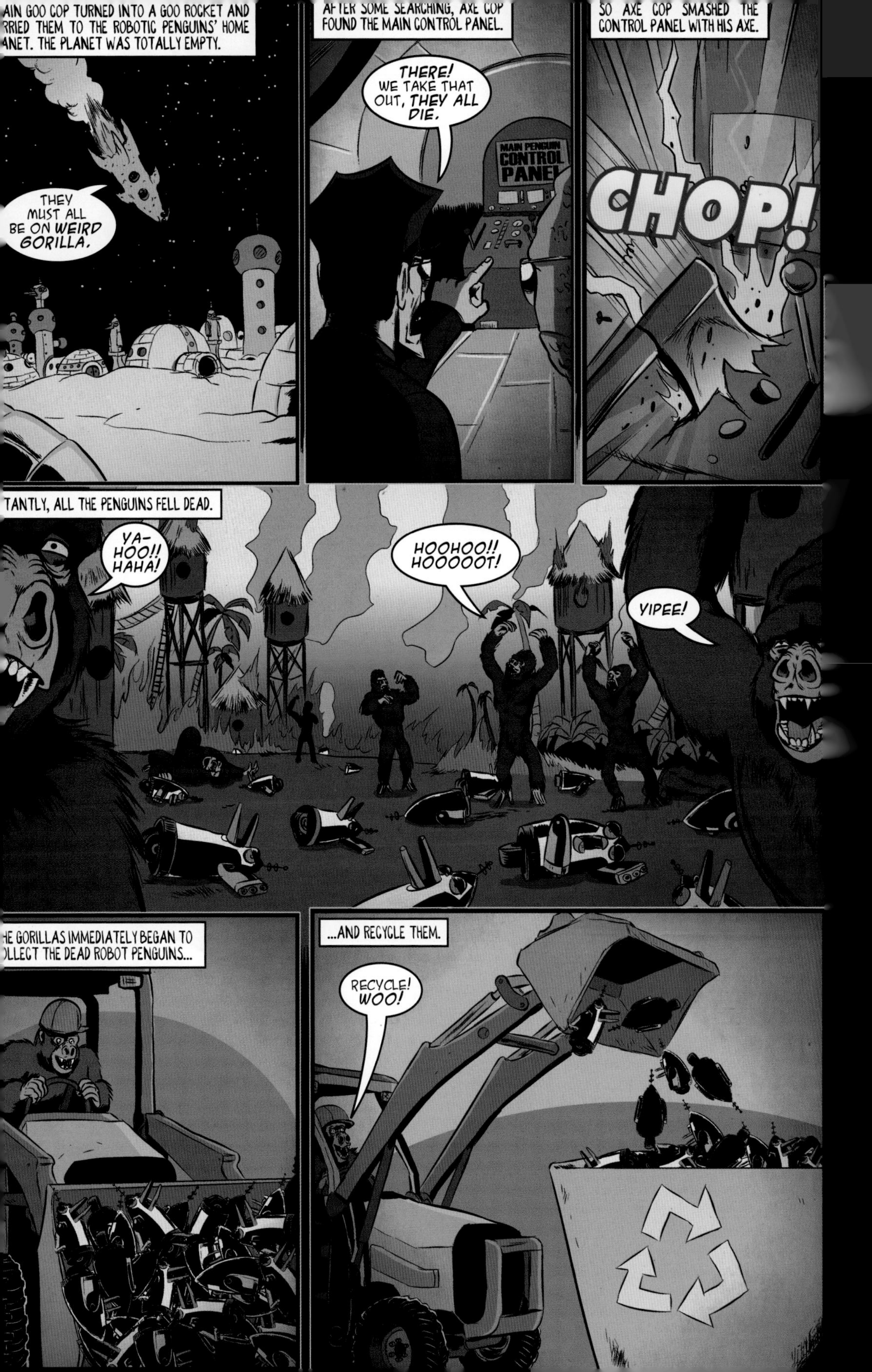
AIN GOO COP TURNED INTO A GOO ROCKET AND RRIED THEM TO THE ROBOTIC PENGUINS' HOME ANET. THE PLANET WAS TOTALLY EMPTY.
THEY MUST ALL BE ON WEIRD GORILLA.
AFTER SOME SEARCHING, AXE COP FOUND THE MAIN CONTROL PANEL.
THERE! WE TAKE THAT OUT, THEY ALL DIE.
MAIN PENGUIN CONTROL PANEL
SO AXE COP SMASHED THE CONTROL PANEL WITH HIS AXE.
CHOP!
TANTLY, ALL THE PENGUINS FELL DEAD.
YA-HOO!! HAHA!
HOOHOO!! HOOOOOT!
YIPEE!
HE GORILLAS IMMEDIATELY BEGAN TO OLLECT THE DEAD ROBOT PENGUINS...
...AND RECYCLE THEM.
RECYCLE! WOO!

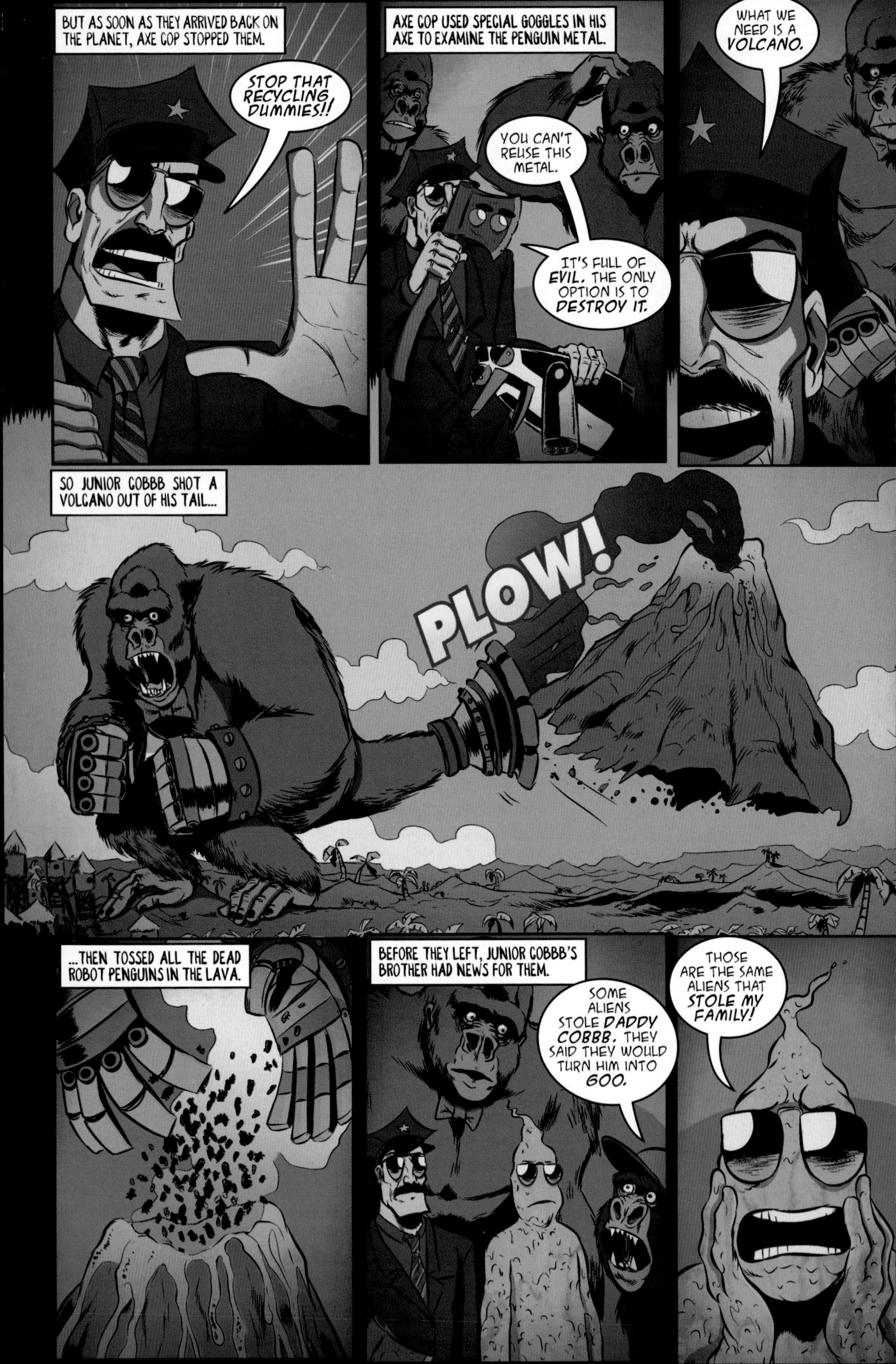
BUT AS SOON AS THEY ARRIVED BACK ON THE PLANET, AXE COP STOPPED THEM.
STOP THAT RECYCLING, DUMMIES!!
AXE COP USED SPECIAL GOGGLES IN HIS AXE TO EXAMINE THE PENGUIN METAL.
YOU CAN'T REUSE THIS METAL.
IT'S FULL OF EVIL. THE ONLY OPTION IS TO DESTROY IT.
WHAT WE NEED IS A VOLCANO.
SO JUNIOR COBBB SHOT A VOLCANO OUT OF HIS TAIL...
PLOW!
...THEN TOSSED ALL THE DEAD ROBOT PENGUINS IN THE LAVA.
BEFORE THEY LEFT, JUNIOR COBBB'S BROTHER HAD NEWS FOR THEM.
SOME ALIENS STOLE DADDY COBBB. THEY SAID THEY WOULD TURN HIM INTO GOO.
THOSE ARE THE SAME ALIENS THAT STOLE MY FAMILY!

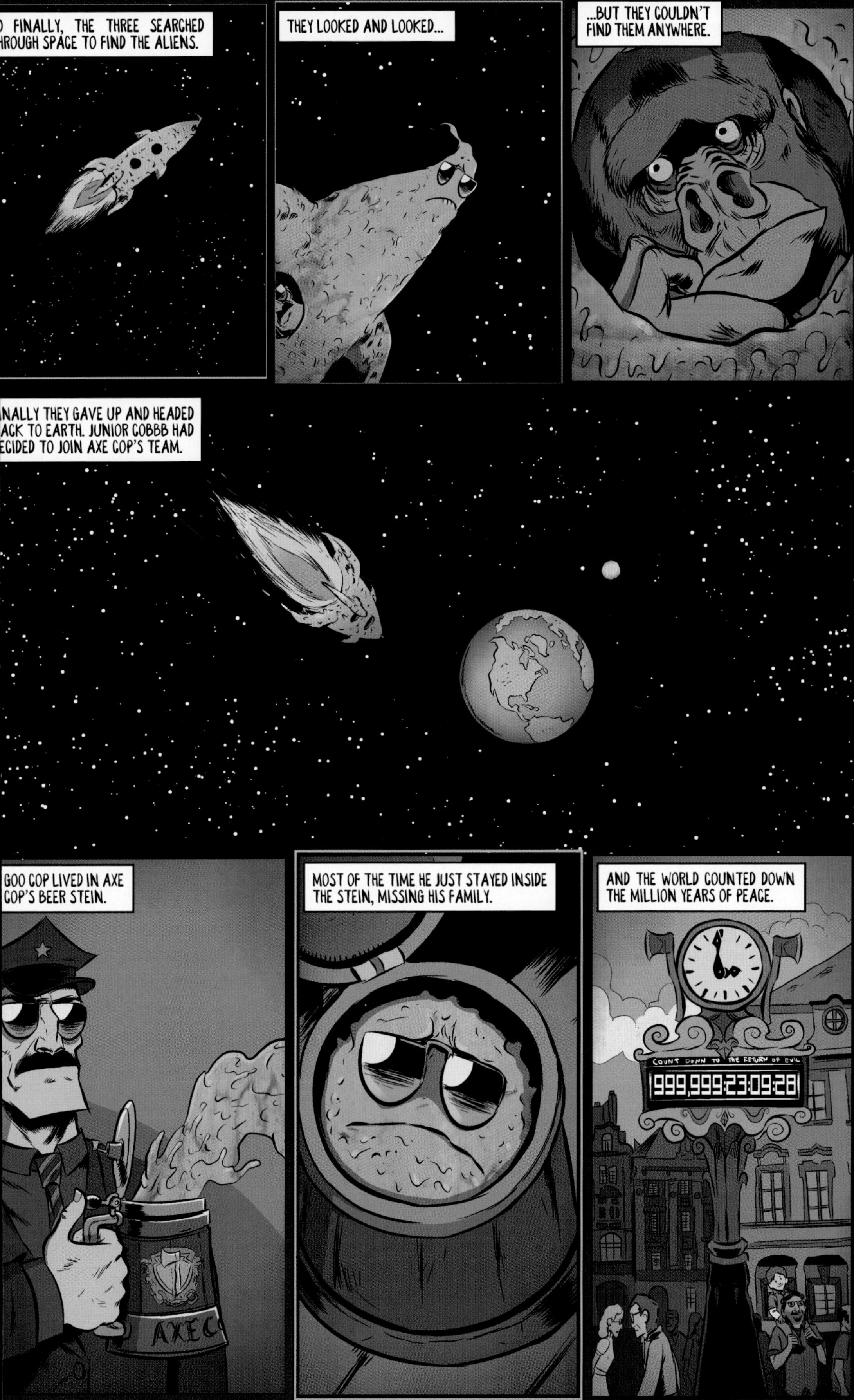
O FINALLY, THE THREE SEARCHED THROUGH SPACE TO FIND THE ALIENS.
THEY LOOKED AND LOOKED...
...BUT THEY COULDN'T FIND THEM ANYWHERE.
INALLY THEY GAVE UP AND HEADED ACK TO EARTH. JUNIOR COBBB HAD ECIDED TO JOIN AXE COP'S TEAM.
GOO COP LIVED IN AXE COP'S BEER STEIN.
AXE C
MOST OF THE TIME HE JUST STAYED INSIDE THE STEIN, MISSING HIS FAMILY.
AND THE WORLD COUNTED DOWN THE MILLION YEARS OF PEACE.
COUNT DOWN TO THE RETURN OF EVIL
999,999:23:09:28

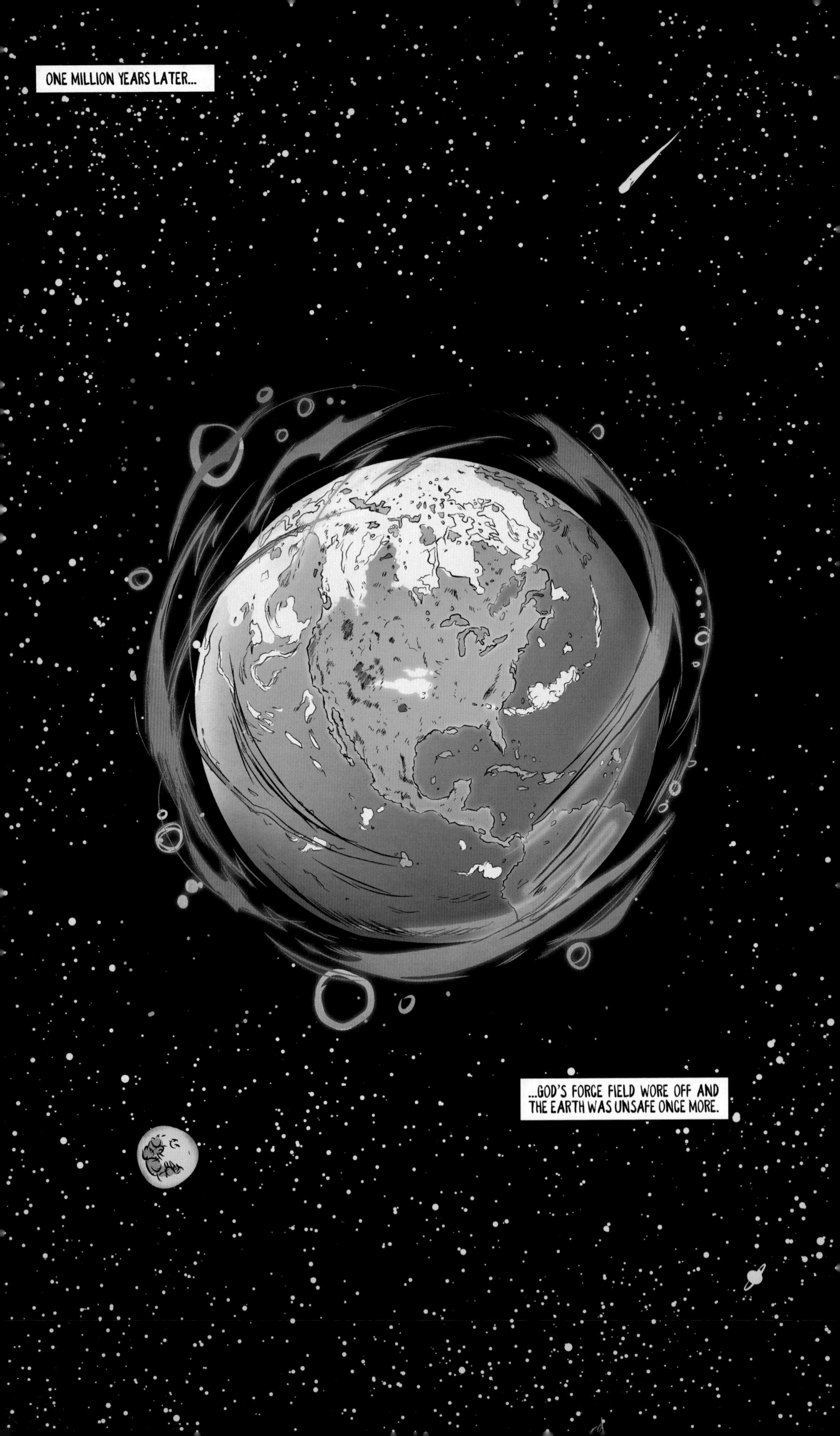
ONE MILLION YEARS LATER...
...GOD'S FORCE FIELD WORE OFF AND THE EARTH WAS UNSAFE ONCE MORE.

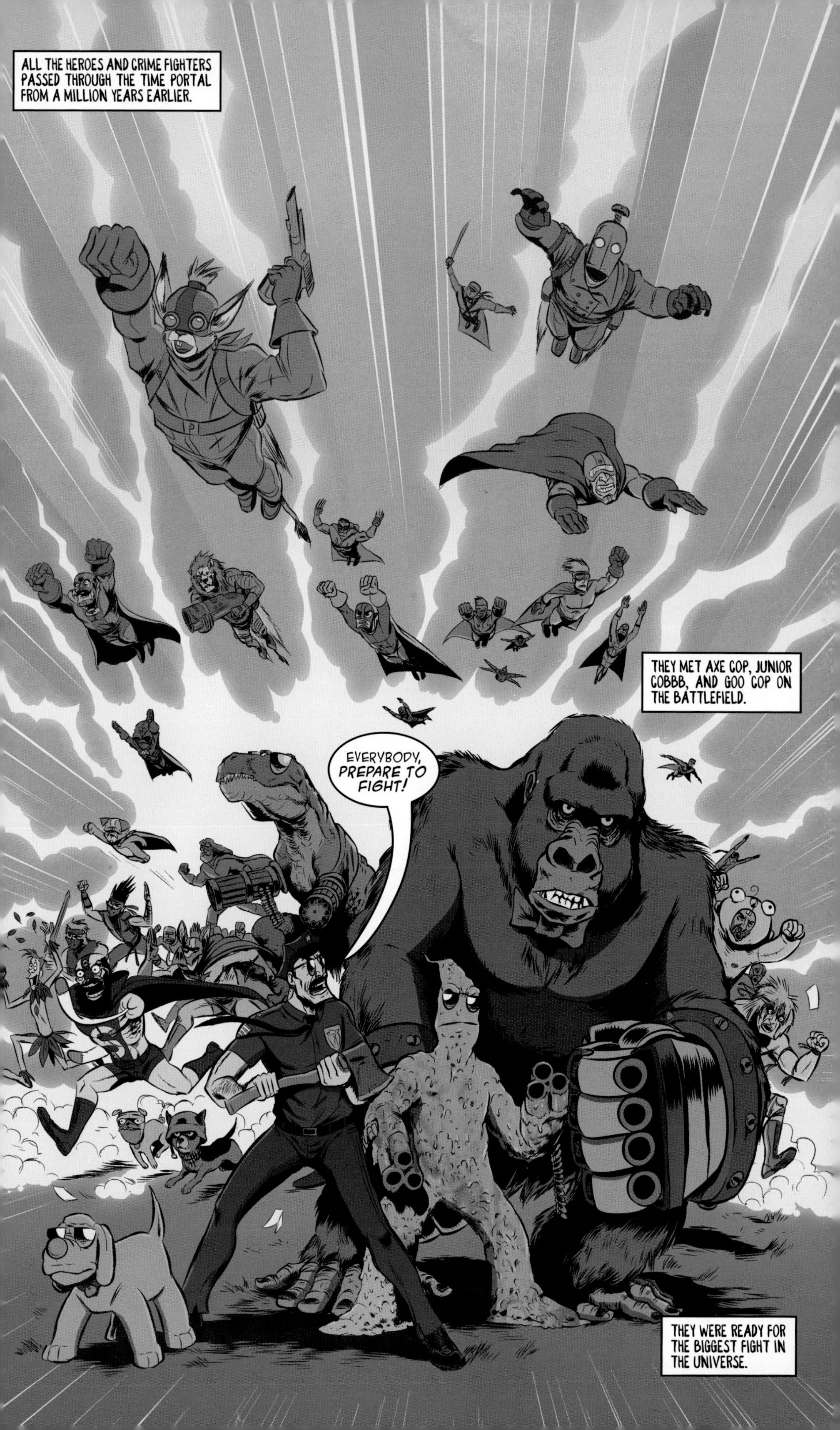
ALL THE HEROES AND CRIME FIGHTERS PASSED THROUGH THE TIME PORTAL FROM A MILLION YEARS EARLIER.
THEY MET AXE COP, JUNIOR COBBB, AND GOO COP ON THE BATTLEFIELD.
EVERYBODY, PREPARE TO FIGHT!
THEY WERE READY FOR THE BIGGEST FIGHT IN THE UNIVERSE.

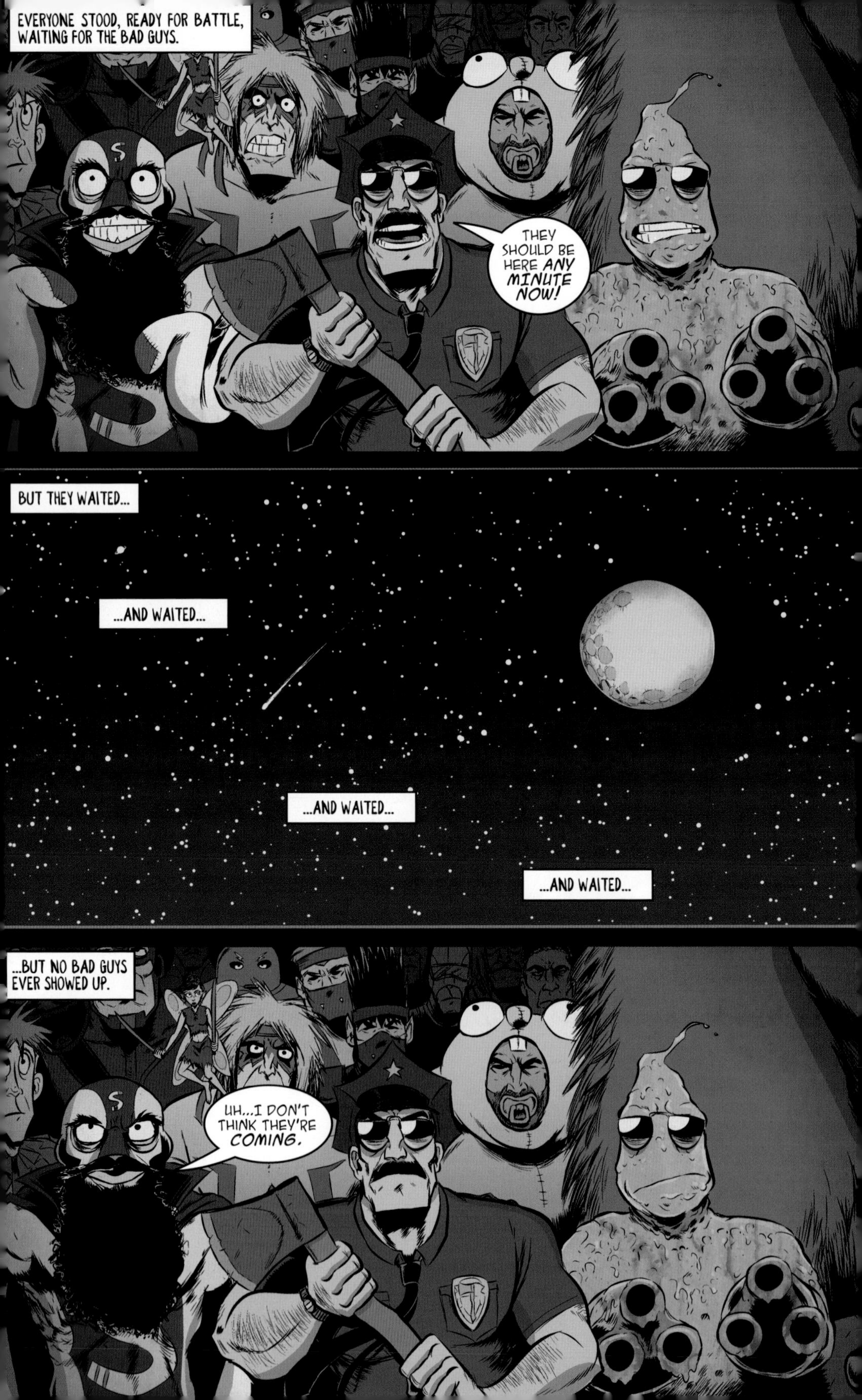
EVERYONE STOOD, READY FOR BATTLE, WAITING FOR THE BAD GUYS.
THEY SHOULD BE HERE ANY MINUTE NOW!
BUT THEY WAITED...
...AND WAITED...
...AND WAITED...
...AND WAITED...
...BUT NO BAD GUYS EVER SHOWED UP.
UH...I DON'T THINK THEY'RE COMING.

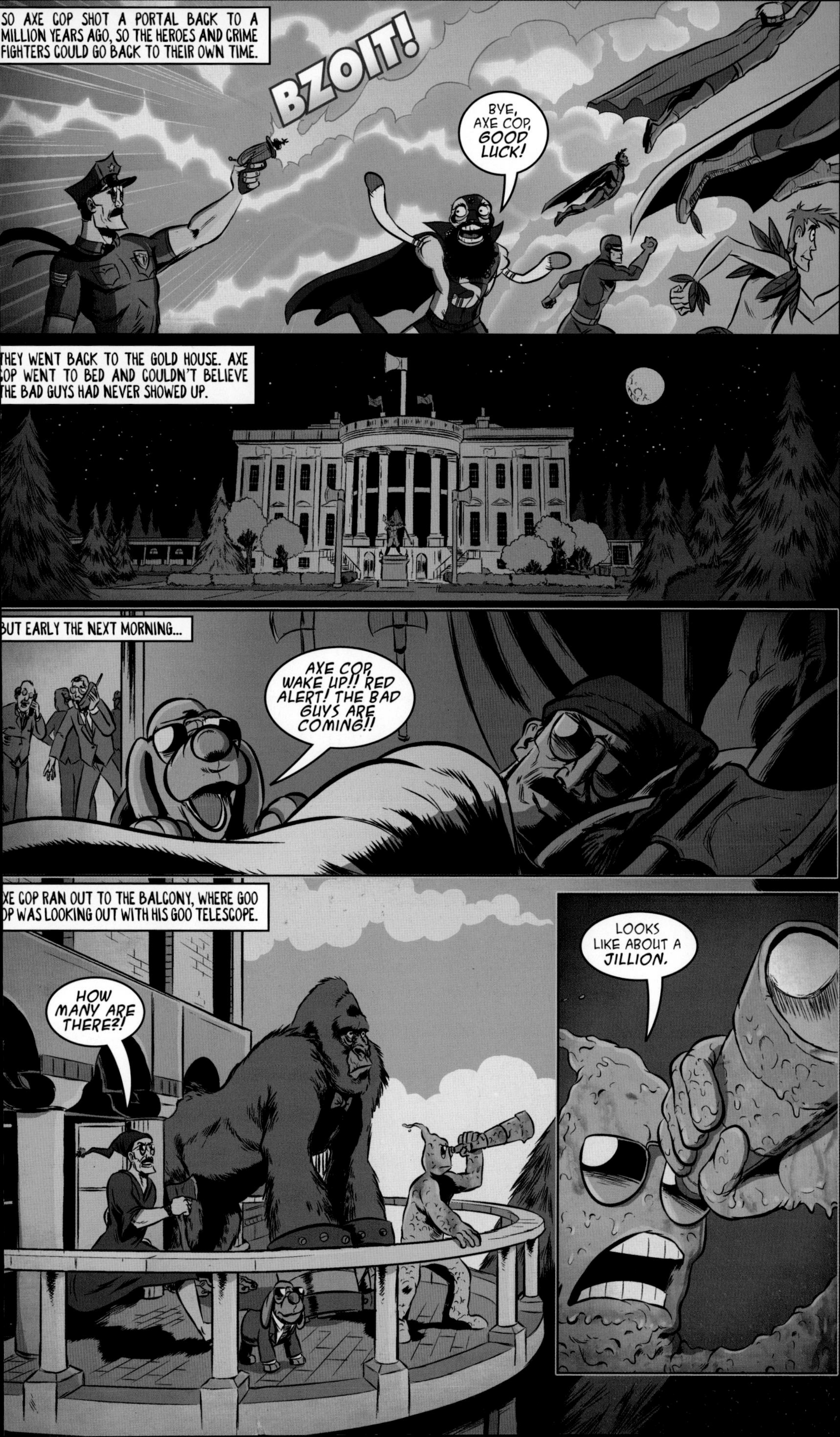
SO AXE COP SHOT A PORTAL BACK TO A MILLION YEARS AGO, SO THE HEROES AND CRIME FIGHTERS COULD GO BACK TO THEIR OWN TIME.
BZOIT!
BYE, AXE COP, GOOD LUCK!
THEY WENT BACK TO THE GOLD HOUSE. AXE COP WENT TO BED AND COULDN'T BELIEVE THE BAD GUYS HAD NEVER SHOWED UP.
BUT EARLY THE NEXT MORNING...
AXE COP, WAKE UP!! RED ALERT! THE BAD GUYS ARE COMING!!
AXE COP RAN OUT TO THE BALCONY, WHERE GOO COP WAS LOOKING OUT WITH HIS GOO TELESCOPE.
HOW MANY ARE THERE?!
LOOKS LIKE ABOUT A JILLION.

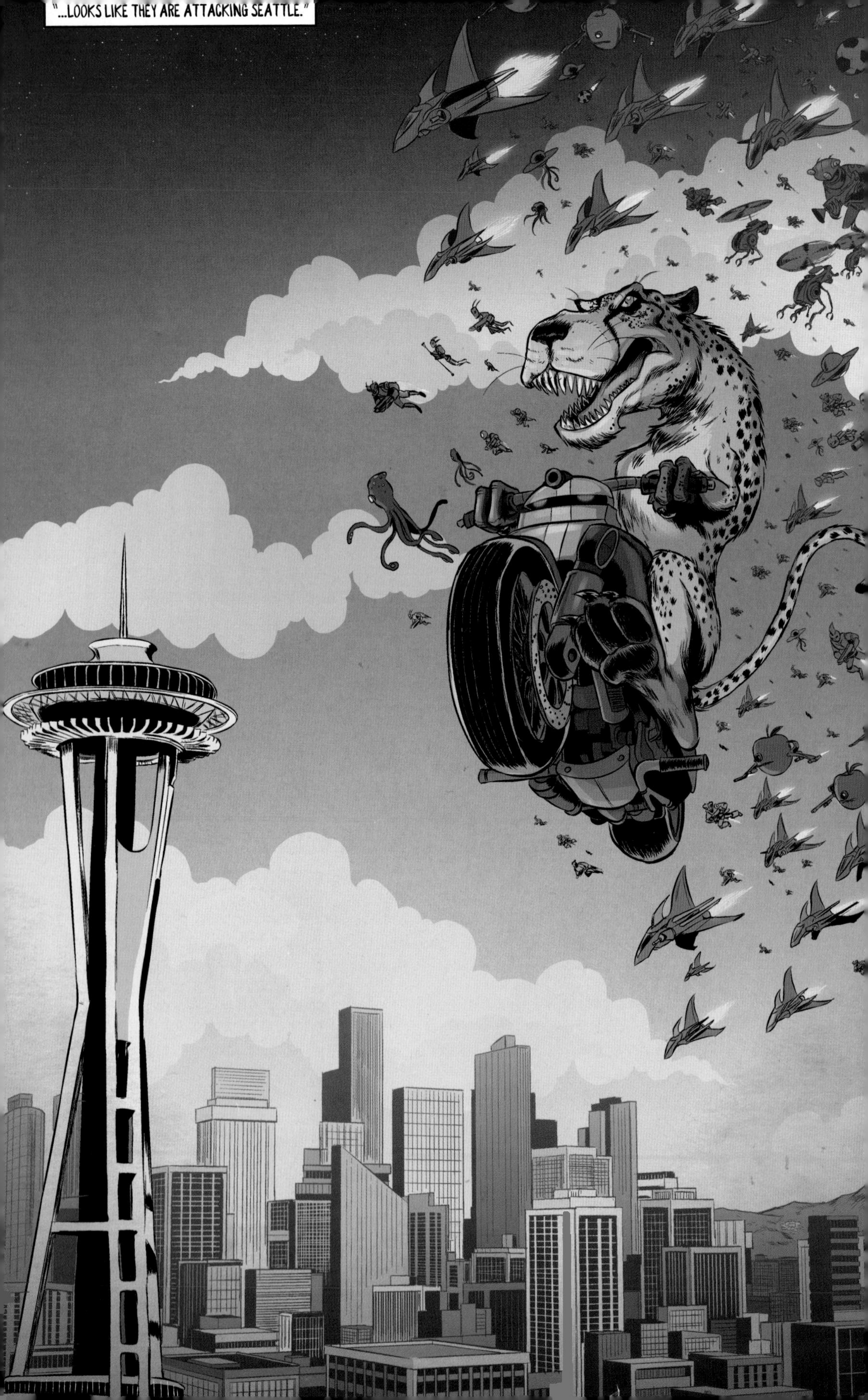
"...LOOKS LIKE THEY ARE ATTACKING SEATTLE."

PENCILED BY **ETHAN NICOLLE** ★ PAINTED BY **BRYNN METHENEY**

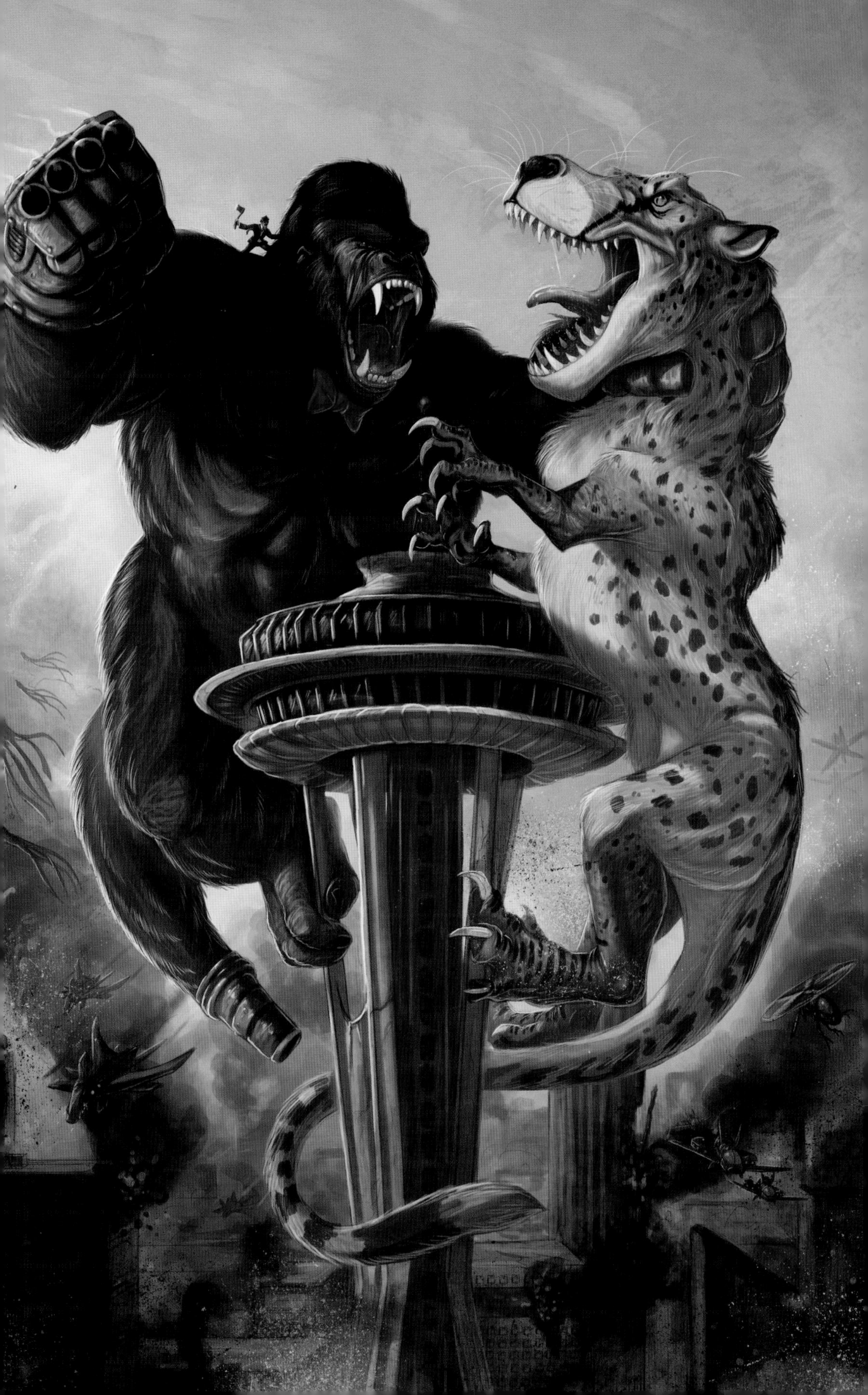

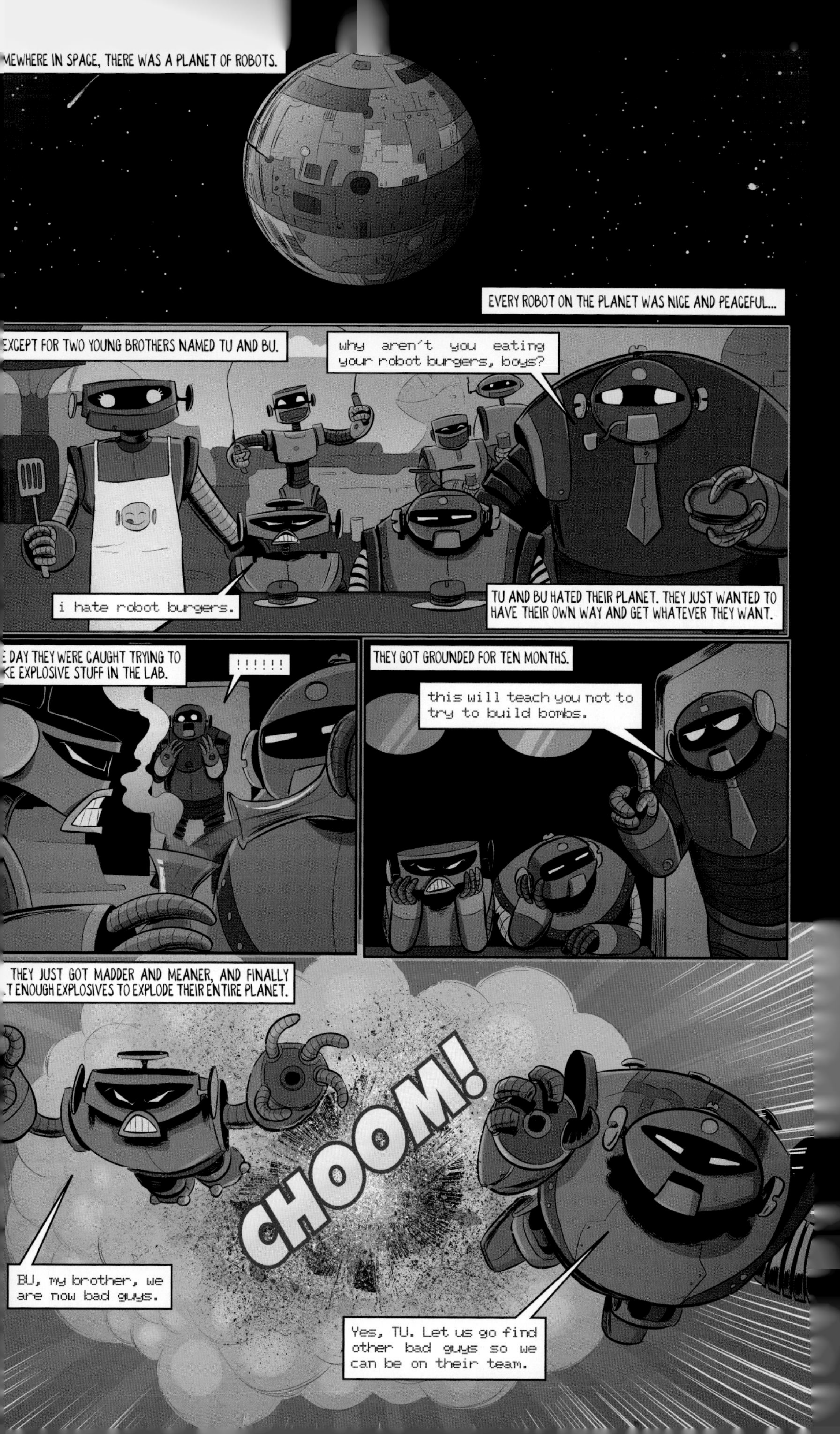
MEWHERE IN SPACE, THERE WAS A PLANET OF ROBOTS.
EVERY ROBOT ON THE PLANET WAS NICE AND PEACEFUL...
EXCEPT FOR TWO YOUNG BROTHERS NAMED TU AND BU.
why aren't you eating your robot burgers, boys?
i hate robot burgers.
TU AND BU HATED THEIR PLANET. THEY JUST WANTED TO HAVE THEIR OWN WAY AND GET WHATEVER THEY WANT.
E DAY THEY WERE CAUGHT TRYING TO KE EXPLOSIVE STUFF IN THE LAB.
!!!!!!
THEY GOT GROUNDED FOR TEN MONTHS.
this will teach you not to try to build bombs.
THEY JUST GOT MADDER AND MEANER, AND FINALLY T ENOUGH EXPLOSIVES TO EXPLODE THEIR ENTIRE PLANET.
CHOOM!
BU, my brother, we are now bad guys.
Yes, TU. Let us go find other bad guys so we can be on their team.

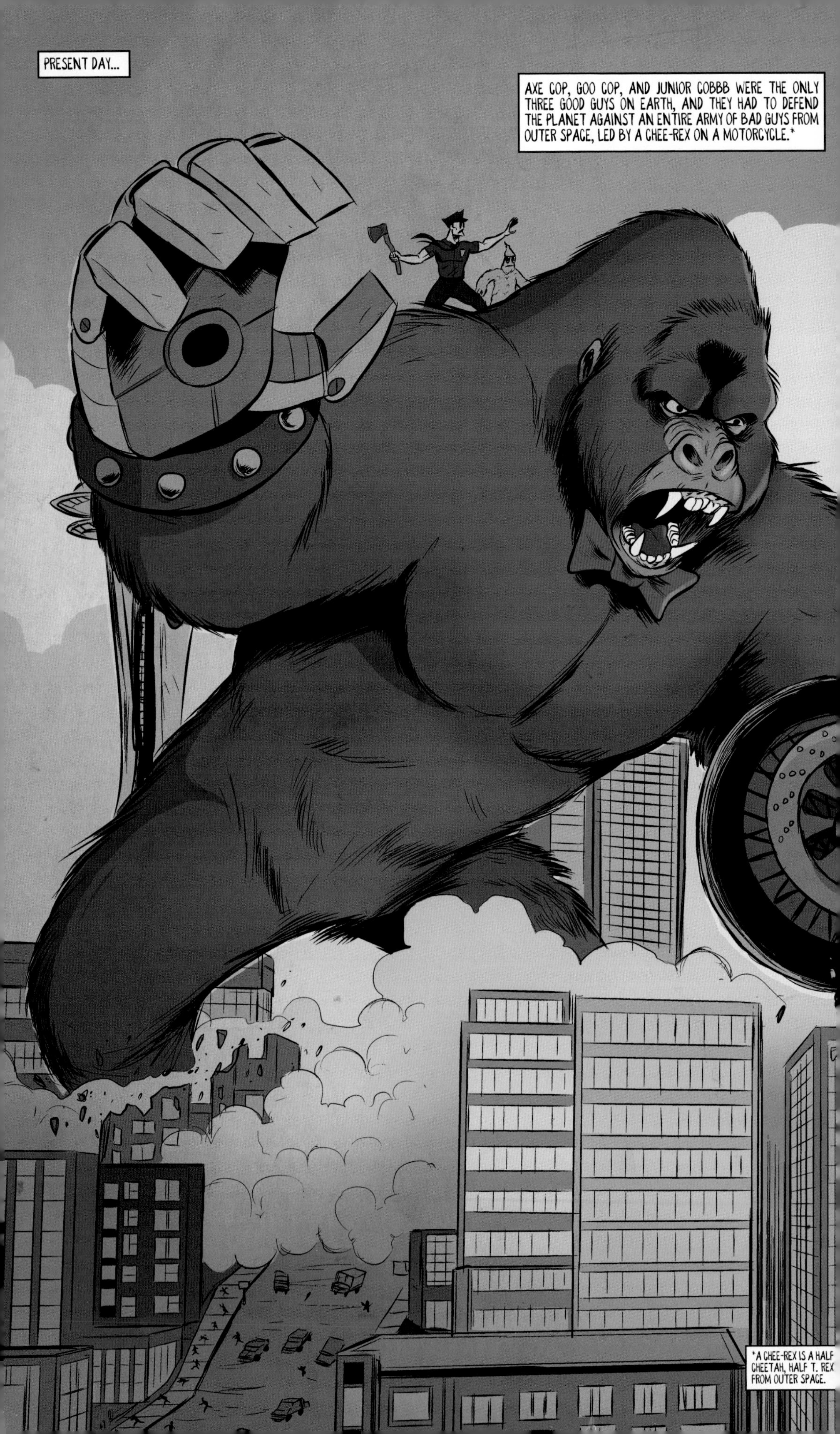
PRESENT DAY...
AXE COP, GOO COP, AND JUNIOR COBBB WERE THE ONLY THREE GOOD GUYS ON EARTH, AND THEY HAD TO DEFEND THE PLANET AGAINST AN ENTIRE ARMY OF BAD GUYS FROM OUTER SPACE, LED BY A CHEE-REX ON A MOTORCYCLE.*
*A CHEE-REX IS A HALF CHEETAH, HALF T. REX FROM OUTER SPACE.

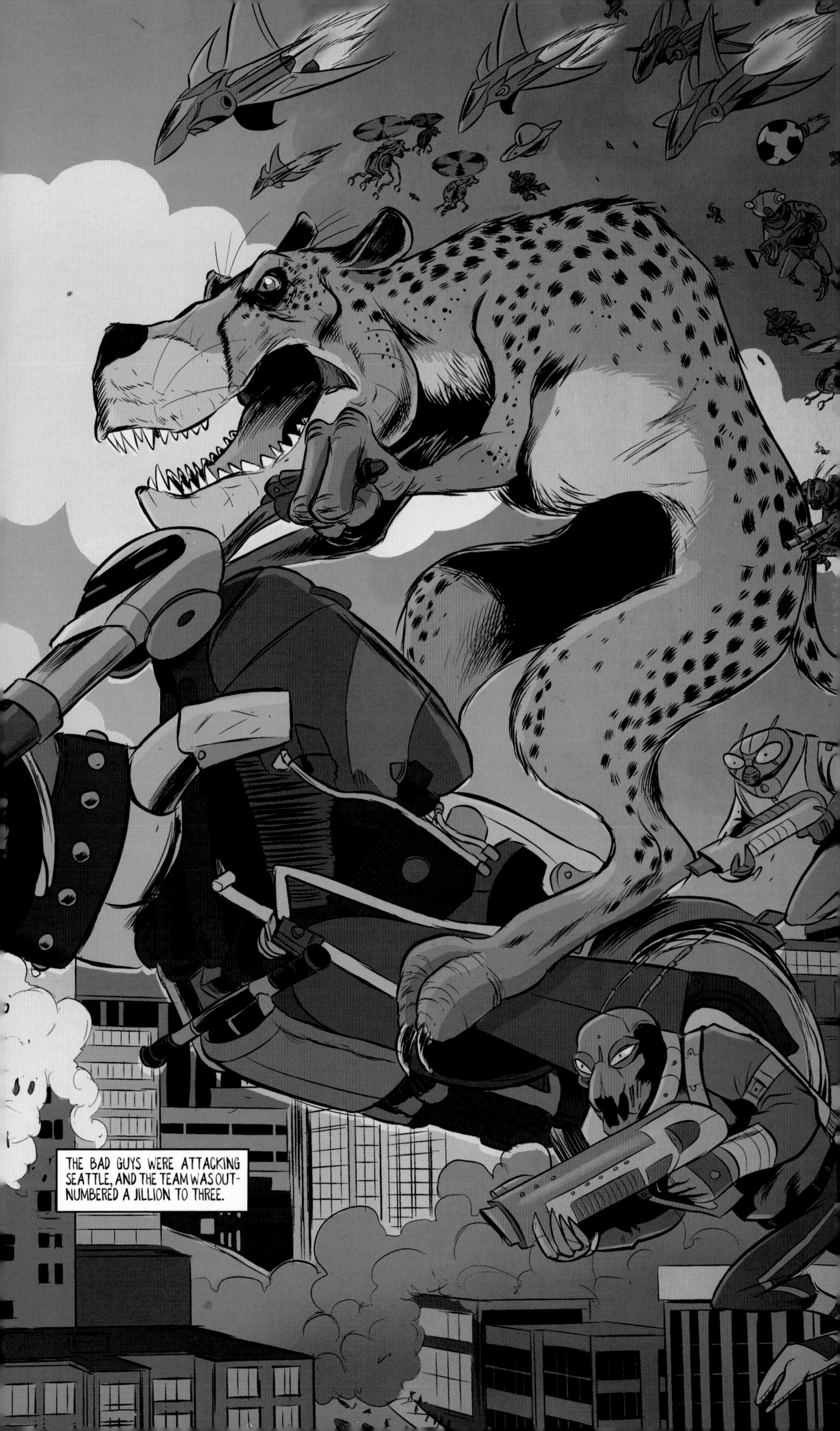
THE BAD GUYS WERE ATTACKING SEATTLE, AND THE TEAM WAS OUT-NUMBERED A JILLION TO THREE.

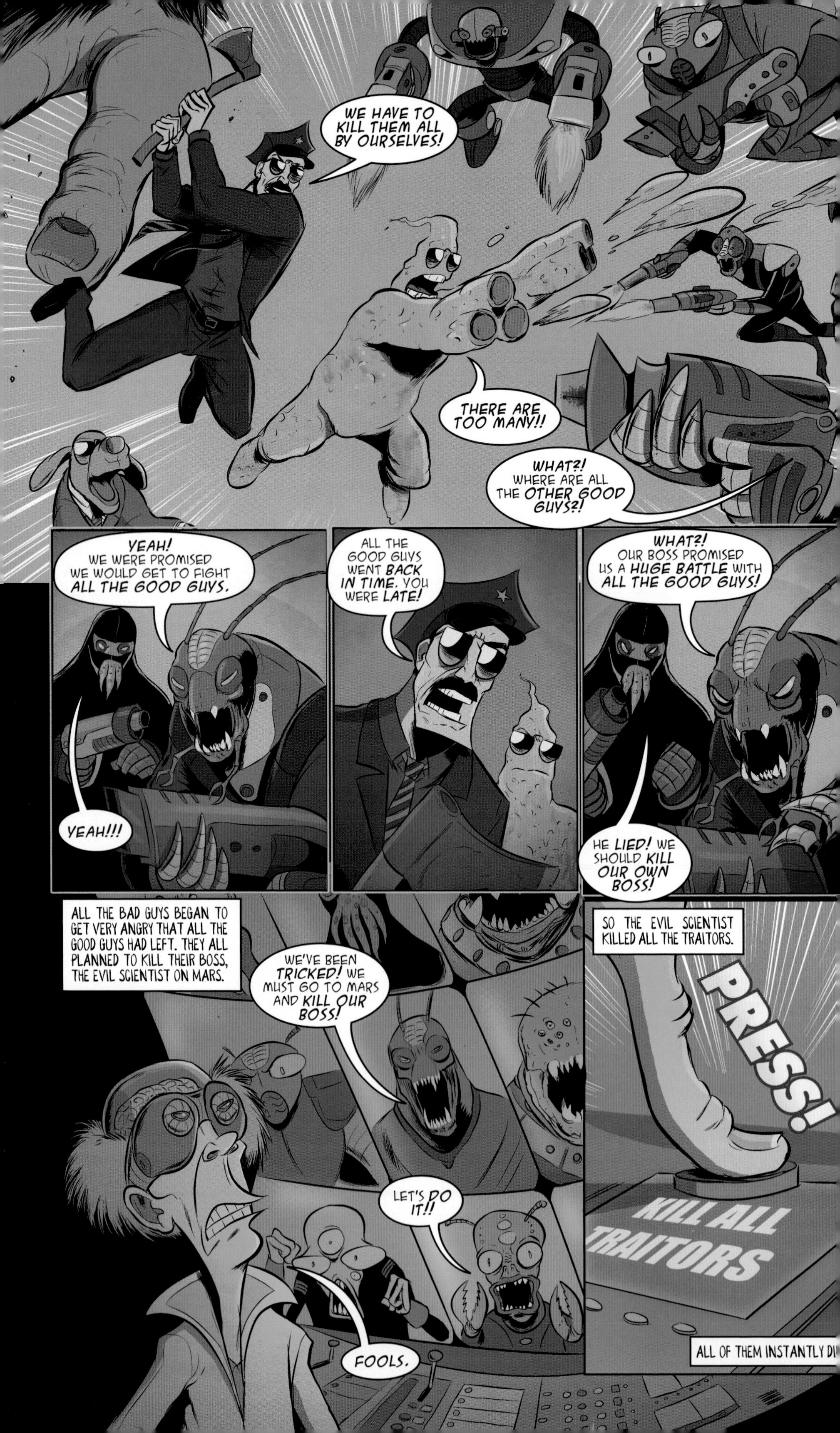
WE HAVE TO KILL THEM ALL BY OURSELVES!
THERE ARE TOO MANY!!
WHAT?! WHERE ARE ALL THE OTHER GOOD GUYS?!
YEAH! WE WERE PROMISED WE WOULD GET TO FIGHT ALL THE GOOD GUYS.
YEAH!!!
ALL THE GOOD GUYS WENT BACK IN TIME. YOU WERE LATE!
WHAT?! OUR BOSS PROMISED US A HUGE BATTLE WITH ALL THE GOOD GUYS!
HE LIED! WE SHOULD KILL OUR OWN BOSS!
ALL THE BAD GUYS BEGAN TO GET VERY ANGRY THAT ALL THE GOOD GUYS HAD LEFT. THEY ALL PLANNED TO KILL THEIR BOSS, THE EVIL SCIENTIST ON MARS.
WE'VE BEEN TRICKED! WE MUST GO TO MARS AND KILL OUR BOSS!
LET'S DO IT!!
FOOLS.
SO THE EVIL SCIENTIST KILLED ALL THE TRAITORS.
PRESS!
KILL ALL TRAITORS
ALL OF THEM INSTANTLY DI

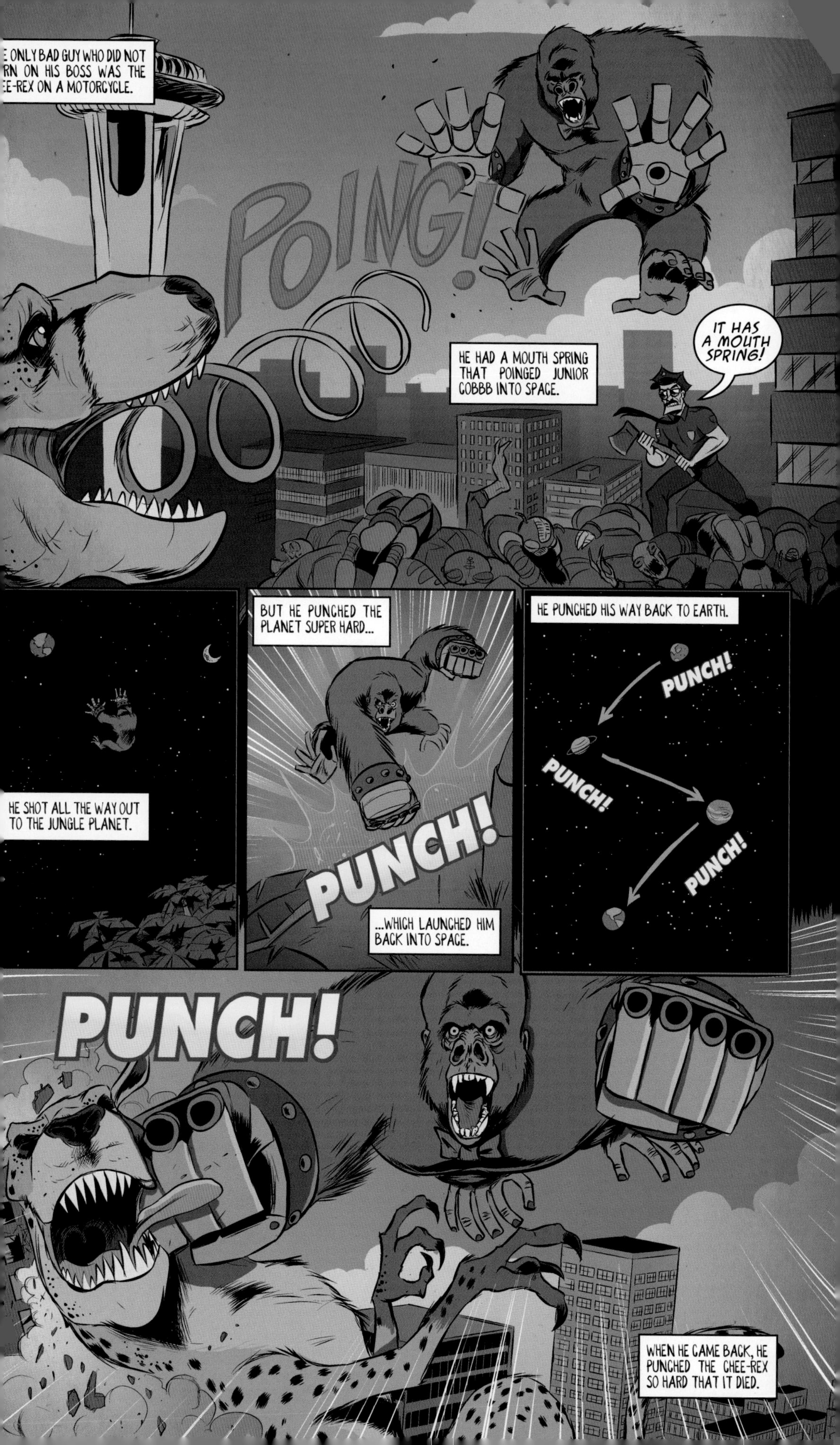

E ONLY BAD GUY WHO DID NOT
RN ON HIS BOSS WAS THE
EE-REX ON A MOTORCYCLE.
POING!
HE HAD A MOUTH SPRING THAT POINGED JUNIOR COBBB INTO SPACE.
IT HAS A MOUTH SPRING!
HE SHOT ALL THE WAY OUT TO THE JUNGLE PLANET.
BUT HE PUNCHED THE PLANET SUPER HARD...
PUNCH!
...WHICH LAUNCHED HIM BACK INTO SPACE.
HE PUNCHED HIS WAY BACK TO EARTH.
PUNCH!
PUNCH!
PUNCH!
PUNCH!
WHEN HE CAME BACK, HE PUNCHED THE CHEE-REX SO HARD THAT IT DIED.

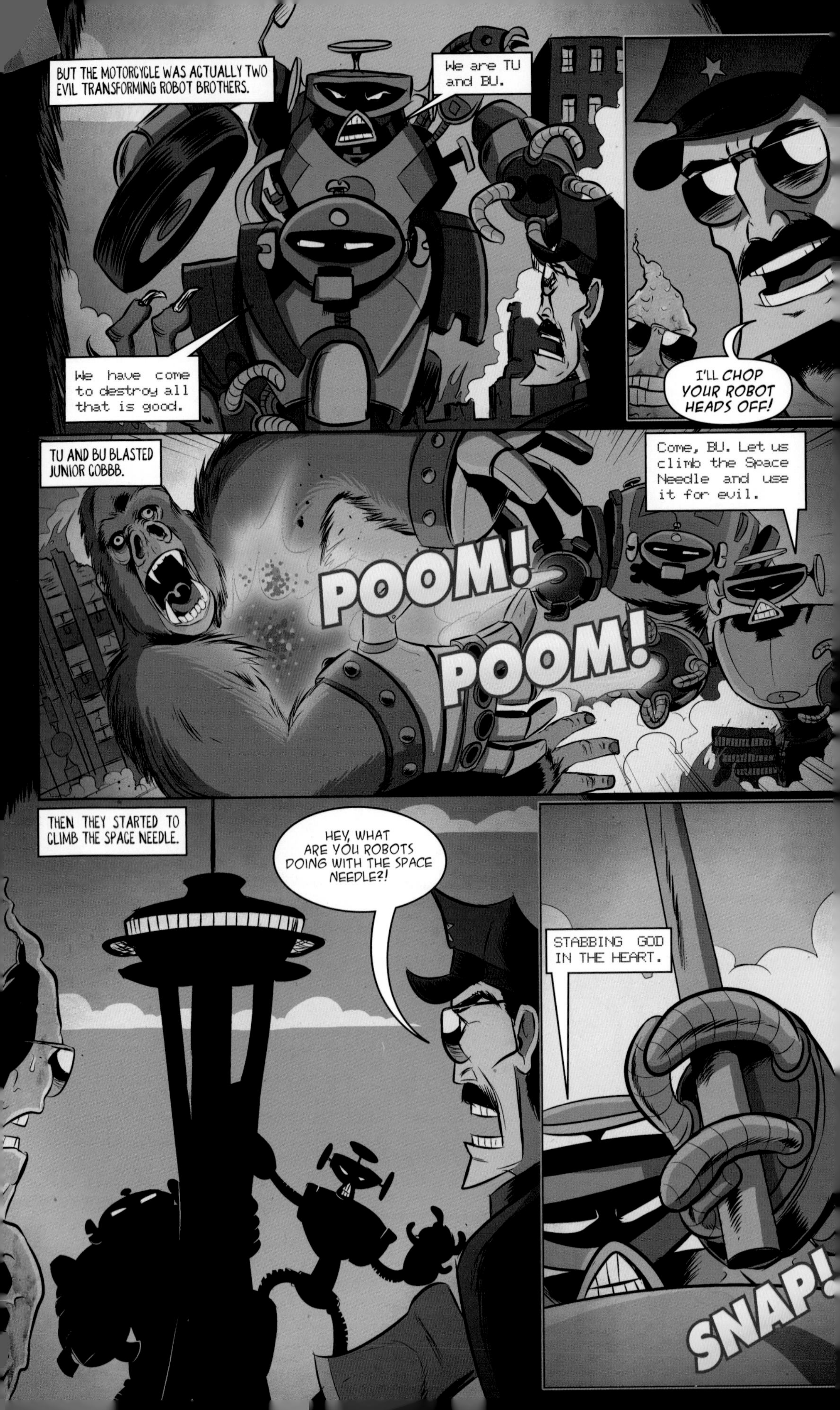
BUT THE MOTORCYCLE WAS ACTUALLY TWO EVIL TRANSFORMING ROBOT BROTHERS.
We are TU and BU.
We have come to destroy all that is good.
I'LL CHOP YOUR ROBOT HEADS OFF!
TU AND BU BLASTED JUNIOR GOBBB.
Come, BU. Let us climb the Space Needle and use it for evil.
POOM!
POOM!
THEN THEY STARTED TO CLIMB THE SPACE NEEDLE.
HEY, WHAT ARE YOU ROBOTS DOING WITH THE SPACE NEEDLE?!
STABBING GOD IN THE HEART.
SNAP!

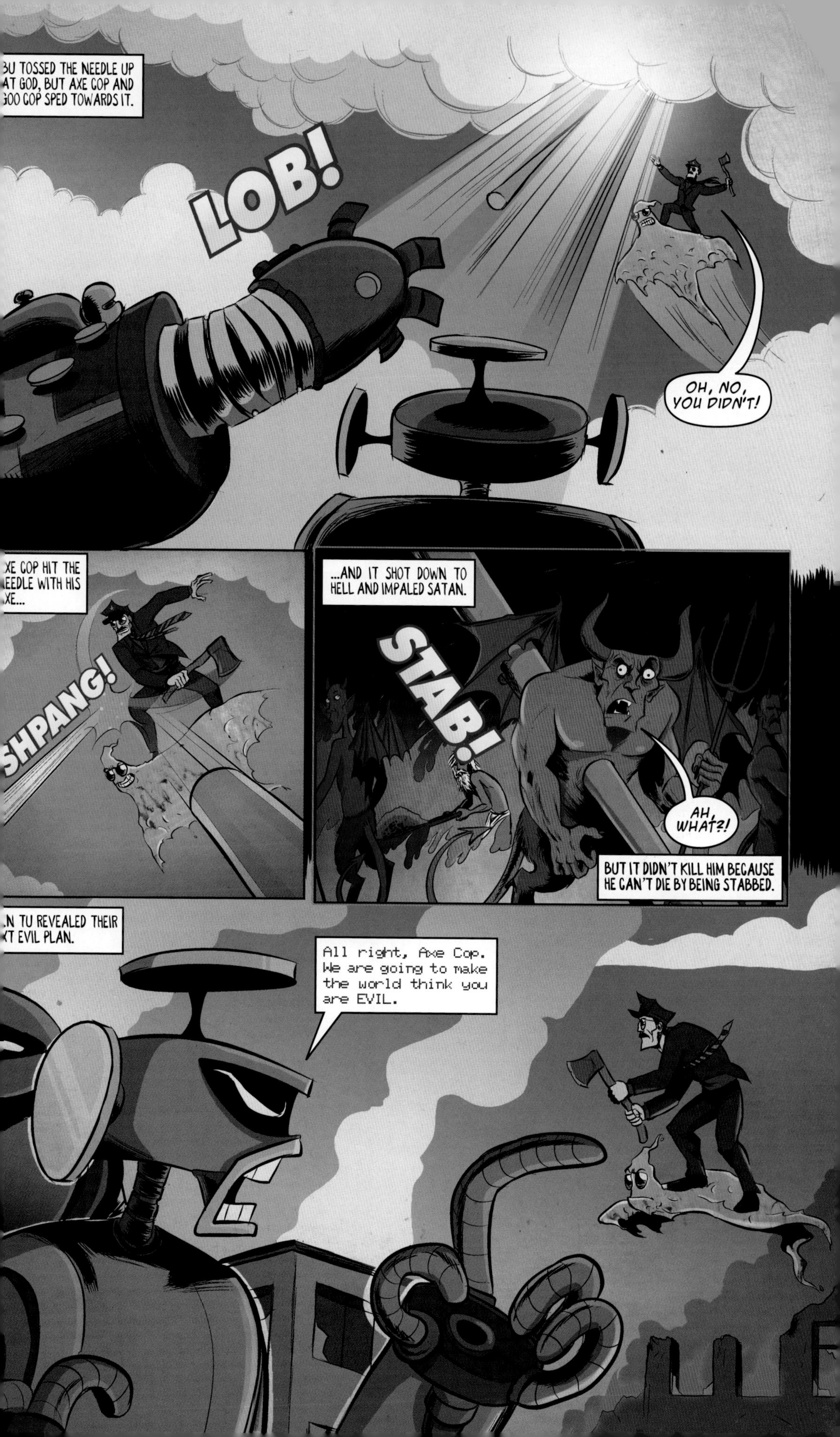
BU TOSSED THE NEEDLE UP
AT GOD, BUT AXE COP AND
GOO COP SPED TOWARDS IT.
LOB!
OH, NO, YOU DIDN'T!
XE COP HIT THE
EEDLE WITH HIS
XE...
SHPANG!
...AND IT SHOT DOWN TO HELL AND IMPALED SATAN.
STAB!
AH, WHAT?!
BUT IT DIDN'T KILL HIM BECAUSE HE CAN'T DIE BY BEING STABBED.
N TU REVEALED THEIR
T EVIL PLAN.
All right, Axe Cop. We are going to make the world think you are EVIL.

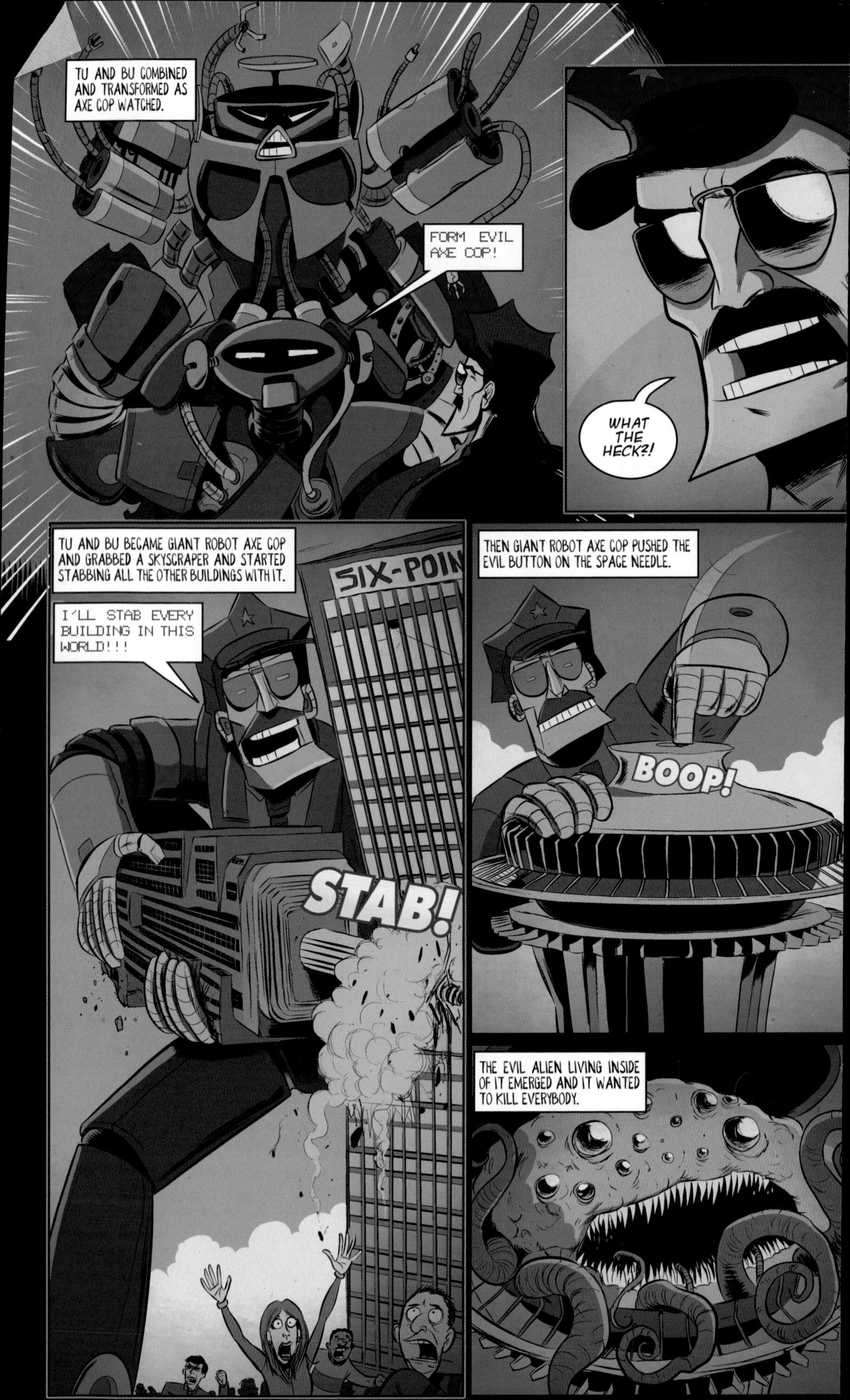
TU AND BU COMBINED AND TRANSFORMED AS AXE COP WATCHED.
FORM EVIL AXE COP!
WHAT THE HECK?!
TU AND BU BECAME GIANT ROBOT AXE COP AND GRABBED A SKYSCRAPER AND STARTED STABBING ALL THE OTHER BUILDINGS WITH IT.
I'LL STAB EVERY BUILDING IN THIS WORLD!!!
SIX-POIN
STAB!
THEN GIANT ROBOT AXE COP PUSHED THE EVIL BUTTON ON THE SPACE NEEDLE.
BOOP!
THE EVIL ALIEN LIVING INSIDE OF IT EMERGED AND IT WANTED TO KILL EVERYBODY.

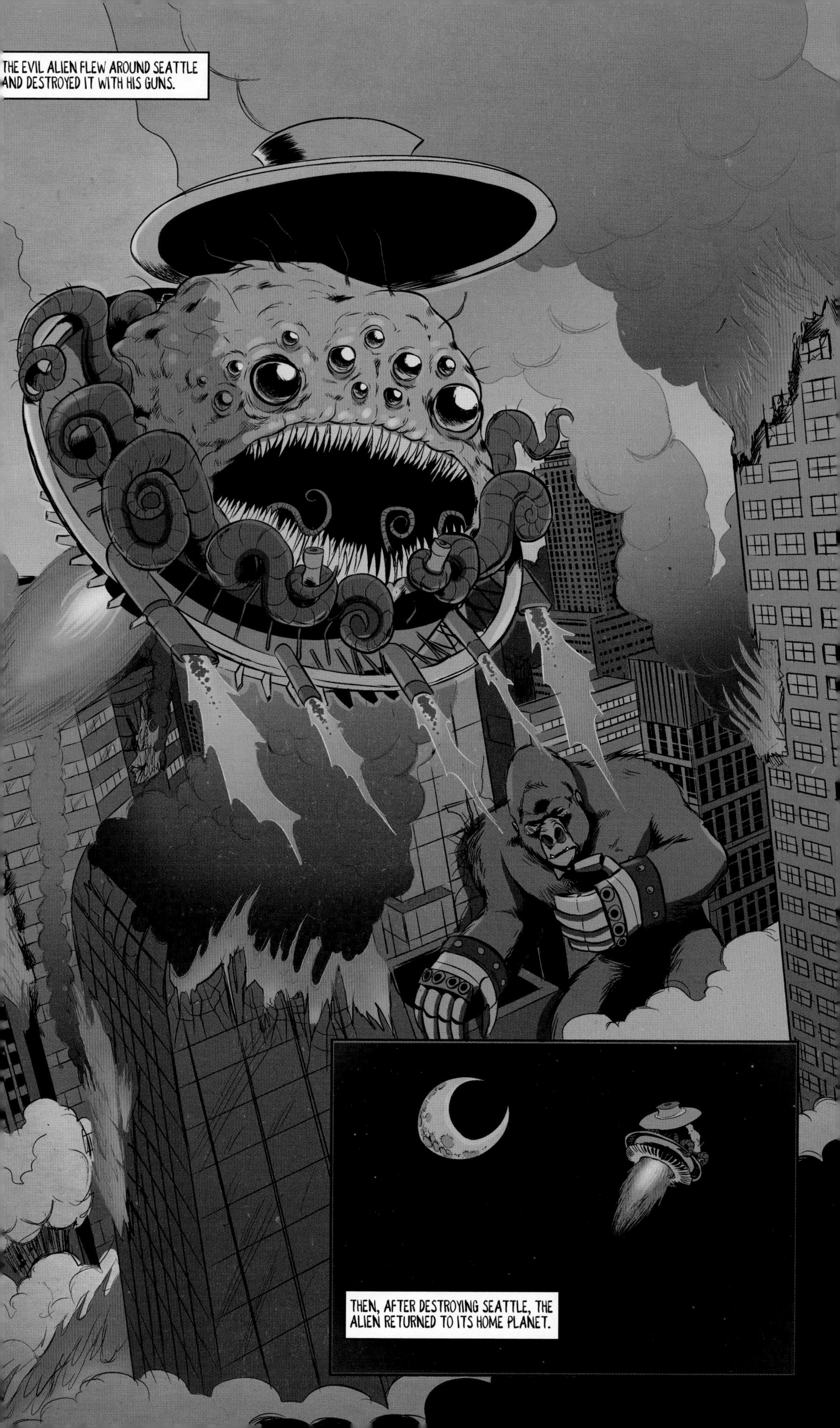
THE EVIL ALIEN FLEW AROUND SEATTLE AND DESTROYED IT WITH HIS GUNS.
THEN, AFTER DESTROYING SEATTLE, THE ALIEN RETURNED TO ITS HOME PLANET.

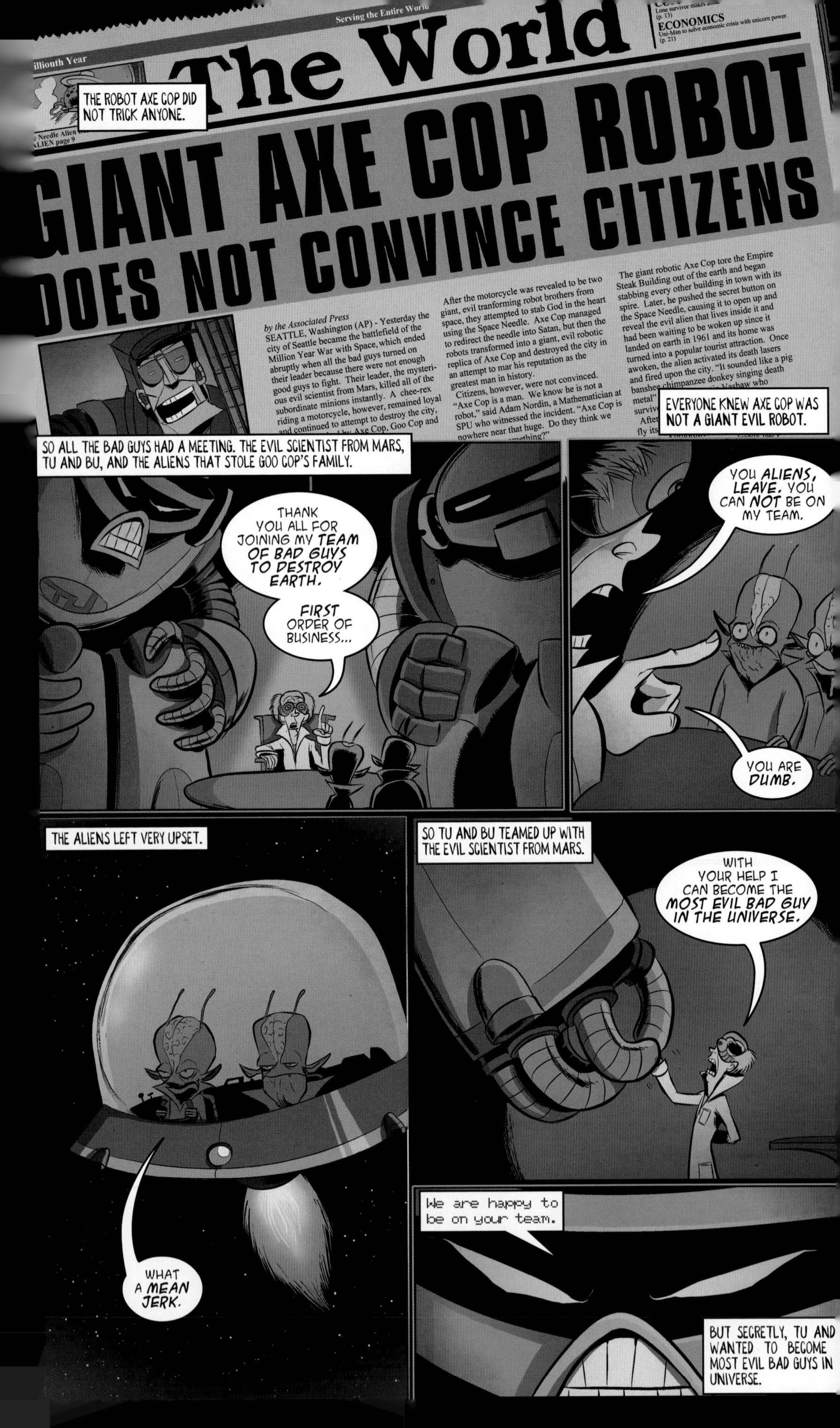

Serving the Entire World
The World
Millionth Year
ECONOMICS
Uni-Man to solve economic crisis with unicorn power.
(p. 21)
THE ROBOT AXE COP DID NOT TRICK ANYONE.
GIANT AXE COP ROBOT DOES NOT CONVINCE CITIZENS
by the Associated Press
SEATTLE, Washington (AP) - Yesterday the city of Seattle became the battlefield of the Million Year War with Space, which ended abruptly when all the bad guys turned on their leader because there were not enough good guys to fight. Their leader, the mysterious evil scientist from Mars, killed all of the subordinate minions instantly. A chee-rex riding a motorcycle, however, remained loyal and continued to attempt to destroy the city,
After the motorcycle was revealed to be two giant, evil tranforming robot brothers from space, they attempted to stab God in the heart using the Space Needle. Axe Cop managed to redirect the needle into Satan, but then the robots transformed into a giant, evil robotic replica of Axe Cop and destroyed the city in an attempt to mar his reputation as the greatest man in history.
Citizens, however, were not convinced. "Axe Cop is a man. We know he is not a robot," said Adam Nordin, a Mathematician at SPU who witnessed the incident. "Axe Cop is nowhere near that huge. Do they think we
The giant robotic Axe Cop tore the Empire Steak Building out of the earth and began stabbing every other building in town with its spire. Later, he pushed the secret button on the Space Needle, causing it to open up and reveal the evil alien that lives inside it and had been waiting to be woken up since it landed on earth in 1961 and its home was turned into a popular tourist attraction. Once awoken, the alien activated its death lasers and fired upon the city. "It sounded like a pig banshee chimpanzee donkey singing death metal"
EVERYONE KNEW AXE COP WAS NOT A GIANT EVIL ROBOT.
SO ALL THE BAD GUYS HAD A MEETING. THE EVIL SCIENTIST FROM MARS, TU AND BU, AND THE ALIENS THAT STOLE GOO COP'S FAMILY.
THANK YOU ALL FOR JOINING MY TEAM OF BAD GUYS TO DESTROY EARTH.
FIRST ORDER OF BUSINESS...
YOU ALIENS, LEAVE. YOU CAN NOT BE ON MY TEAM.
YOU ARE DUMB.
THE ALIENS LEFT VERY UPSET.
WHAT A MEAN JERK.
SO TU AND BU TEAMED UP WITH THE EVIL SCIENTIST FROM MARS.
WITH YOUR HELP I CAN BECOME THE MOST EVIL BAD GUY IN THE UNIVERSE.
We are happy to be on your team.
BUT SECRETLY, TU AND BU WANTED TO BECOME THE MOST EVIL BAD GUYS IN THE UNIVERSE.

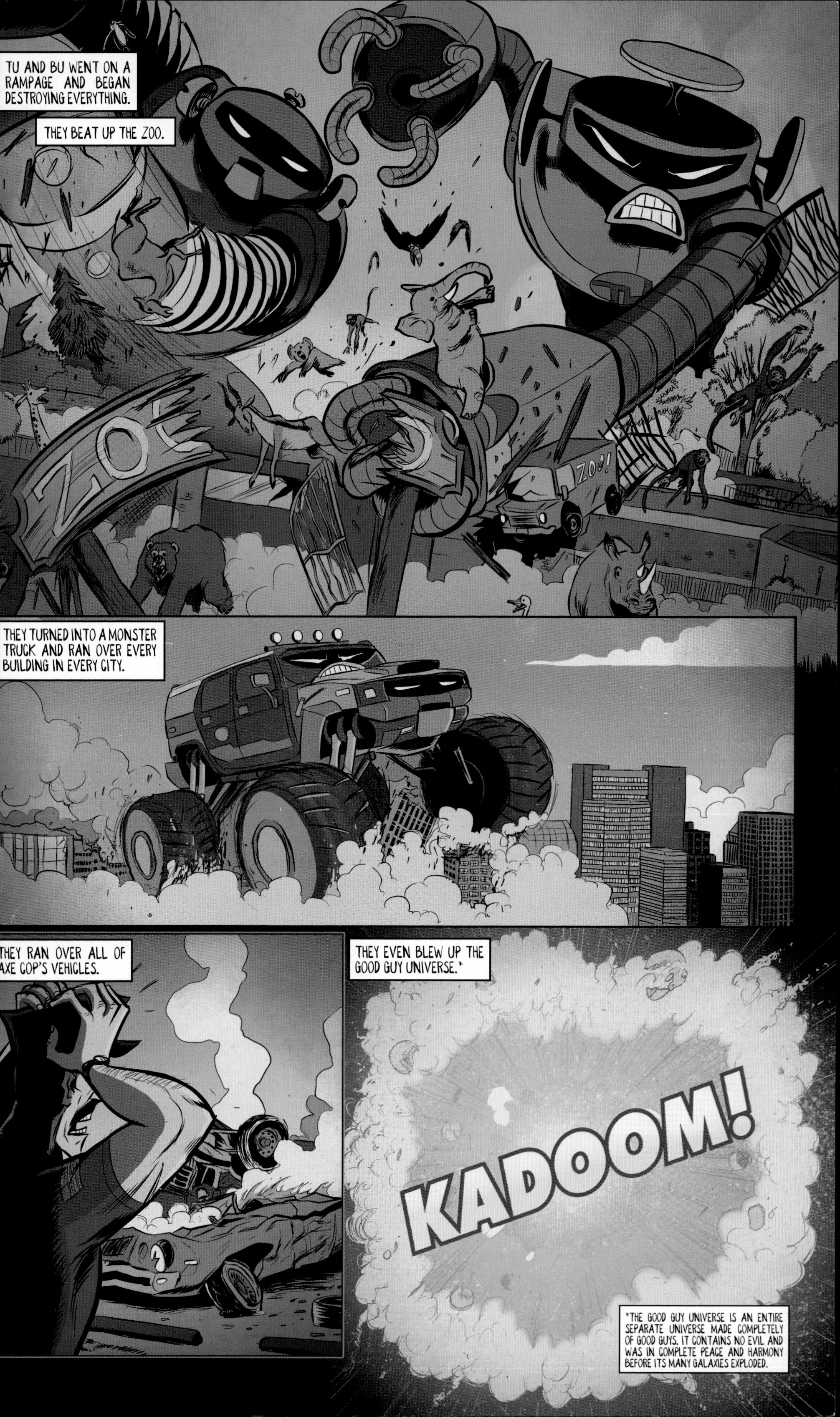
TU AND BU WENT ON A RAMPAGE AND BEGAN DESTROYING EVERYTHING.
THEY BEAT UP THE ZOO.
ZOO
ZOO!
THEY TURNED INTO A MONSTER TRUCK AND RAN OVER EVERY BUILDING IN EVERY CITY.
THEY RAN OVER ALL OF AXE COP'S VEHICLES.
THEY EVEN BLEW UP THE GOOD GUY UNIVERSE.*
KADOOM!
*THE GOOD GUY UNIVERSE IS AN ENTIRE SEPARATE UNIVERSE MADE COMPLETELY OF GOOD GUYS. IT CONTAINS NO EVIL AND WAS IN COMPLETE PEACE AND HARMONY BEFORE ITS MANY GALAXIES EXPLODED.

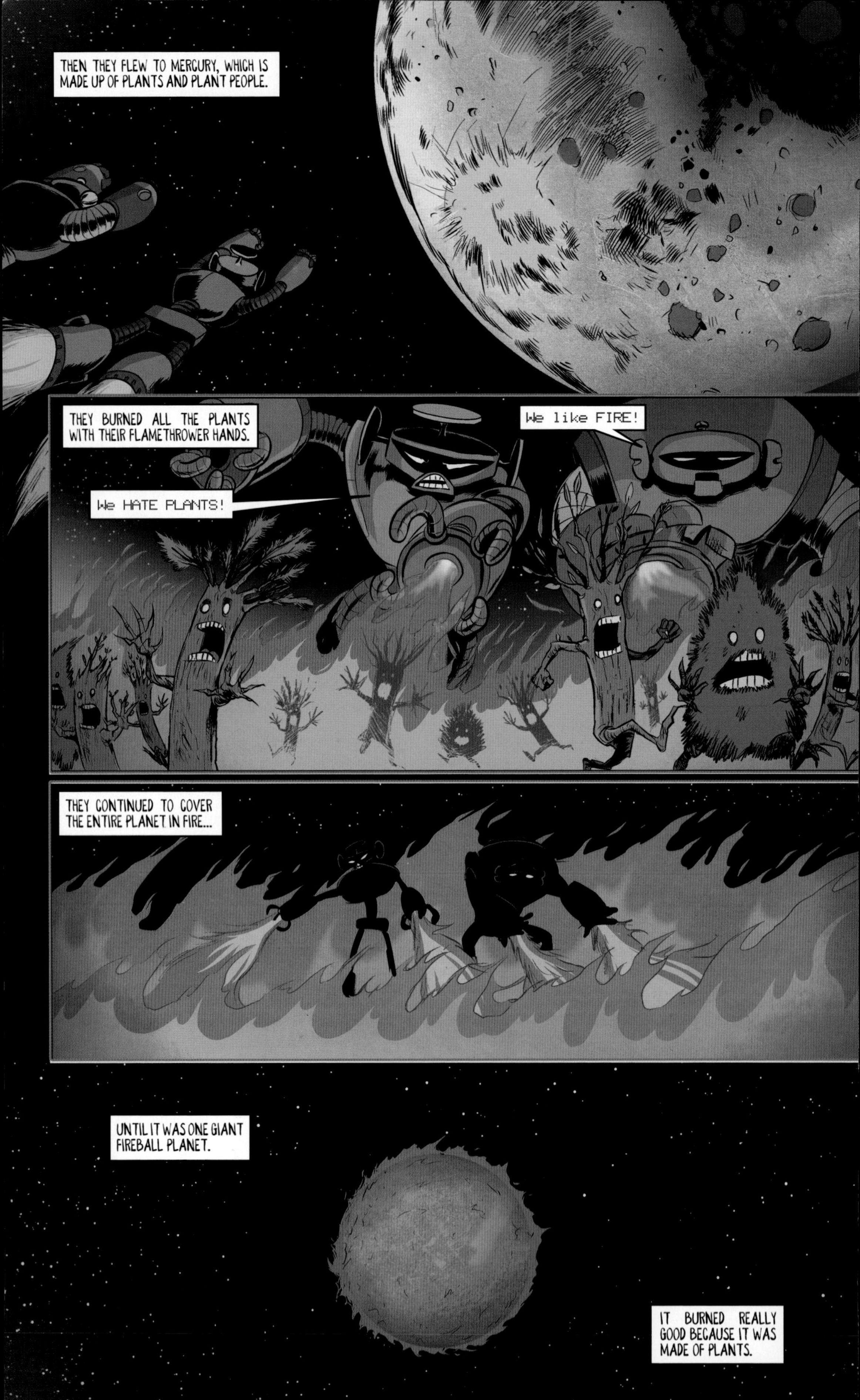
THEN THEY FLEW TO MERCURY, WHICH IS MADE UP OF PLANTS AND PLANT PEOPLE.
THEY BURNED ALL THE PLANTS WITH THEIR FLAMETHROWER HANDS.
We HATE PLANTS!
We like FIRE!
THEY CONTINUED TO COVER THE ENTIRE PLANET IN FIRE...
UNTIL IT WAS ONE GIANT FIREBALL PLANET.
IT BURNED REALLY GOOD BECAUSE IT WAS MADE OF PLANTS.

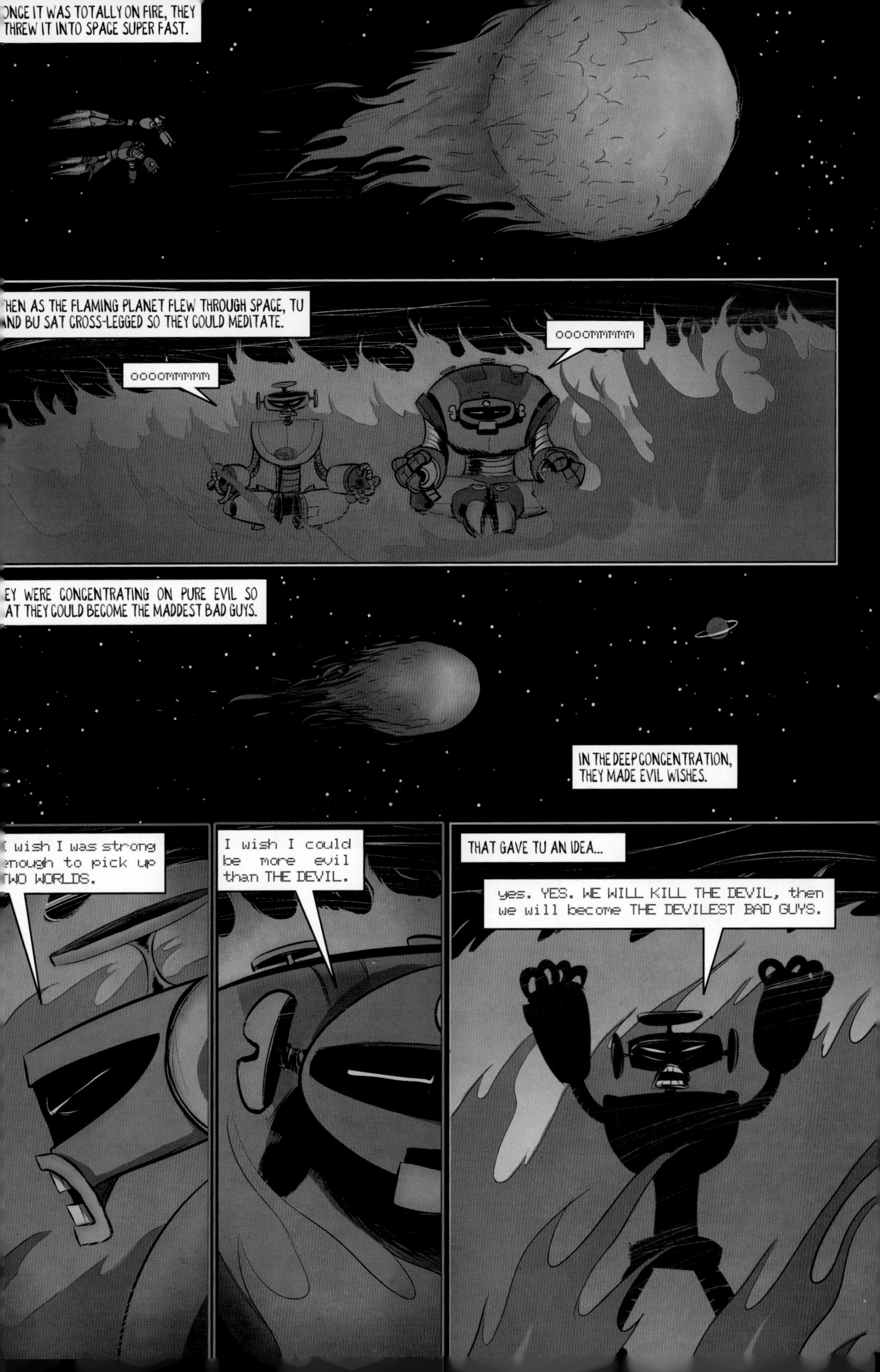
ONCE IT WAS TOTALLY ON FIRE, THEY THREW IT INTO SPACE SUPER FAST.
HEN AS THE FLAMING PLANET FLEW THROUGH SPACE, TU ND BU SAT CROSS-LEGGED SO THEY COULD MEDITATE.
OOOOMMMMM
OOOOMMMMM
EY WERE CONCENTRATING ON PURE EVIL SO AT THEY COULD BECOME THE MADDEST BAD GUYS.
IN THE DEEP CONCENTRATION, THEY MADE EVIL WISHES.
I wish I was strong enough to pick up TWO WORLDS.
I wish I could be more evil than THE DEVIL.
THAT GAVE TU AN IDEA...
yes. YES. WE WILL KILL THE DEVIL, then we will become THE DEVILEST BAD GUYS.

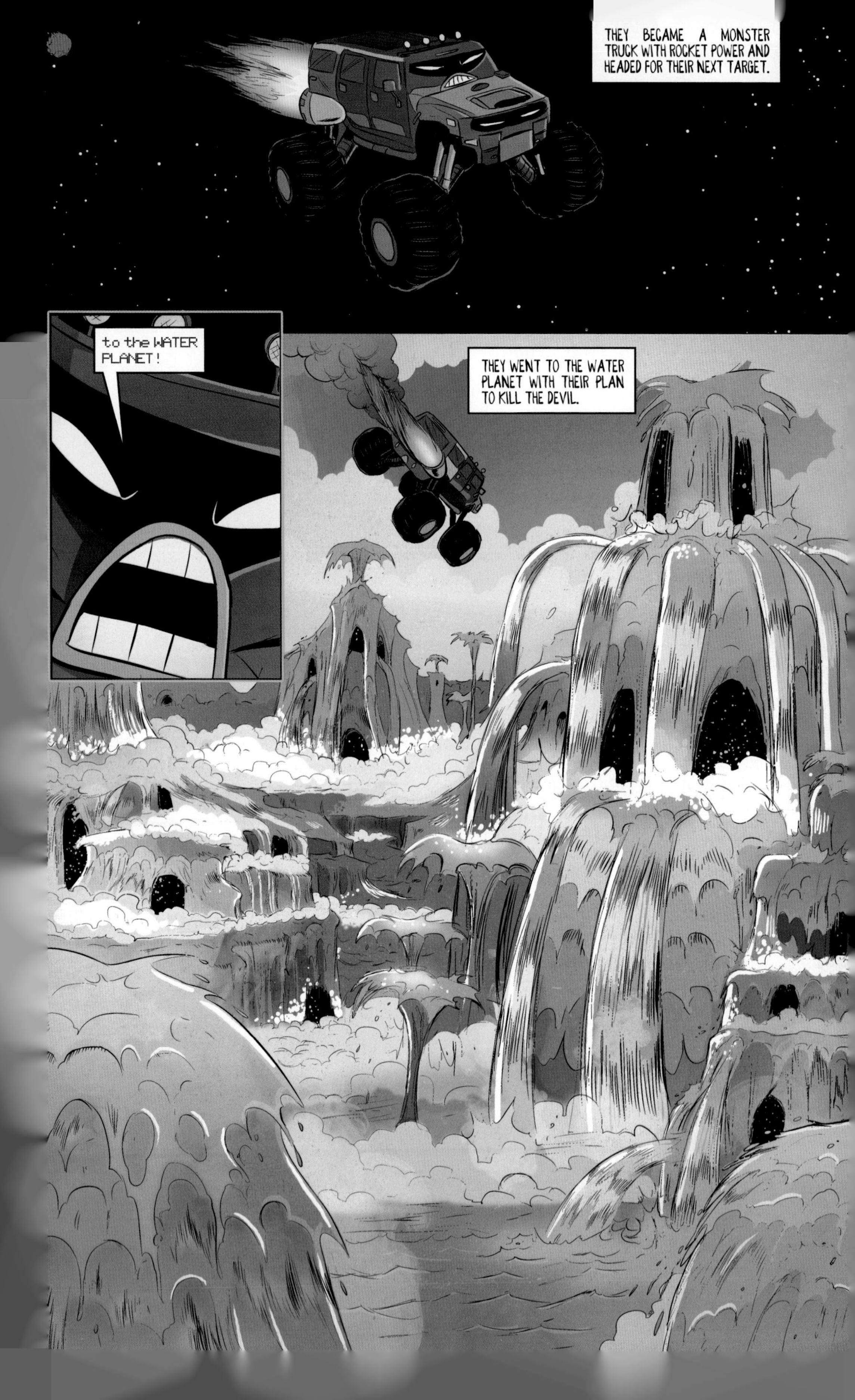
THEY BECAME A MONSTER TRUCK WITH ROCKET POWER AND HEADED FOR THEIR NEXT TARGET.
to the WATER PLANET!
THEY WENT TO THE WATER PLANET WITH THEIR PLAN TO KILL THE DEVIL.

THEY USED HUGE STRAWS AND DRANK ALL THE WATER ON THE WATER PLANET.

SLURRP! SLURRP!

now we kidnap the Water Queen.

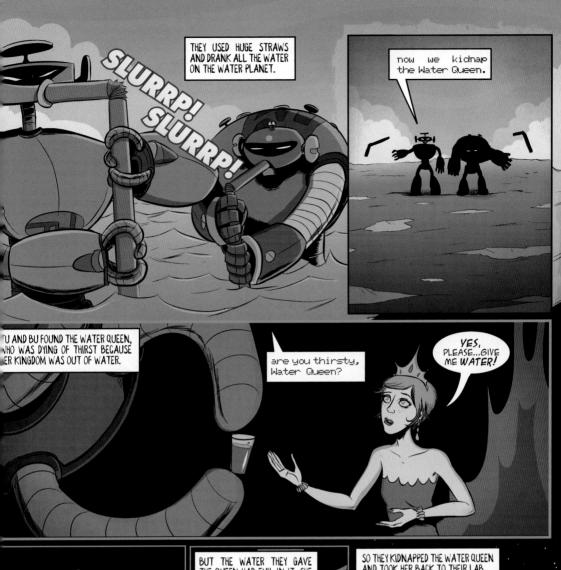

TU AND BU FOUND THE WATER QUEEN, WHO WAS DYING OF THIRST BECAUSE HER KINGDOM WAS OUT OF WATER.

are you thirsty, Water Queen?

YES, PLEASE...GIVE ME WATER!

GLUG! GLUG! GLUG!

BUT THE WATER THEY GAVE THE QUEEN HAD EVIL IN IT. SHE IMMEDIATELY TURNED BAD.

SO THEY KIDNAPPED THE WATER QUEEN AND TOOK HER BACK TO THEIR LAB.

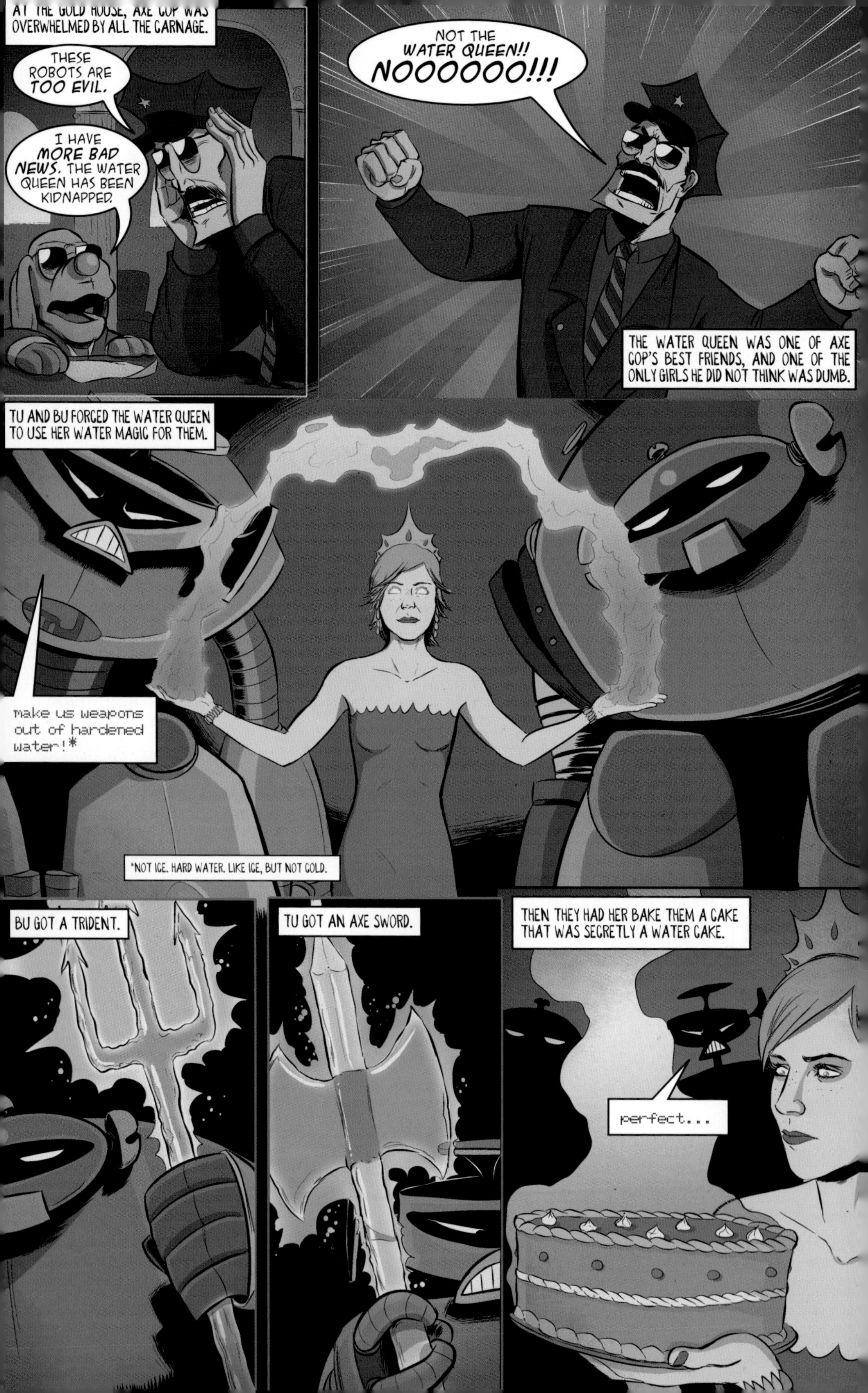
AT THE GOLD HOUSE, AXE COP WAS OVERWHELMED BY ALL THE CARNAGE.
THESE ROBOTS ARE TOO EVIL.
I HAVE MORE BAD NEWS. THE WATER QUEEN HAS BEEN KIDNAPPED.
NOT THE WATER QUEEN!! NOOOOOO!!!
THE WATER QUEEN WAS ONE OF AXE COP'S BEST FRIENDS, AND ONE OF THE ONLY GIRLS HE DID NOT THINK WAS DUMB.
TU AND BU FORCED THE WATER QUEEN TO USE HER WATER MAGIC FOR THEM.
make us weapons out of hardened water!*
*NOT ICE. HARD WATER. LIKE ICE, BUT NOT COLD.
BU GOT A TRIDENT.
TU GOT AN AXE SWORD.
THEN THEY HAD HER BAKE THEM A CAKE THAT WAS SECRETLY A WATER CAKE.
perfect...

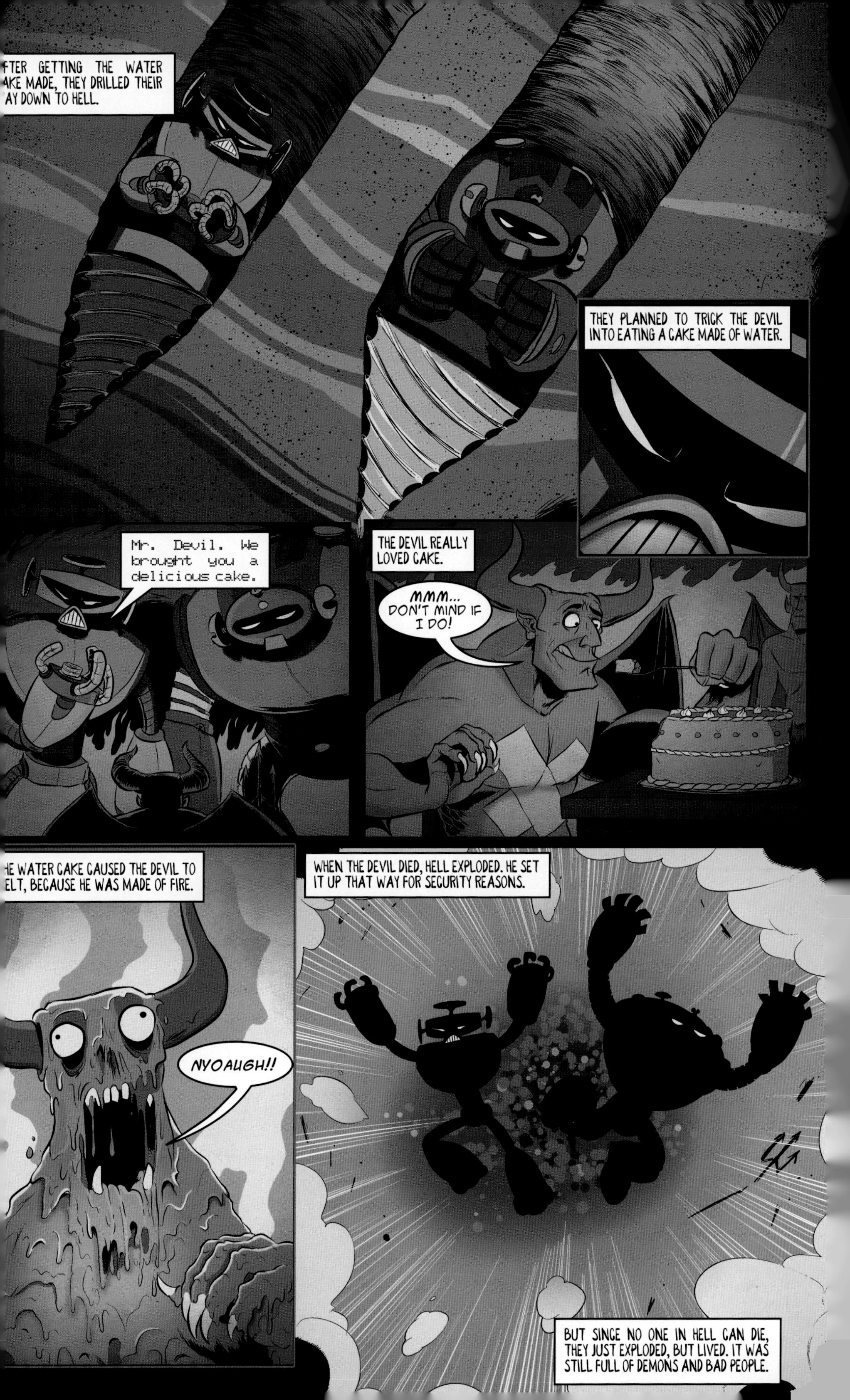
FTER GETTING THE WATER
AKE MADE, THEY DRILLED THEIR
AY DOWN TO HELL.
THEY PLANNED TO TRICK THE DEVIL INTO EATING A CAKE MADE OF WATER.
Mr. Devil. We brought you a delicious cake.
THE DEVIL REALLY LOVED CAKE.
MMM... DON'T MIND IF I DO!
HE WATER CAKE CAUSED THE DEVIL TO ELT, BECAUSE HE WAS MADE OF FIRE.
NYOAUGH!!
WHEN THE DEVIL DIED, HELL EXPLODED. HE SET IT UP THAT WAY FOR SECURITY REASONS.
BUT SINCE NO ONE IN HELL CAN DIE, THEY JUST EXPLODED, BUT LIVED. IT WAS STILL FULL OF DEMONS AND BAD PEOPLE.

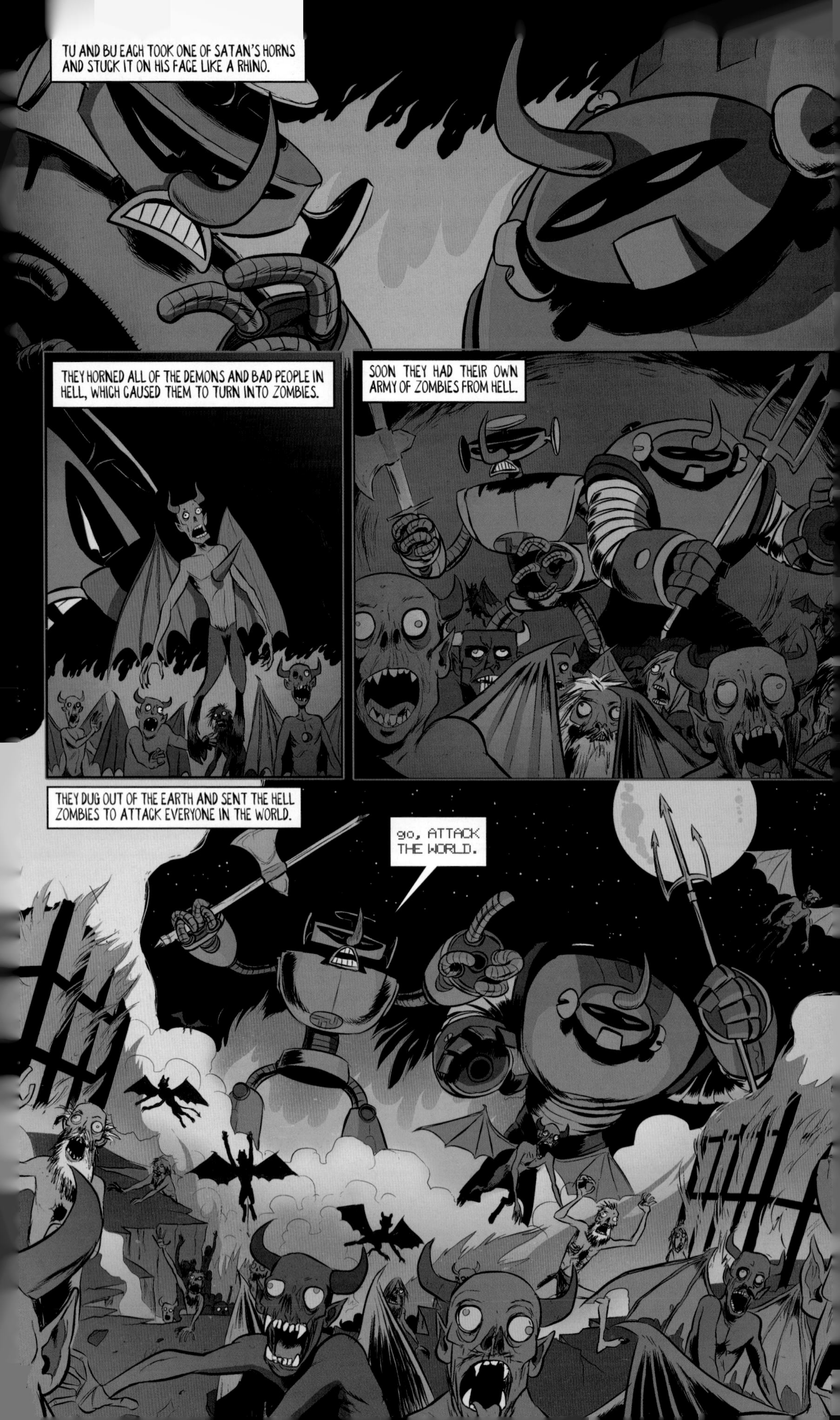
TU AND BU EACH TOOK ONE OF SATAN'S HORNS AND STUCK IT ON HIS FACE LIKE A RHINO.
THEY HORNED ALL OF THE DEMONS AND BAD PEOPLE IN HELL, WHICH CAUSED THEM TO TURN INTO ZOMBIES.
SOON THEY HAD THEIR OWN ARMY OF ZOMBIES FROM HELL.
THEY DUG OUT OF THE EARTH AND SENT THE HELL ZOMBIES TO ATTACK EVERYONE IN THE WORLD.
go, ATTACK THE WORLD.

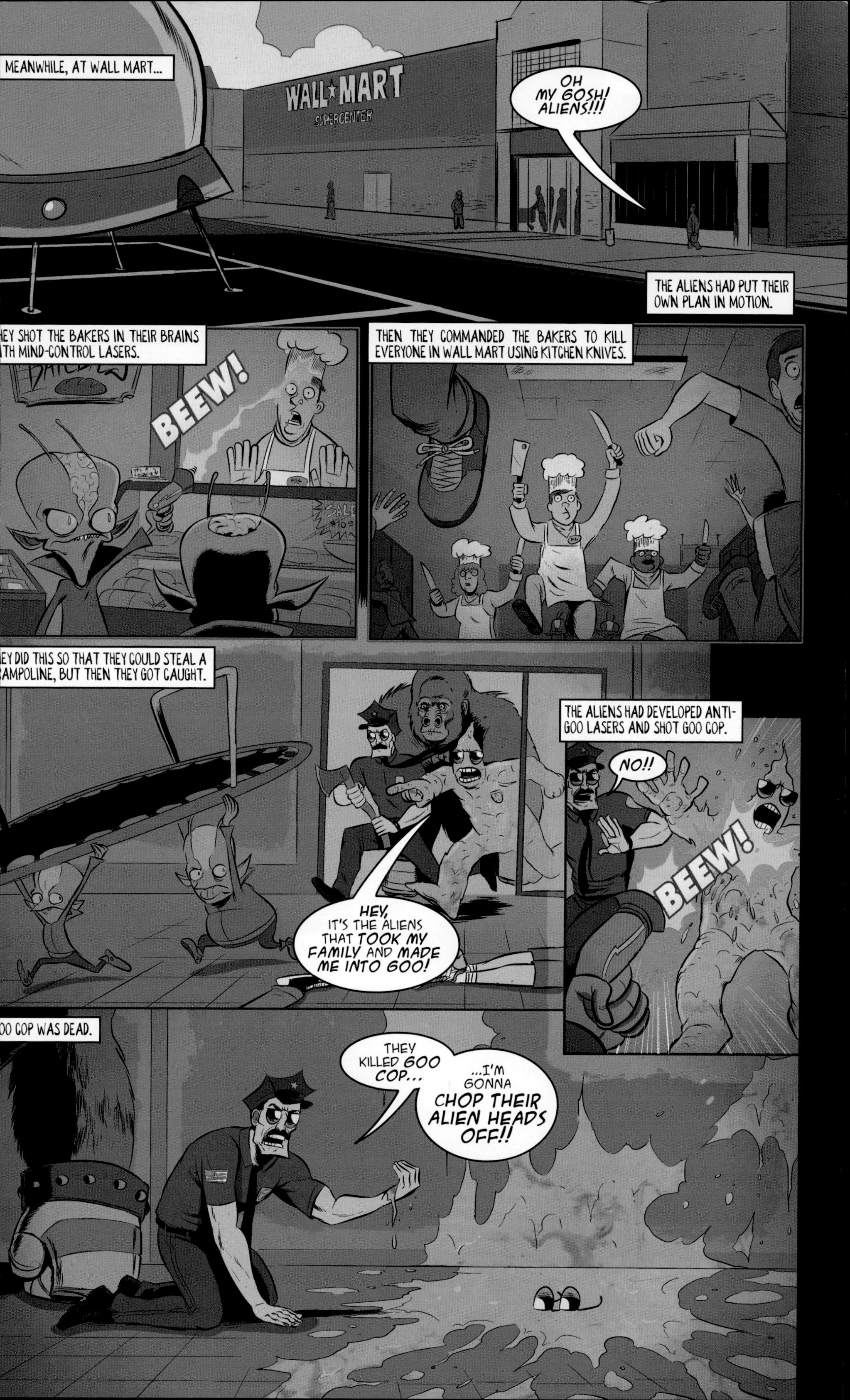

MEANWHILE, AT WALL MART...
WALL★MART
SUPERCENTER
OH MY GOSH! ALIENS!!!
THE ALIENS HAD PUT THEIR OWN PLAN IN MOTION.
HEY SHOT THE BAKERS IN THEIR BRAINS
ITH MIND-CONTROL LASERS.
BEEW!
THEN THEY COMMANDED THE BAKERS TO KILL EVERYONE IN WALL MART USING KITCHEN KNIVES.
EY DID THIS SO THAT THEY COULD STEAL A
RAMPOLINE, BUT THEN THEY GOT CAUGHT.
HEY, IT'S THE ALIENS THAT TOOK MY FAMILY AND MADE ME INTO GOO!
THE ALIENS HAD DEVELOPED ANTI-GOO LASERS AND SHOT GOO COP.
NO!!
BEEW!
OO COP WAS DEAD.
THEY KILLED GOO COP...
...I'M GONNA CHOP THEIR ALIEN HEADS OFF!!

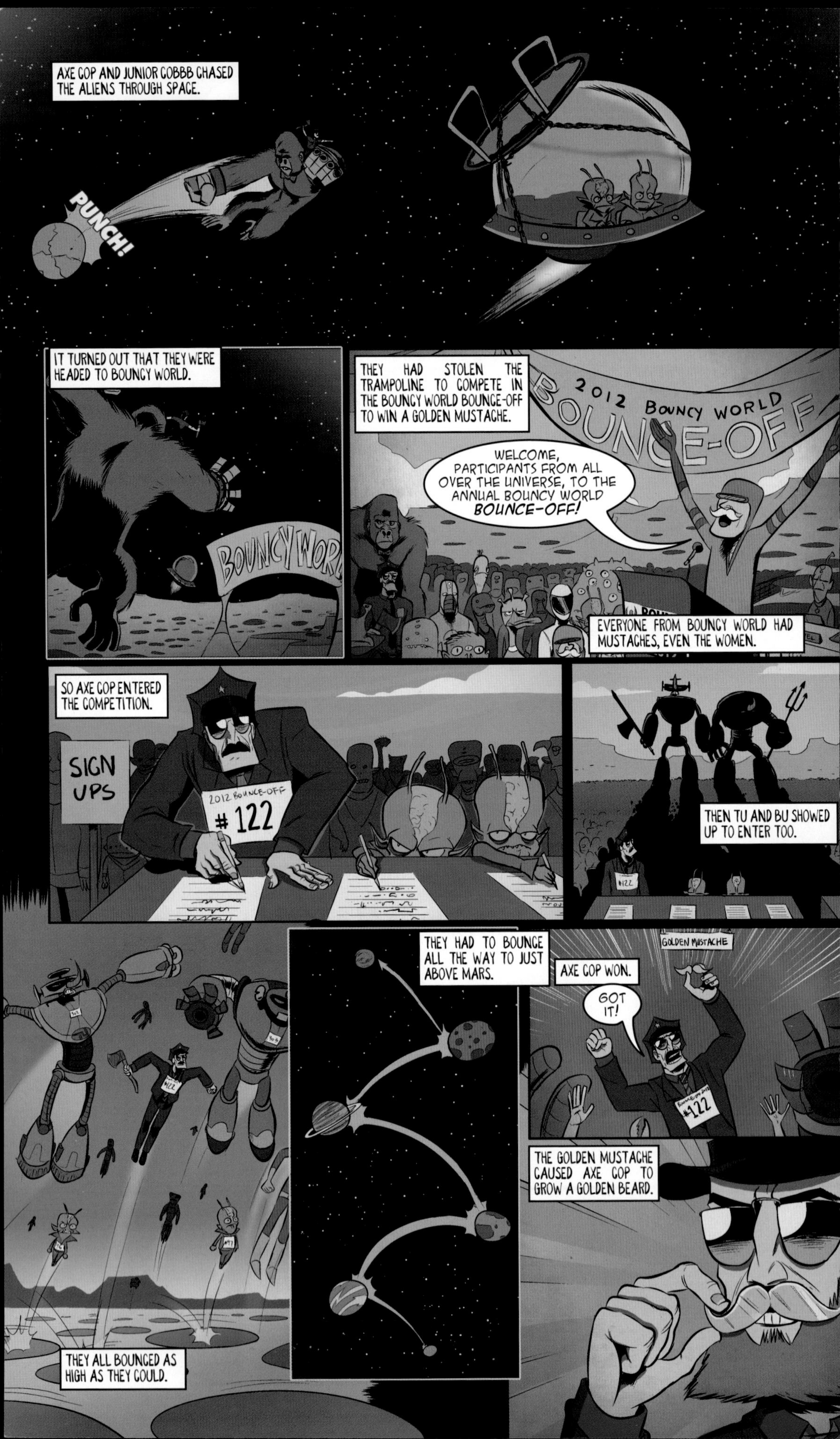
AXE COP AND JUNIOR COBBB CHASED THE ALIENS THROUGH SPACE.
PUNCH!
IT TURNED OUT THAT THEY WERE HEADED TO BOUNCY WORLD.
BOUNCY WORLD
THEY HAD STOLEN THE TRAMPOLINE TO COMPETE IN THE BOUNCY WORLD BOUNCE-OFF TO WIN A GOLDEN MUSTACHE.
2012 BOUNCY WORLD BOUNCE-OFF
WELCOME, PARTICIPANTS FROM ALL OVER THE UNIVERSE, TO THE ANNUAL BOUNCY WORLD BOUNCE-OFF!
EVERYONE FROM BOUNCY WORLD HAD MUSTACHES, EVEN THE WOMEN.
SO AXE COP ENTERED THE COMPETITION.
SIGN UPS
2012 BOUNCE-OFF
122
THEN TU AND BU SHOWED UP TO ENTER TOO.
THEY ALL BOUNCED AS HIGH AS THEY COULD.
THEY HAD TO BOUNCE ALL THE WAY TO JUST ABOVE MARS.
AXE COP WON.
GOLDEN MUSTACHE
GOT IT!
#122
THE GOLDEN MUSTACHE CAUSED AXE COP TO GROW A GOLDEN BEARD.

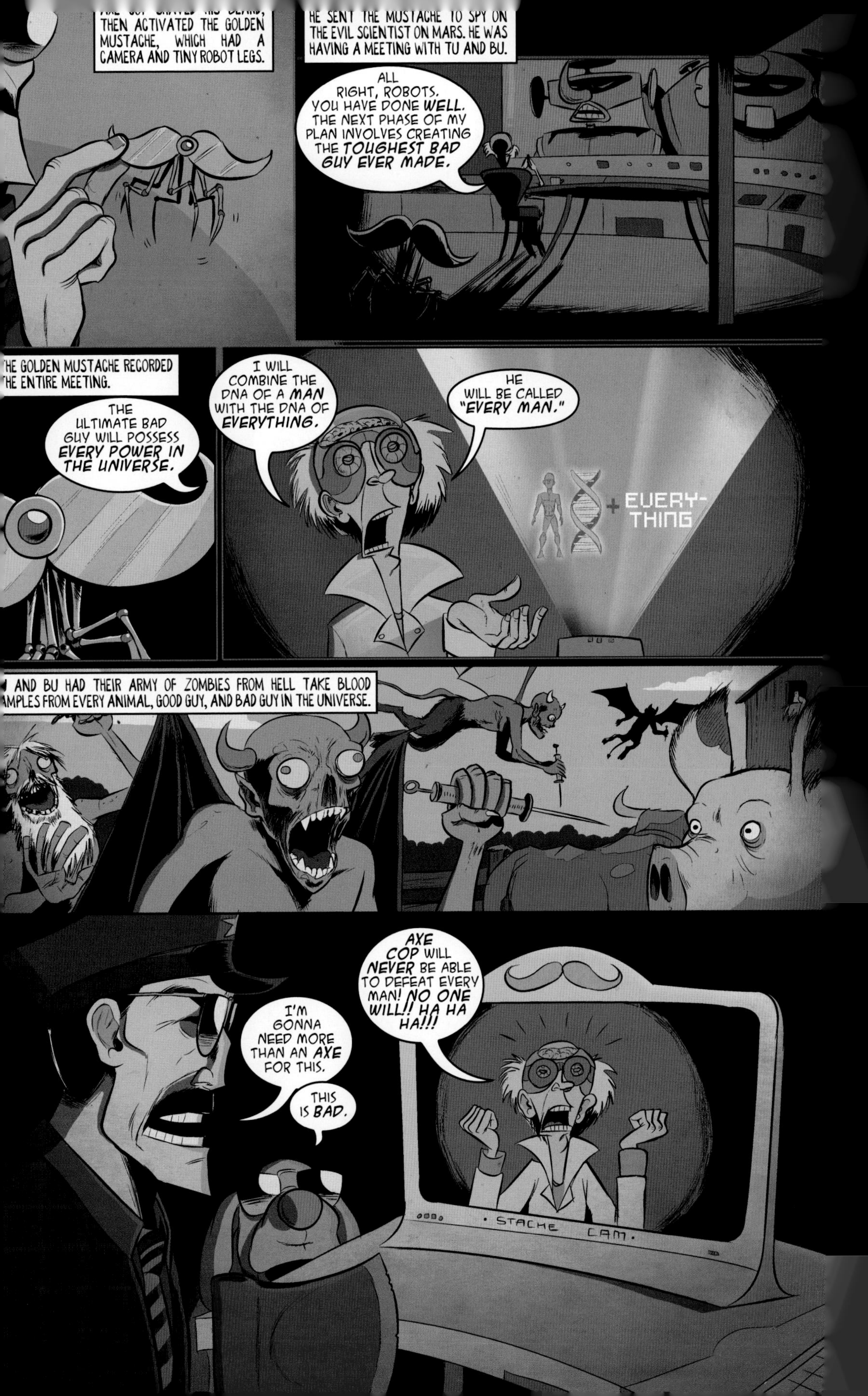

THEN ACTIVATED THE GOLDEN MUSTACHE, WHICH HAD A CAMERA AND TINY ROBOT LEGS.
HE SENT THE MUSTACHE TO SPY ON THE EVIL SCIENTIST ON MARS. HE WAS HAVING A MEETING WITH TU AND BU.
ALL RIGHT, ROBOTS. YOU HAVE DONE WELL. THE NEXT PHASE OF MY PLAN INVOLVES CREATING THE TOUGHEST BAD GUY EVER MADE.
THE GOLDEN MUSTACHE RECORDED THE ENTIRE MEETING.
THE ULTIMATE BAD GUY WILL POSSESS EVERY POWER IN THE UNIVERSE.
I WILL COMBINE THE DNA OF A MAN WITH THE DNA OF EVERYTHING.
HE WILL BE CALLED "EVERY MAN."
+ EVERY-THING
AND BU HAD THEIR ARMY OF ZOMBIES FROM HELL TAKE BLOOD AMPLES FROM EVERY ANIMAL, GOOD GUY, AND BAD GUY IN THE UNIVERSE.
AXE COP WILL NEVER BE ABLE TO DEFEAT EVERY MAN! NO ONE WILL!! HA HA HA!!!
I'M GONNA NEED MORE THAN AN AXE FOR THIS.
THIS IS BAD.
STACHE CAM.

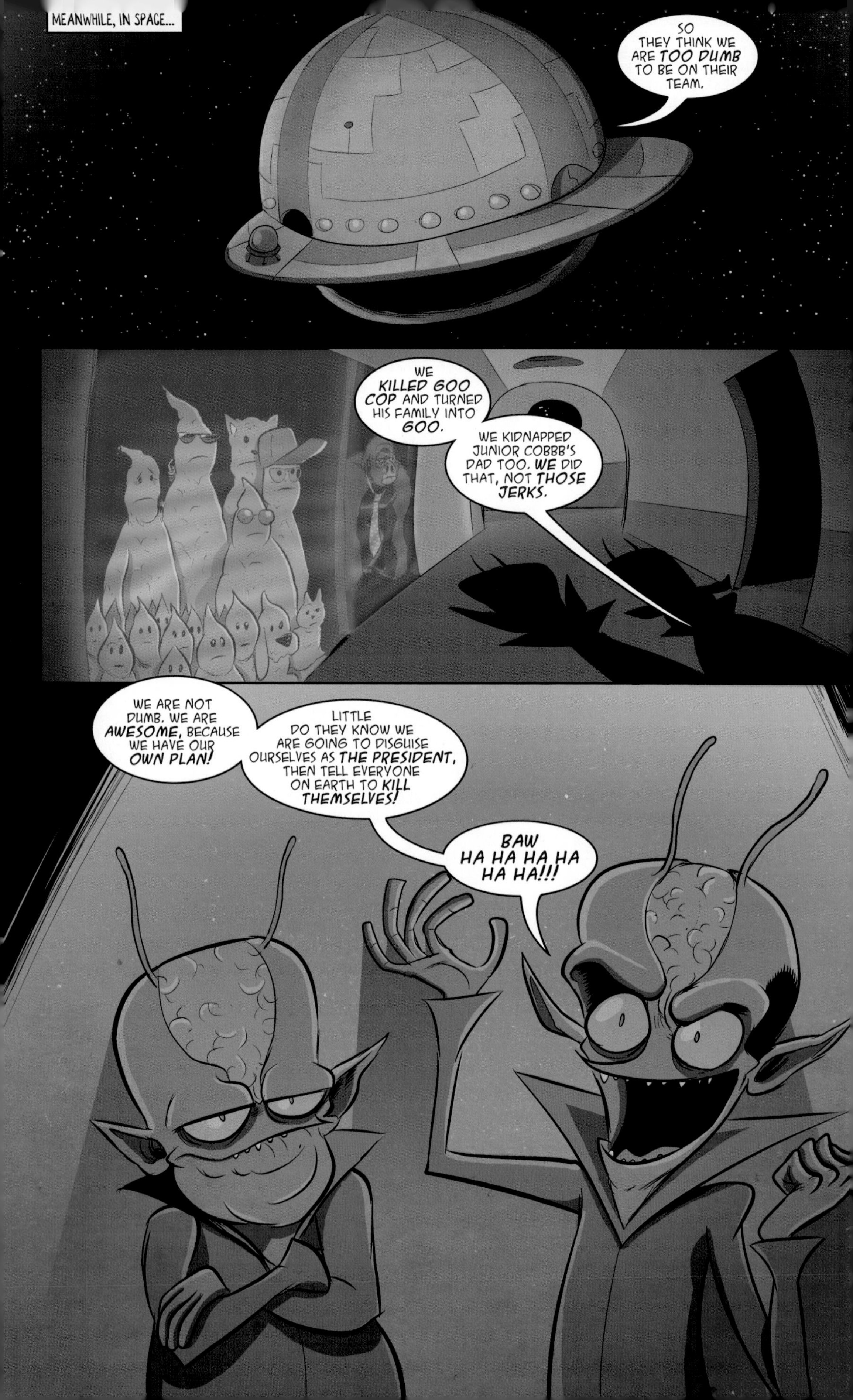
MEANWHILE, IN SPACE...
SO THEY THINK WE ARE TOO DUMB TO BE ON THEIR TEAM.
WE KILLED GOO COP AND TURNED HIS FAMILY INTO GOO.
WE KIDNAPPED JUNIOR COBBB'S DAD TOO. WE DID THAT, NOT THOSE JERKS.
WE ARE NOT DUMB. WE ARE AWESOME, BECAUSE WE HAVE OUR OWN PLAN!
LITTLE DO THEY KNOW WE ARE GOING TO DISGUISE OURSELVES AS THE PRESIDENT, THEN TELL EVERYONE ON EARTH TO KILL THEMSELVES!
BAW HA HA HA HA HA HA!!!

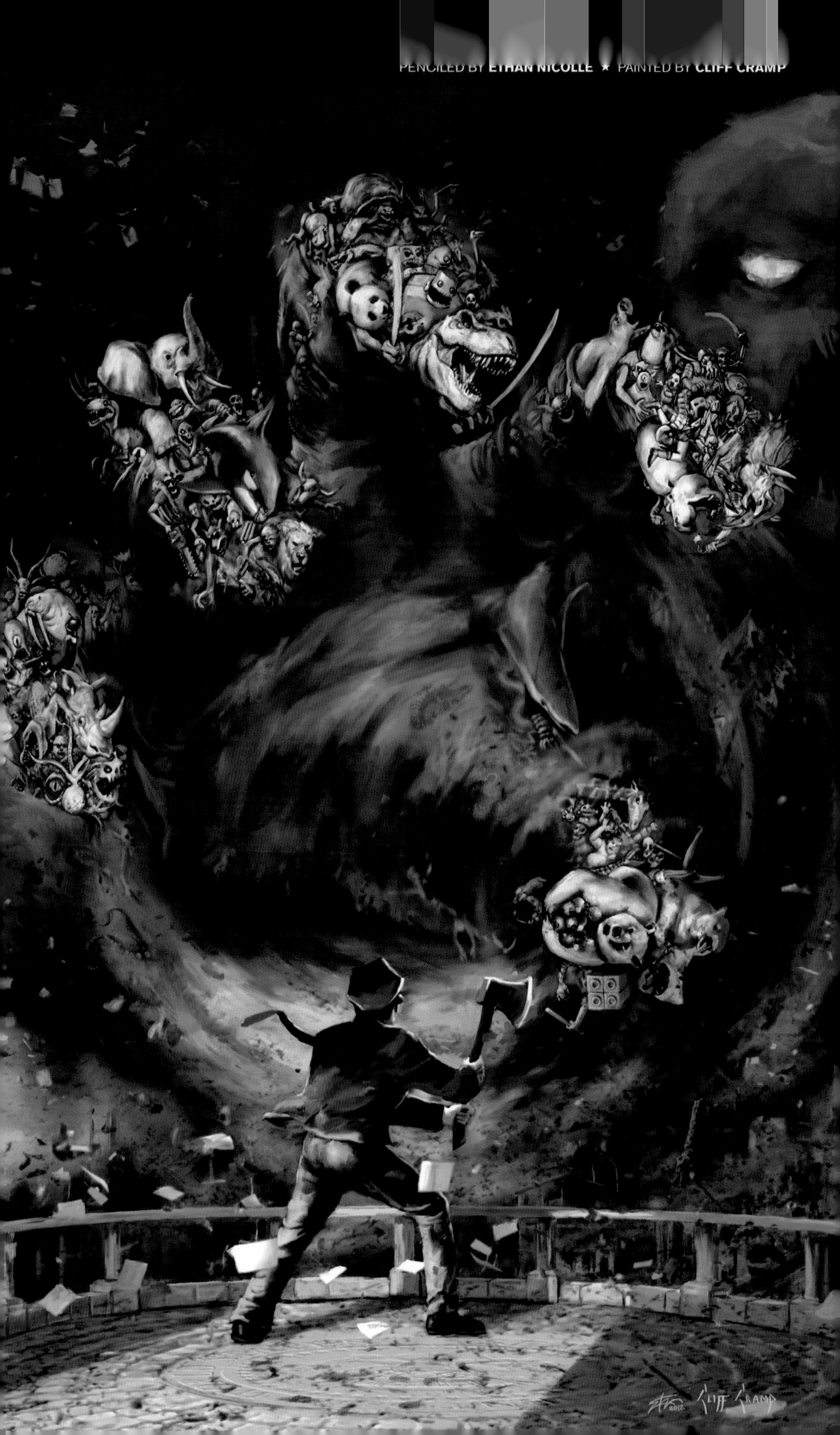
PENCILED BY ETHAN NICOLLE ★ PAINTED BY CLIFF CRAMP

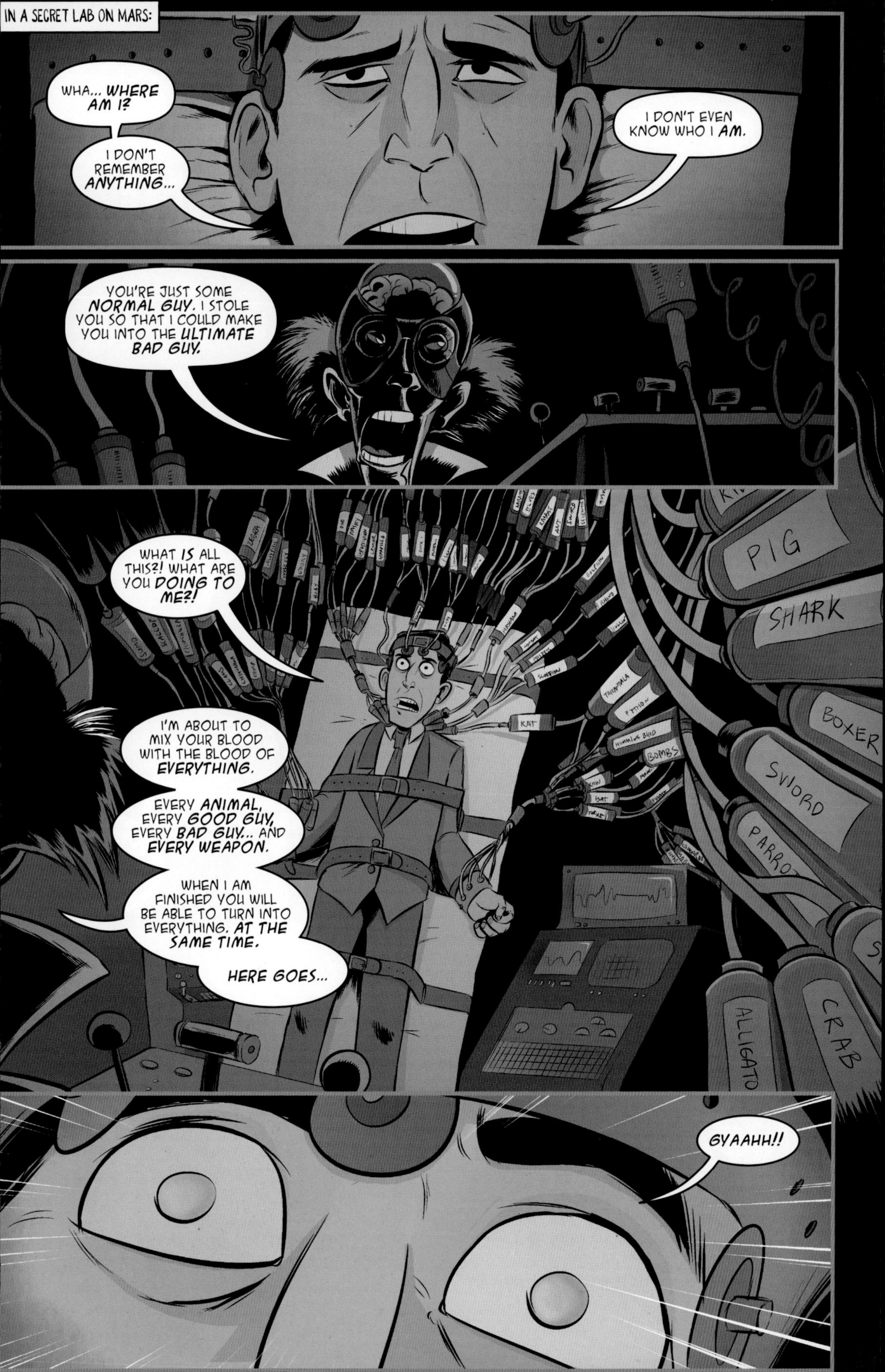
IN A SECRET LAB ON MARS:
WHA... WHERE AM I?
I DON'T REMEMBER ANYTHING...
I DON'T EVEN KNOW WHO I AM.
YOU'RE JUST SOME NORMAL GUY. I STOLE YOU SO THAT I COULD MAKE YOU INTO THE ULTIMATE BAD GUY.
WHAT IS ALL THIS?! WHAT ARE YOU DOING TO ME?!
I'M ABOUT TO MIX YOUR BLOOD WITH THE BLOOD OF EVERYTHING.
EVERY ANIMAL, EVERY GOOD GUY, EVERY BAD GUY... AND EVERY WEAPON.
WHEN I AM FINISHED YOU WILL BE ABLE TO TURN INTO EVERYTHING. AT THE SAME TIME.
HERE GOES...
PIG
SHARK
BOXER
SWORD
RAT
BOMBS
CRAB
GYAAHH!!

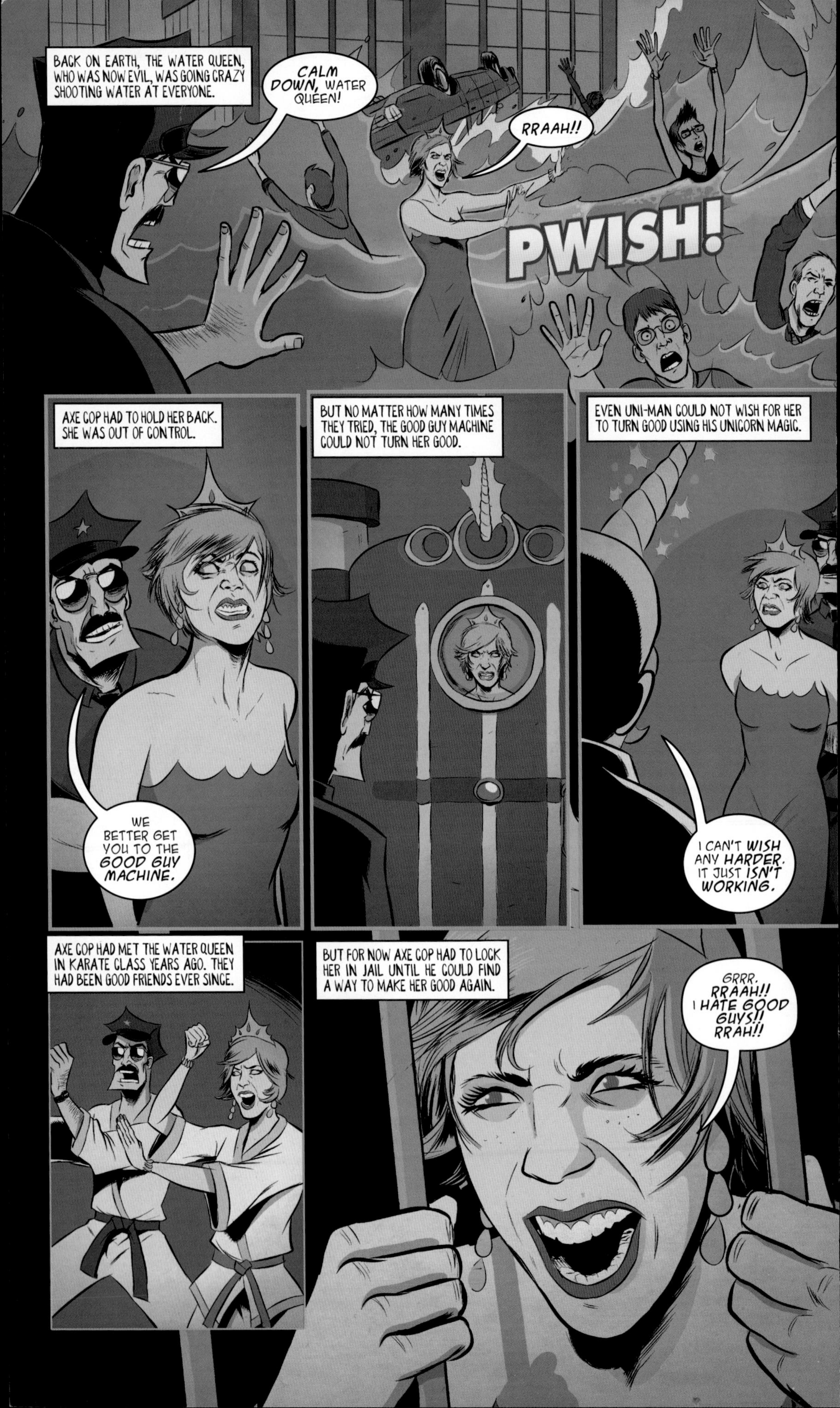
BACK ON EARTH, THE WATER QUEEN, WHO WAS NOW EVIL, WAS GOING CRAZY SHOOTING WATER AT EVERYONE.
CALM DOWN, WATER QUEEN!
RRAAH!!
PWISH!
AXE COP HAD TO HOLD HER BACK. SHE WAS OUT OF CONTROL.
WE BETTER GET YOU TO THE GOOD GUY MACHINE.
BUT NO MATTER HOW MANY TIMES THEY TRIED, THE GOOD GUY MACHINE COULD NOT TURN HER GOOD.
EVEN UNI-MAN COULD NOT WISH FOR HER TO TURN GOOD USING HIS UNICORN MAGIC.
I CAN'T WISH ANY HARDER. IT JUST ISN'T WORKING.
AXE COP HAD MET THE WATER QUEEN IN KARATE CLASS YEARS AGO. THEY HAD BEEN GOOD FRIENDS EVER SINCE.
BUT FOR NOW AXE COP HAD TO LOCK HER IN JAIL UNTIL HE COULD FIND A WAY TO MAKE HER GOOD AGAIN.
GRRR. RRAAH!! I HATE GOOD GUYS!! RRAH!!

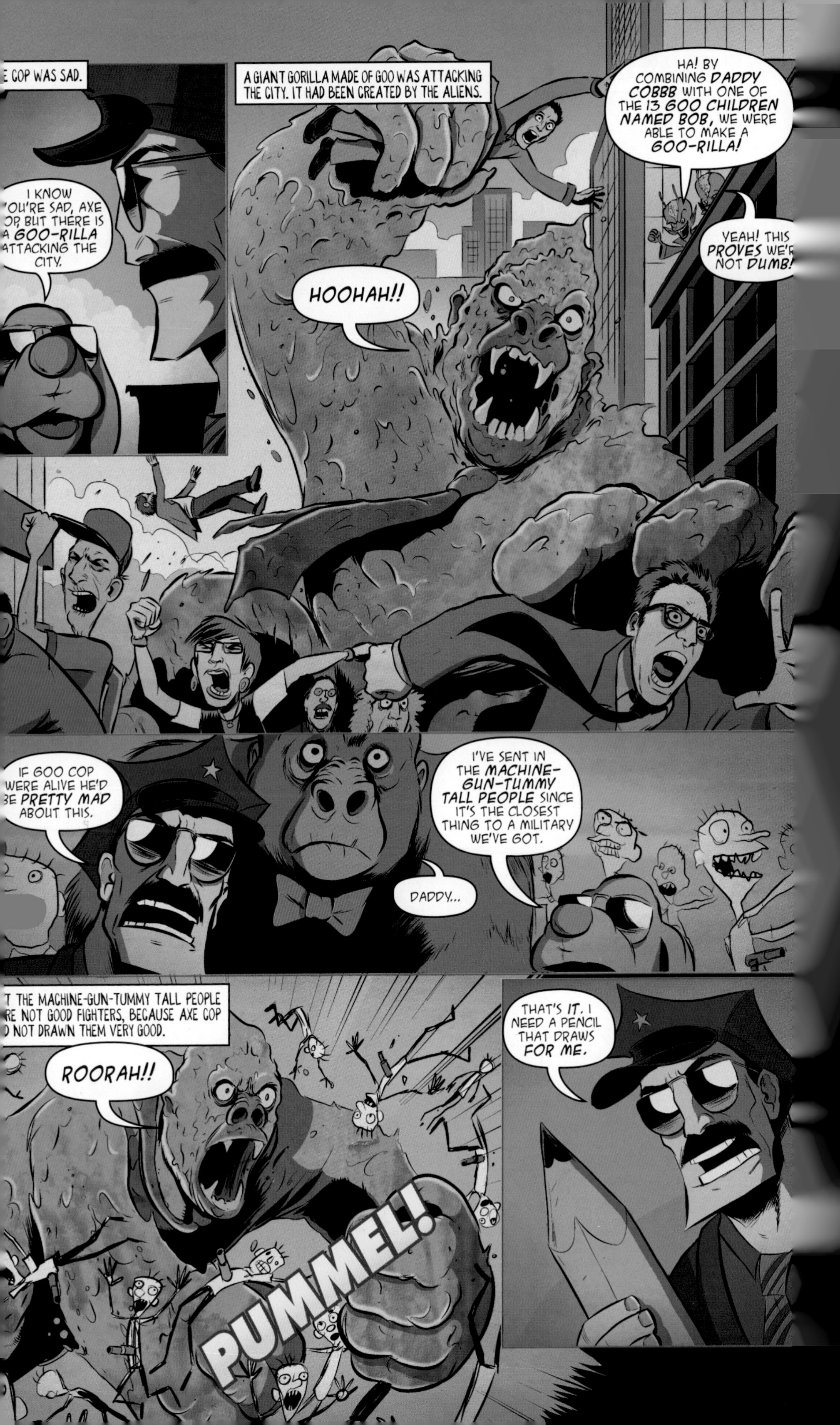

E COP WAS SAD.
I KNOW OU'RE SAD, AXE OP, BUT THERE IS A GOO-RILLA ATTACKING THE CITY.
A GIANT GORILLA MADE OF GOO WAS ATTACKING THE CITY. IT HAD BEEN CREATED BY THE ALIENS.
HA! BY COMBINING DADDY COBBB WITH ONE OF THE 13 GOO CHILDREN NAMED BOB, WE WERE ABLE TO MAKE A GOO-RILLA!
YEAH! THIS PROVES WE'R NOT DUMB!
HOOHAH!!
IF GOO COP WERE ALIVE HE'D BE PRETTY MAD ABOUT THIS.
DADDY...
I'VE SENT IN THE MACHINE-GUN-TUMMY TALL PEOPLE SINCE IT'S THE CLOSEST THING TO A MILITARY WE'VE GOT.
T THE MACHINE-GUN-TUMMY TALL PEOPLE RE NOT GOOD FIGHTERS, BECAUSE AXE COP D NOT DRAWN THEM VERY GOOD.
ROORAH!!
PUMMEL!
THAT'S IT. I NEED A PENCIL THAT DRAWS FOR ME.

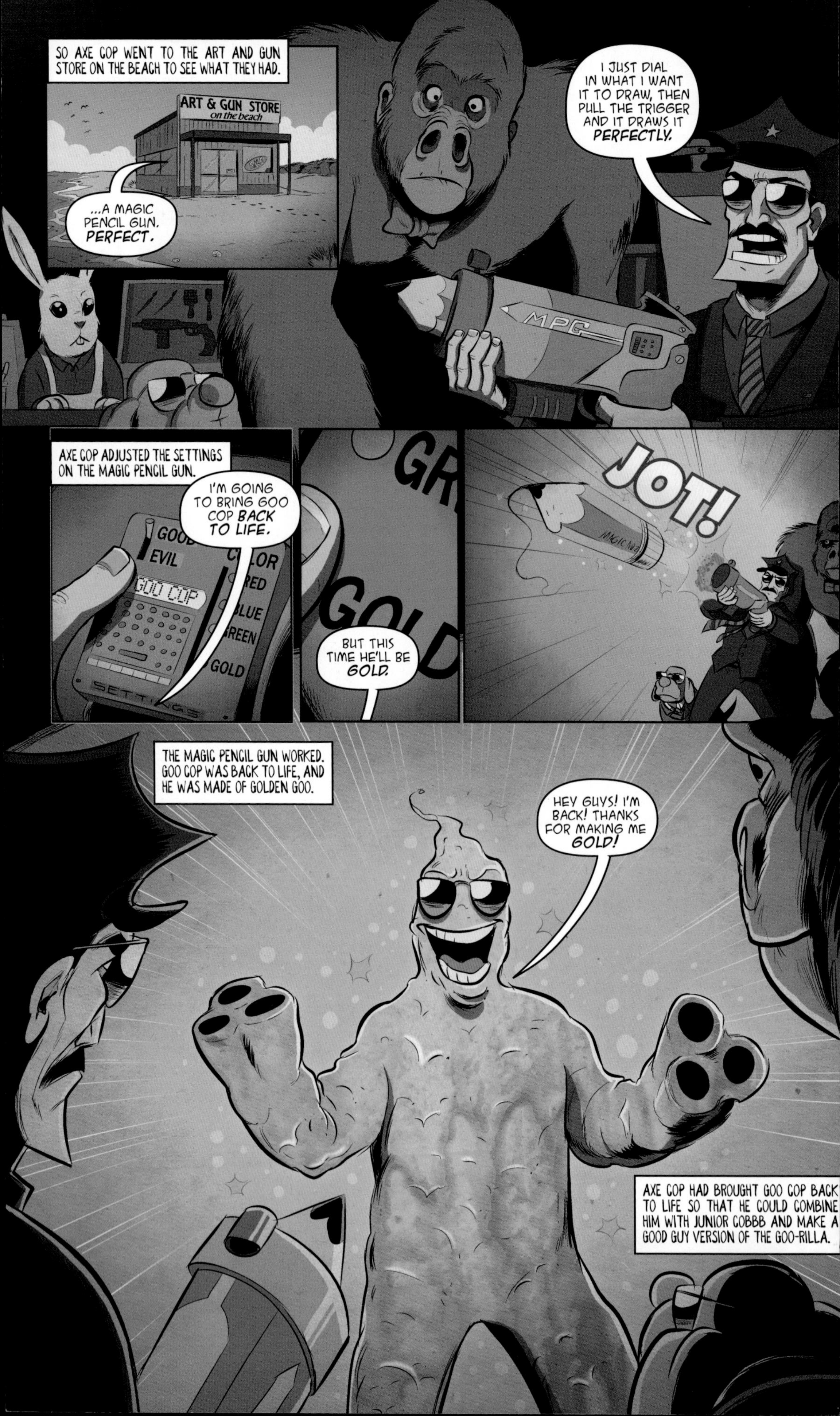
SO AXE COP WENT TO THE ART AND GUN STORE ON THE BEACH TO SEE WHAT THEY HAD.
ART & GUN STORE on the beach
...A MAGIC PENCIL GUN. PERFECT.
I JUST DIAL IN WHAT I WANT IT TO DRAW, THEN PULL THE TRIGGER AND IT DRAWS IT PERFECTLY.
MPG
AXE COP ADJUSTED THE SETTINGS ON THE MAGIC PENCIL GUN.
I'M GOING TO BRING GOO COP BACK TO LIFE.
GOOD
EVIL
GOO COP
COLOR
RED
BLUE
GREEN
GOLD
SETTINGS
BUT THIS TIME HE'LL BE GOLD.
JOT!
THE MAGIC PENCIL GUN WORKED. GOO COP WAS BACK TO LIFE, AND HE WAS MADE OF GOLDEN GOO.
HEY GUYS! I'M BACK! THANKS FOR MAKING ME GOLD!
AXE COP HAD BROUGHT GOO COP BACK TO LIFE SO THAT HE COULD COMBINE HIM WITH JUNIOR COBBB AND MAKE A GOOD GUY VERSION OF THE GOO-RILLA.

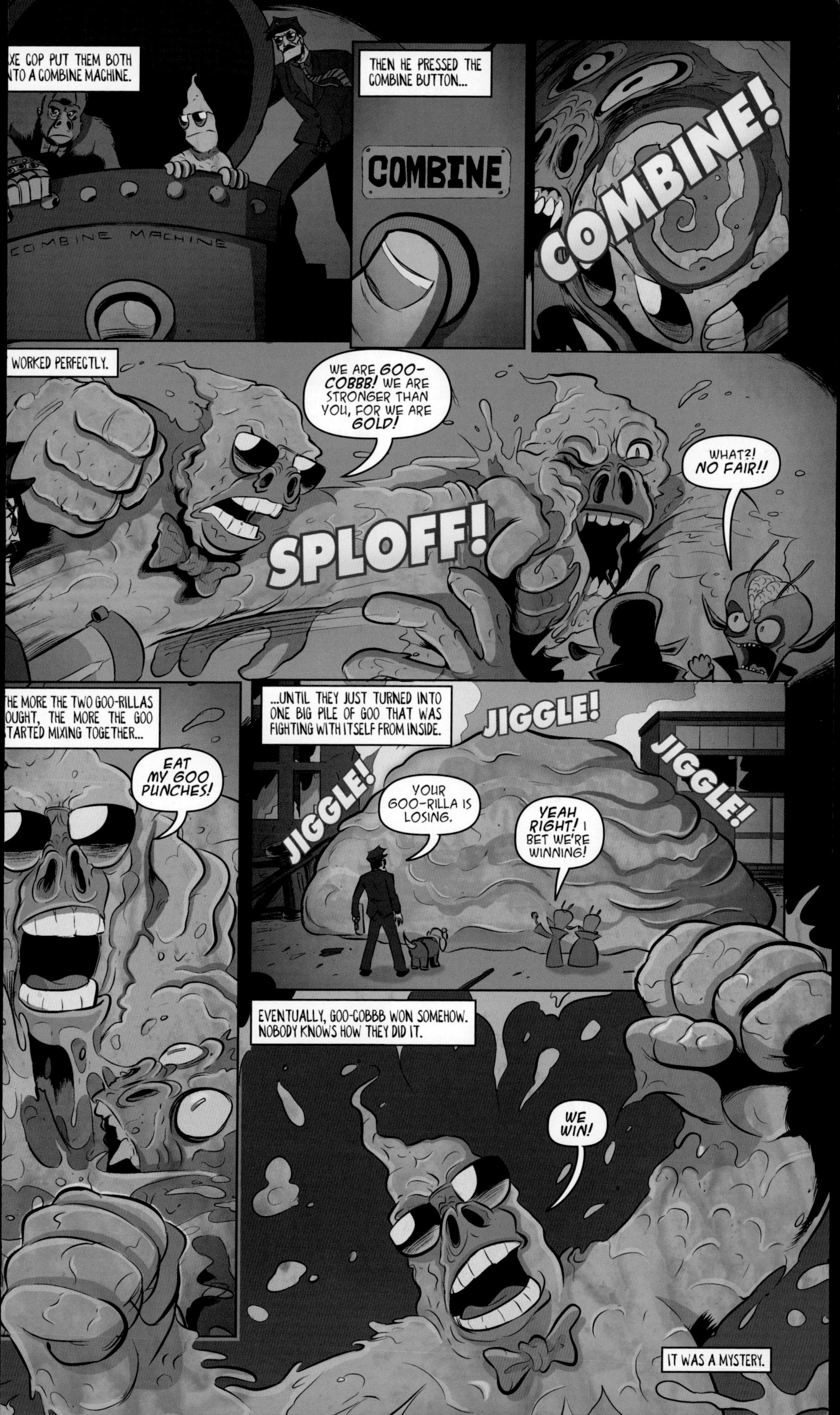

XE COP PUT THEM BOTH
NTO A COMBINE MACHINE.
COMBINE MACHINE
THEN HE PRESSED THE COMBINE BUTTON...
COMBINE
COMBINE!
WORKED PERFECTLY.
WE ARE GOO-COBBB! WE ARE STRONGER THAN YOU, FOR WE ARE GOLD!
SPLOFF!
WHAT?! NO FAIR!!
THE MORE THE TWO GOO-RILLAS FOUGHT, THE MORE THE GOO STARTED MIXING TOGETHER...
EAT MY GOO PUNCHES!
...UNTIL THEY JUST TURNED INTO ONE BIG PILE OF GOO THAT WAS FIGHTING WITH ITSELF FROM INSIDE.
JIGGLE!
JIGGLE!
JIGGLE!
YOUR GOO-RILLA IS LOSING.
YEAH RIGHT! I BET WE'RE WINNING!
EVENTUALLY, GOO-COBBB WON SOMEHOW. NOBODY KNOWS HOW THEY DID IT.
WE WIN!
IT WAS A MYSTERY.

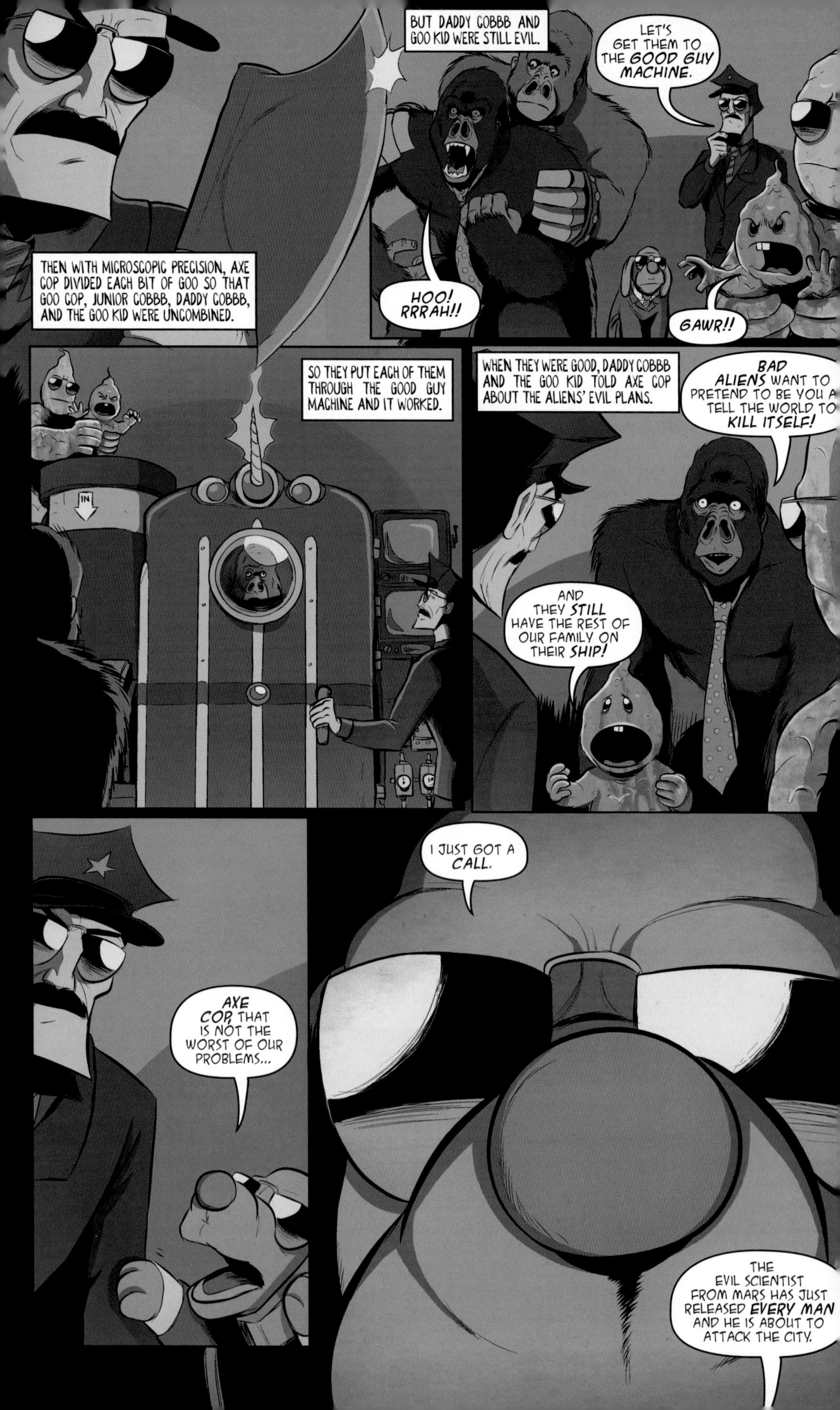
THEN WITH MICROSCOPIC PRECISION, AXE COP DIVIDED EACH BIT OF GOO SO THAT GOO COP, JUNIOR COBBB, DADDY COBBB, AND THE GOO KID WERE UNCOMBINED.
BUT DADDY COBBB AND GOO KID WERE STILL EVIL.
HOO! RRRAH!!
LET'S GET THEM TO THE GOOD GUY MACHINE.
GAWR!!
SO THEY PUT EACH OF THEM THROUGH THE GOOD GUY MACHINE AND IT WORKED.
IN
WHEN THEY WERE GOOD, DADDY COBBB AND THE GOO KID TOLD AXE COP ABOUT THE ALIENS' EVIL PLANS.
BAD ALIENS WANT TO PRETEND TO BE YOU A TELL THE WORLD TO KILL ITSELF!
AND THEY STILL HAVE THE REST OF OUR FAMILY ON THEIR SHIP!
AXE COP, THAT IS NOT THE WORST OF OUR PROBLEMS...
I JUST GOT A CALL.
THE EVIL SCIENTIST FROM MARS HAS JUST RELEASED EVERY MAN AND HE IS ABOUT TO ATTACK THE CITY.

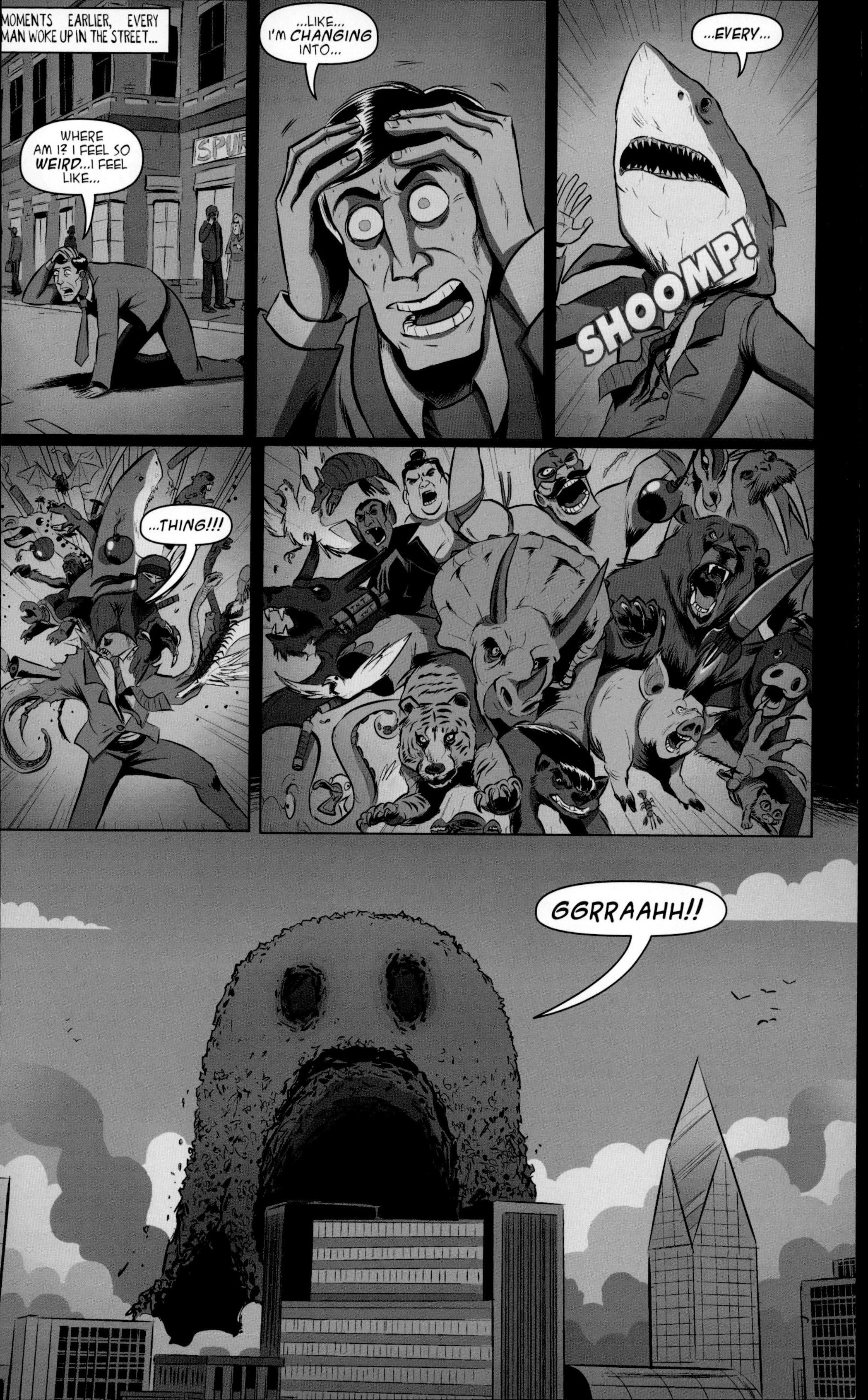
MOMENTS EARLIER, EVERY MAN WOKE UP IN THE STREET...
WHERE AM I? I FEEL SO WEIRD...I FEEL LIKE...
SPUR
...LIKE... I'M CHANGING INTO...
...EVERY...
SHOOMP!
...THING!!!
GGRRAAHH!!

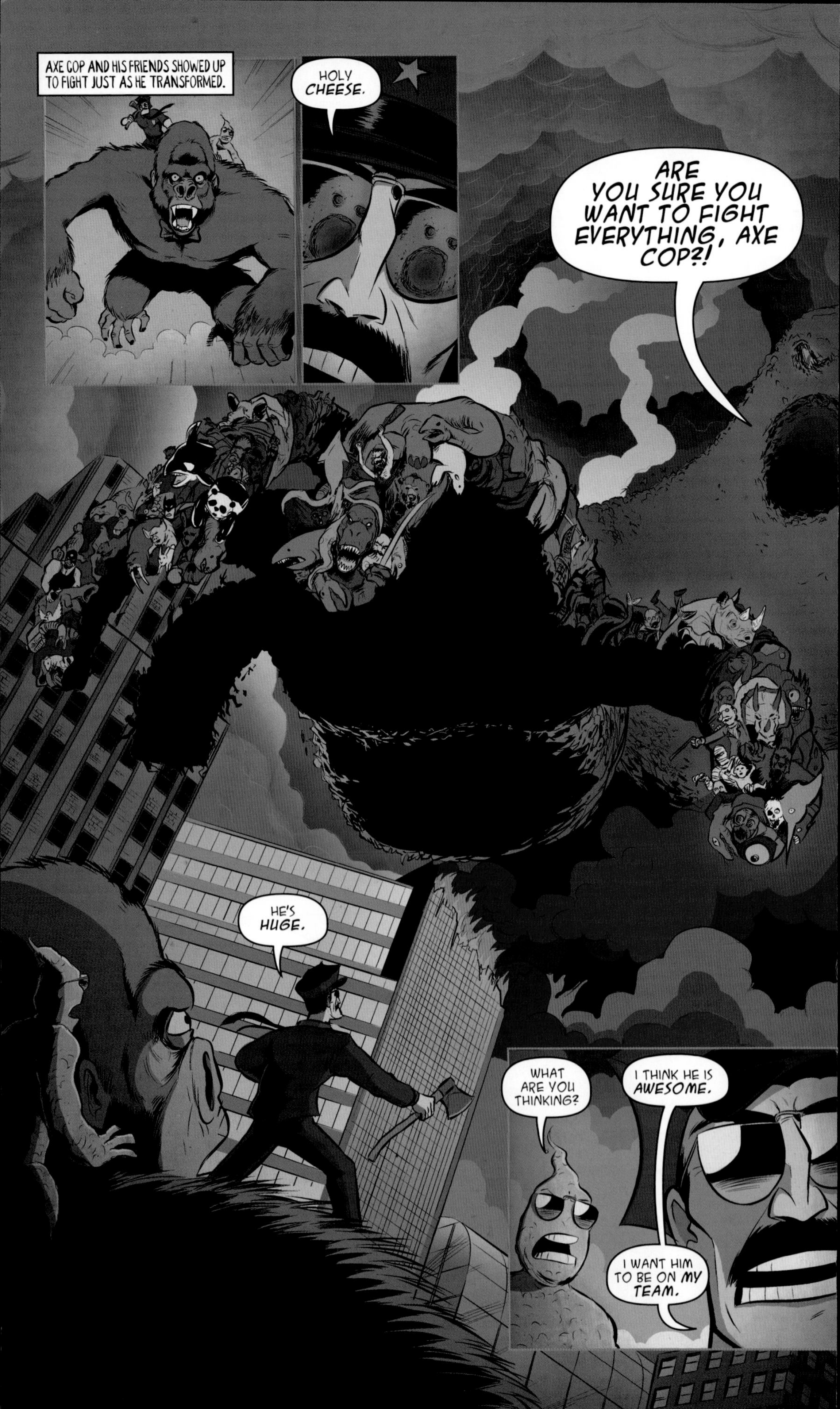
AXE COP AND HIS FRIENDS SHOWED UP TO FIGHT JUST AS HE TRANSFORMED.
HOLY CHEESE.
ARE YOU SURE YOU WANT TO FIGHT EVERYTHING, AXE COP?!
HE'S HUGE.
WHAT ARE YOU THINKING?
I THINK HE IS AWESOME.
I WANT HIM TO BE ON MY TEAM.

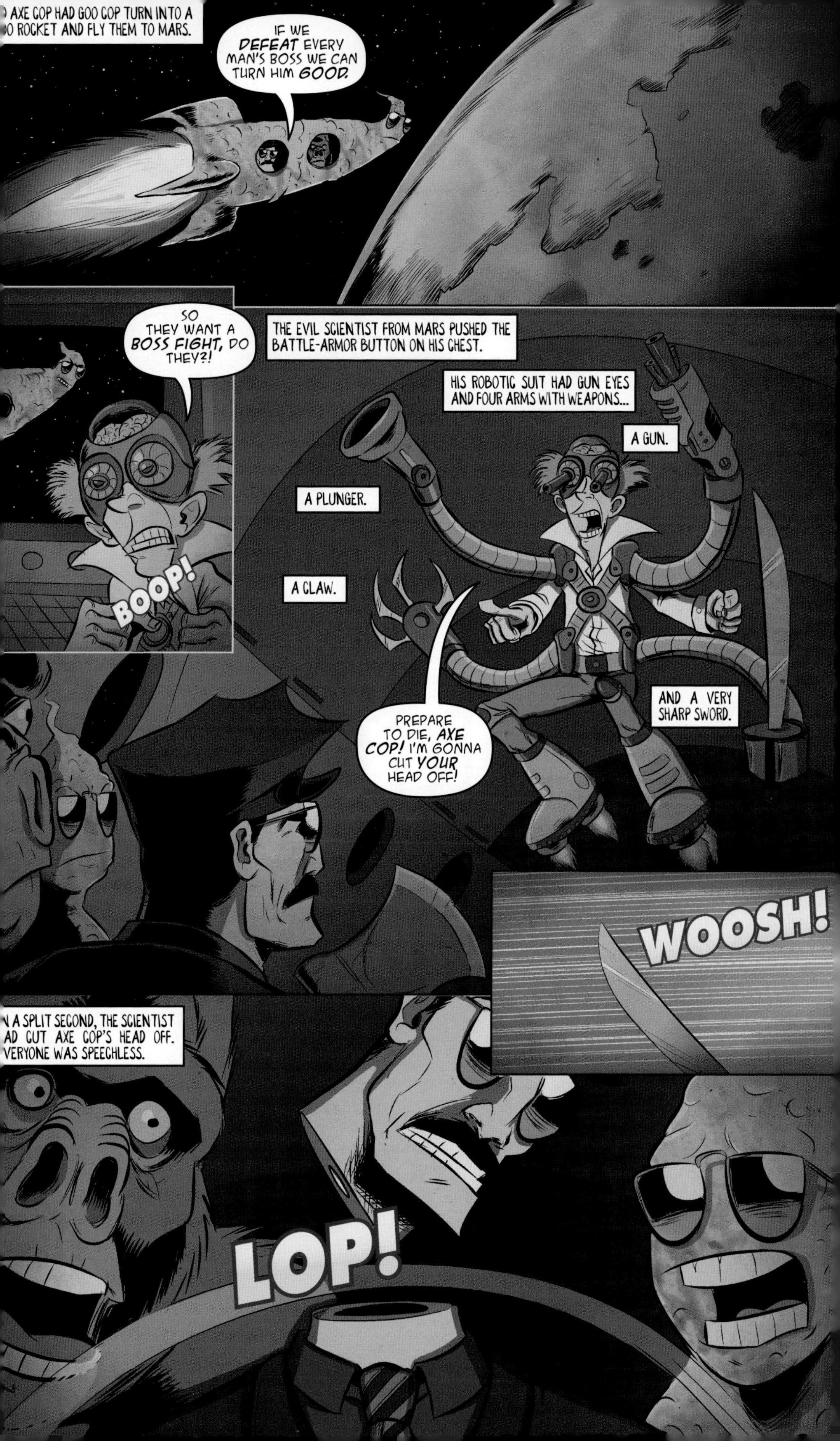

AXE COP HAD GOO COP TURN INTO A
O ROCKET AND FLY THEM TO MARS.
IF WE DEFEAT EVERY MAN'S BOSS WE CAN TURN HIM GOOD.
SO THEY WANT A BOSS FIGHT, DO THEY?!
BOOP!
THE EVIL SCIENTIST FROM MARS PUSHED THE BATTLE-ARMOR BUTTON ON HIS CHEST.
HIS ROBOTIC SUIT HAD GUN EYES AND FOUR ARMS WITH WEAPONS...
A GUN.
A PLUNGER.
A CLAW.
AND A VERY SHARP SWORD.
PREPARE TO DIE, AXE COP! I'M GONNA CUT YOUR HEAD OFF!
WOOSH!
N A SPLIT SECOND, THE SCIENTIST
AD CUT AXE COP'S HEAD OFF.
VERYONE WAS SPEECHLESS.
LOP!

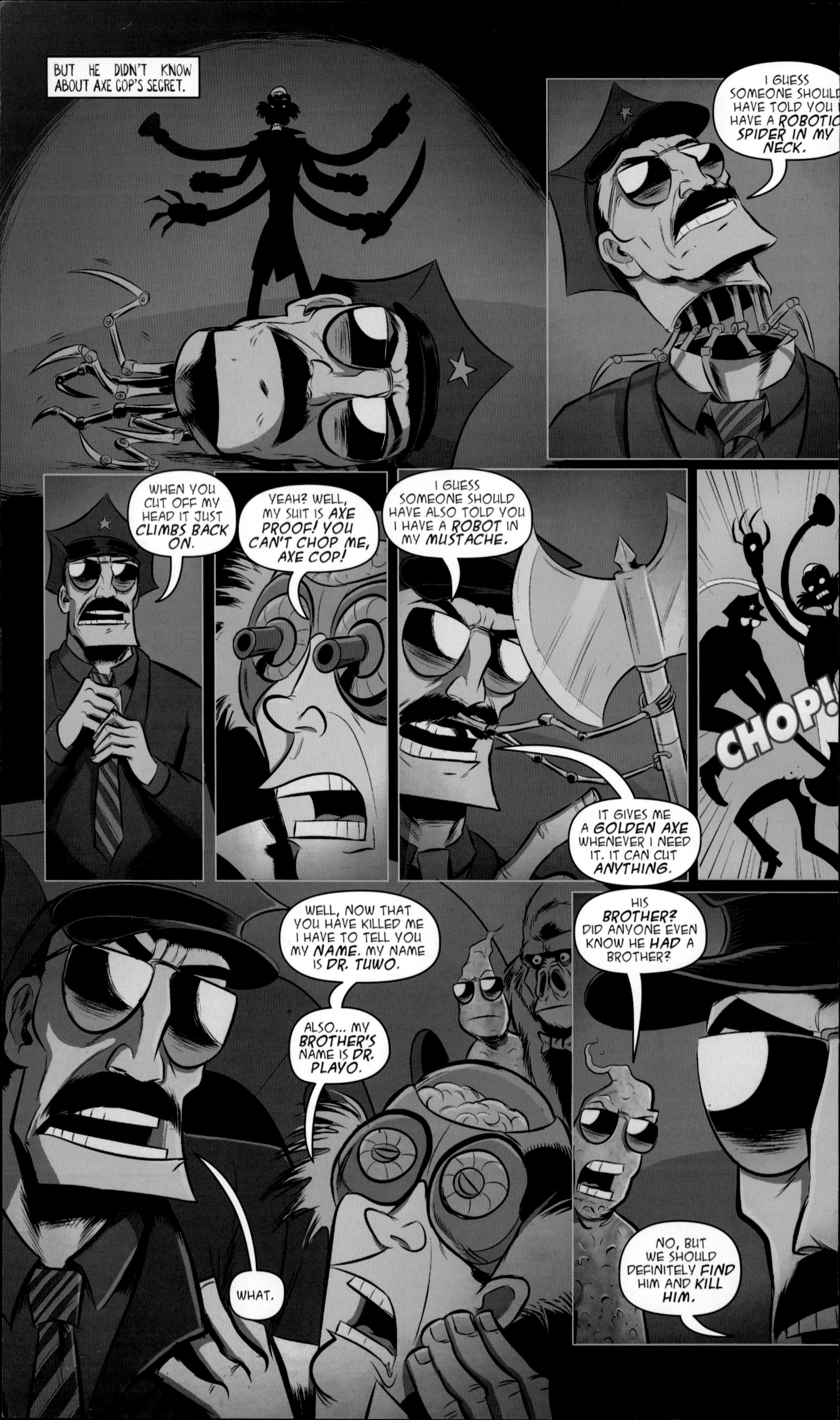
BUT HE DIDN'T KNOW ABOUT AXE COP'S SECRET.
I GUESS SOMEONE SHOULD HAVE TOLD YOU I HAVE A ROBOTIC SPIDER IN MY NECK.
WHEN YOU CUT OFF MY HEAD IT JUST CLIMBS BACK ON.
YEAH? WELL, MY SUIT IS AXE PROOF! YOU CAN'T CHOP ME, AXE COP!
I GUESS SOMEONE SHOULD HAVE ALSO TOLD YOU I HAVE A ROBOT IN MY MUSTACHE.
IT GIVES ME A GOLDEN AXE WHENEVER I NEED IT. IT CAN CUT ANYTHING.
CHOP!
WELL, NOW THAT YOU HAVE KILLED ME I HAVE TO TELL YOU MY NAME. MY NAME IS DR. TUWO.
ALSO... MY BROTHER'S NAME IS DR. PLAYO.
WHAT.
HIS BROTHER? DID ANYONE EVEN KNOW HE HAD A BROTHER?
NO, BUT WE SHOULD DEFINITELY FIND HIM AND KILL HIM.

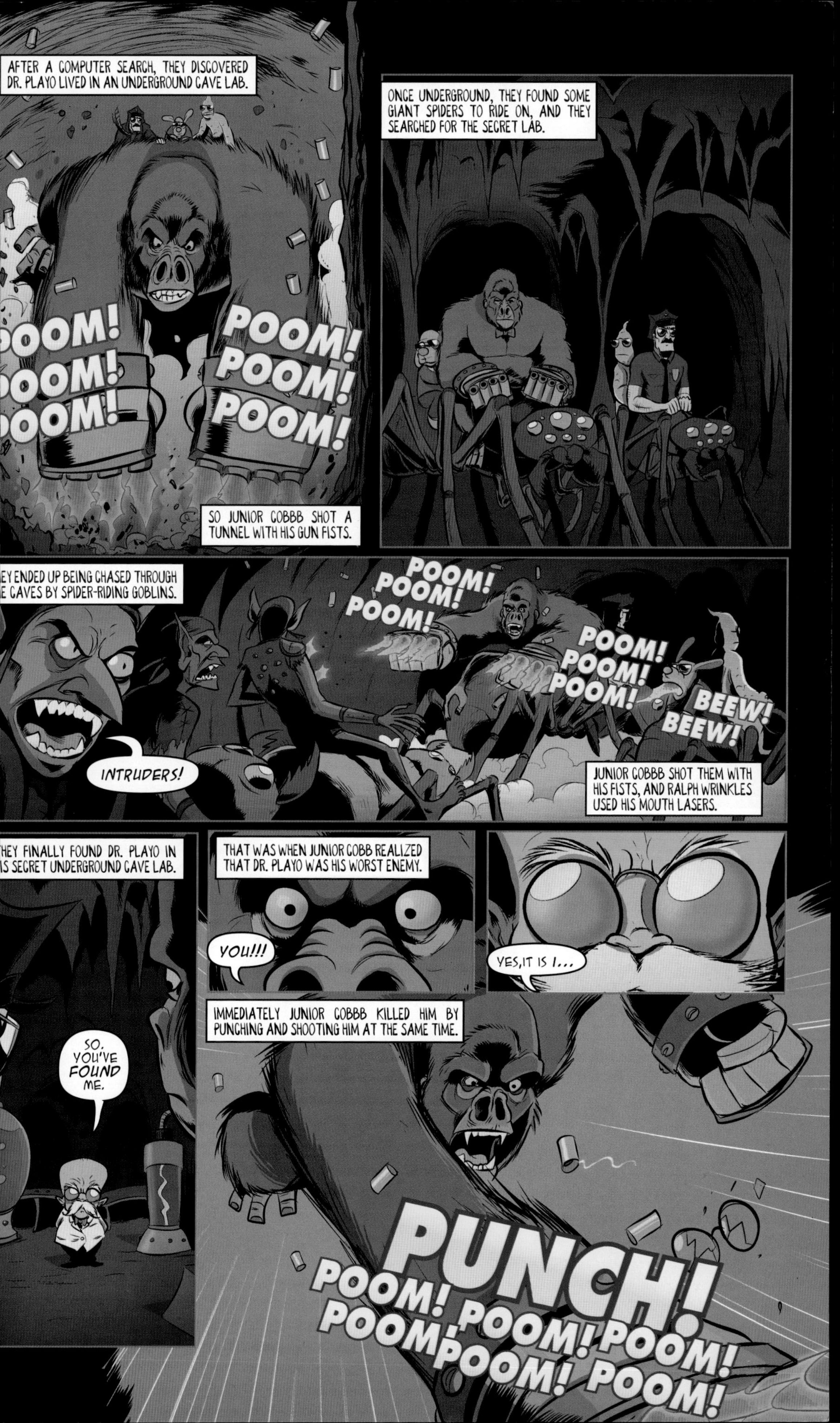
AFTER A COMPUTER SEARCH, THEY DISCOVERED DR. PLAYO LIVED IN AN UNDERGROUND CAVE LAB.
POOM! POOM! POOM!
POOM! POOM! POOM!
SO JUNIOR COBBB SHOT A TUNNEL WITH HIS GUN FISTS.
ONCE UNDERGROUND, THEY FOUND SOME GIANT SPIDERS TO RIDE ON, AND THEY SEARCHED FOR THE SECRET LAB.
EY ENDED UP BEING CHASED THROUGH
E CAVES BY SPIDER-RIDING GOBLINS.
INTRUDERS!
POOM! POOM! POOM!
POOM! POOM! POOM!
BEEW! BEEW!
JUNIOR COBBB SHOT THEM WITH HIS FISTS, AND RALPH WRINKLES USED HIS MOUTH LASERS.
HEY FINALLY FOUND DR. PLAYO IN
S SECRET UNDERGROUND CAVE LAB.
SO. YOU'VE FOUND ME.
THAT WAS WHEN JUNIOR COBB REALIZED THAT DR. PLAYO WAS HIS WORST ENEMY.
YOU!!!
YES,IT IS I...
IMMEDIATELY JUNIOR COBBB KILLED HIM BY PUNCHING AND SHOOTING HIM AT THE SAME TIME.
PUNCH!
POOM! POOM! POOM!
POOM! POOM! POOM!

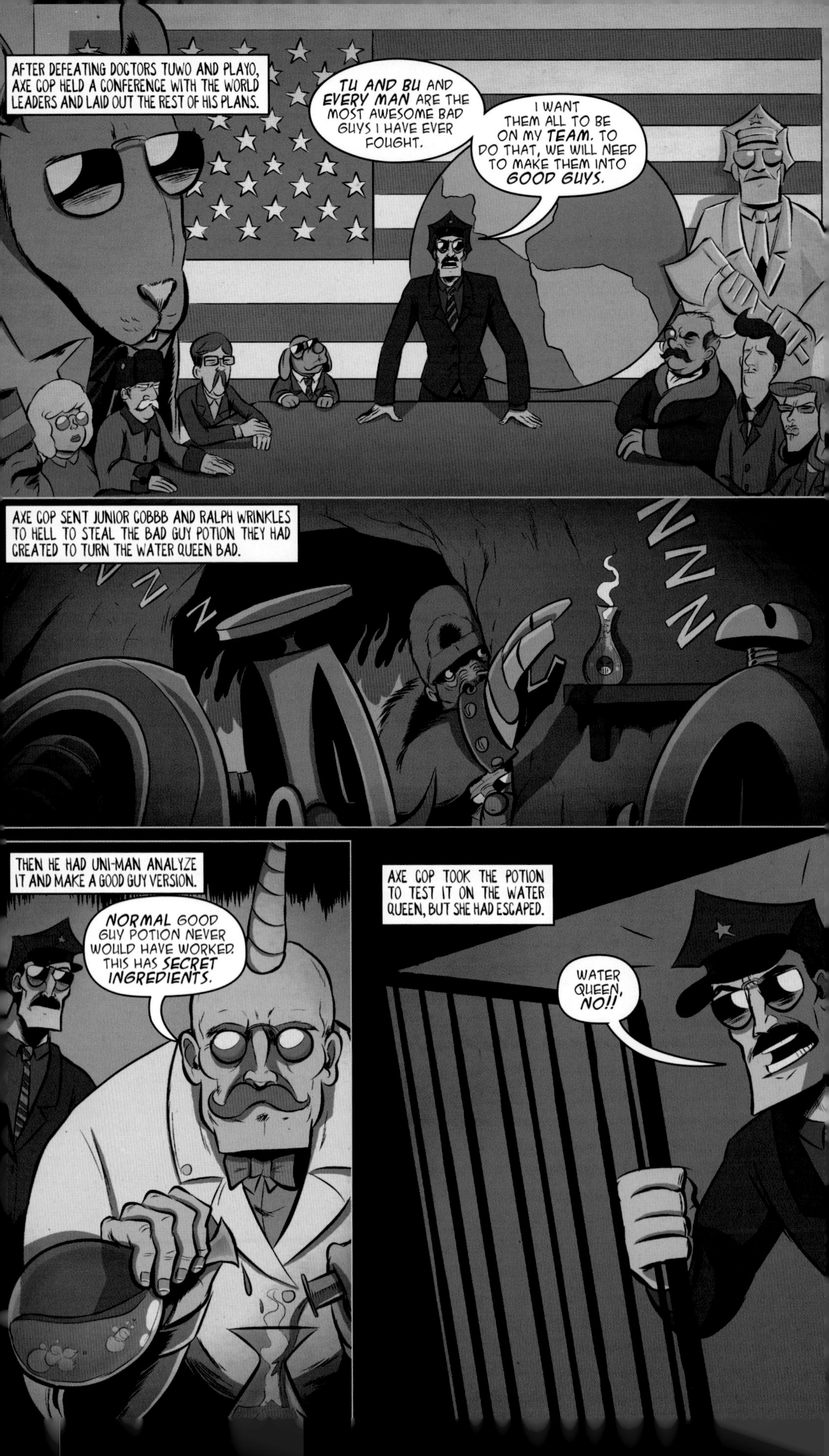

AFTER DEFEATING DOCTORS TUWO AND PLAYO, AXE COP HELD A CONFERENCE WITH THE WORLD LEADERS AND LAID OUT THE REST OF HIS PLANS.
TU AND BU AND EVERY MAN ARE THE MOST AWESOME BAD GUYS I HAVE EVER FOUGHT.
I WANT THEM ALL TO BE ON MY TEAM. TO DO THAT, WE WILL NEED TO MAKE THEM INTO GOOD GUYS.
AXE COP SENT JUNIOR COBBB AND RALPH WRINKLES TO HELL TO STEAL THE BAD GUY POTION THEY HAD CREATED TO TURN THE WATER QUEEN BAD.
Z Z
Z Z Z
THEN HE HAD UNI-MAN ANALYZE IT AND MAKE A GOOD GUY VERSION.
NORMAL GOOD GUY POTION NEVER WOULD HAVE WORKED. THIS HAS SECRET INGREDIENTS.
AXE COP TOOK THE POTION TO TEST IT ON THE WATER QUEEN, BUT SHE HAD ESCAPED.
WATER QUEEN, NO!!

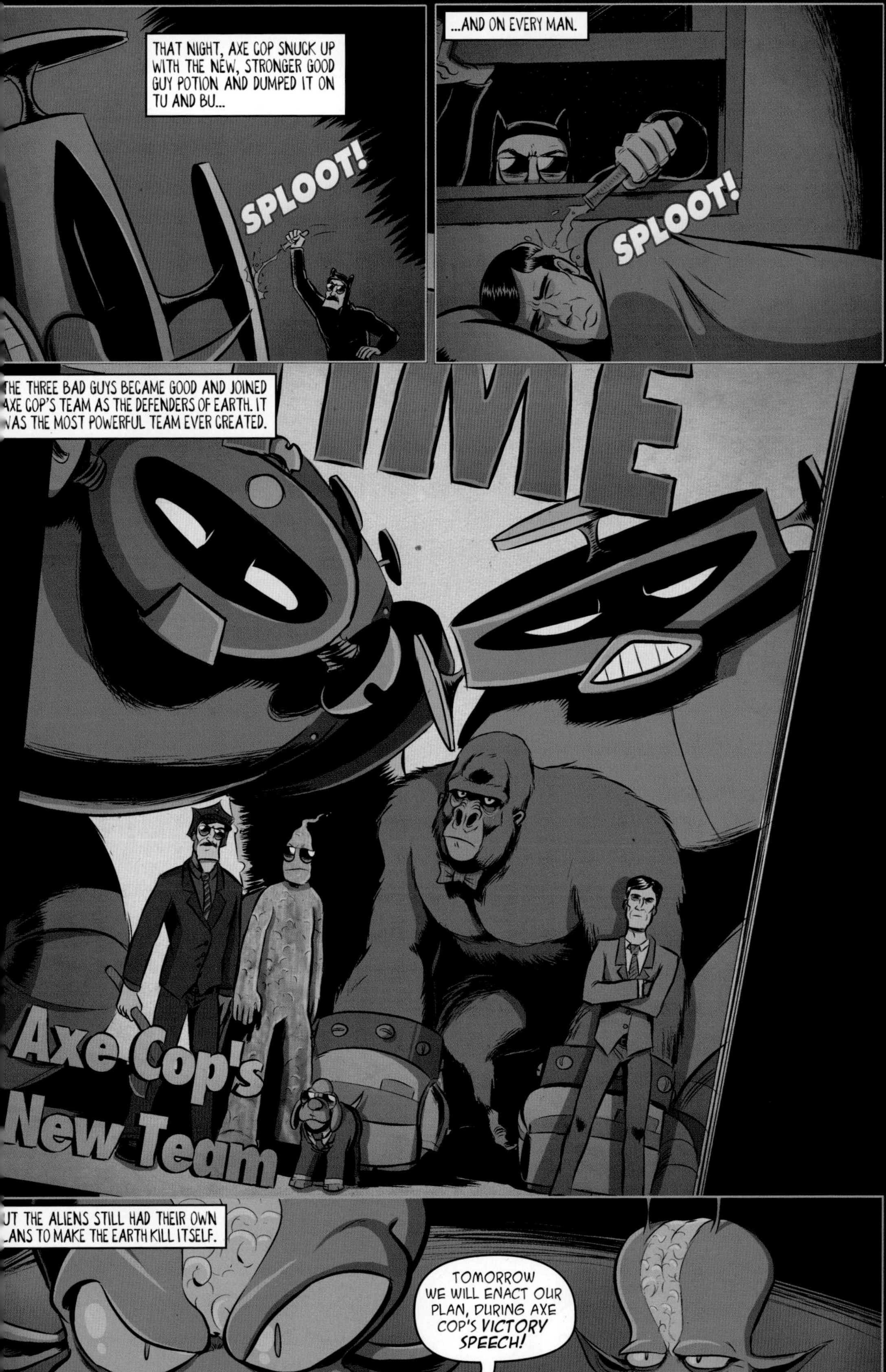
THAT NIGHT, AXE COP SNUCK UP WITH THE NEW, STRONGER GOOD GUY POTION AND DUMPED IT ON TU AND BU...
SPLOOT!
...AND ON EVERY MAN.
SPLOOT!
THE THREE BAD GUYS BECAME GOOD AND JOINED AXE COP'S TEAM AS THE DEFENDERS OF EARTH. IT WAS THE MOST POWERFUL TEAM EVER CREATED.
IME
Axe Cop's New Team
UT THE ALIENS STILL HAD THEIR OWN LANS TO MAKE THE EARTH KILL ITSELF.
TOMORROW WE WILL ENACT OUR PLAN, DURING AXE COP'S VICTORY SPEECH!

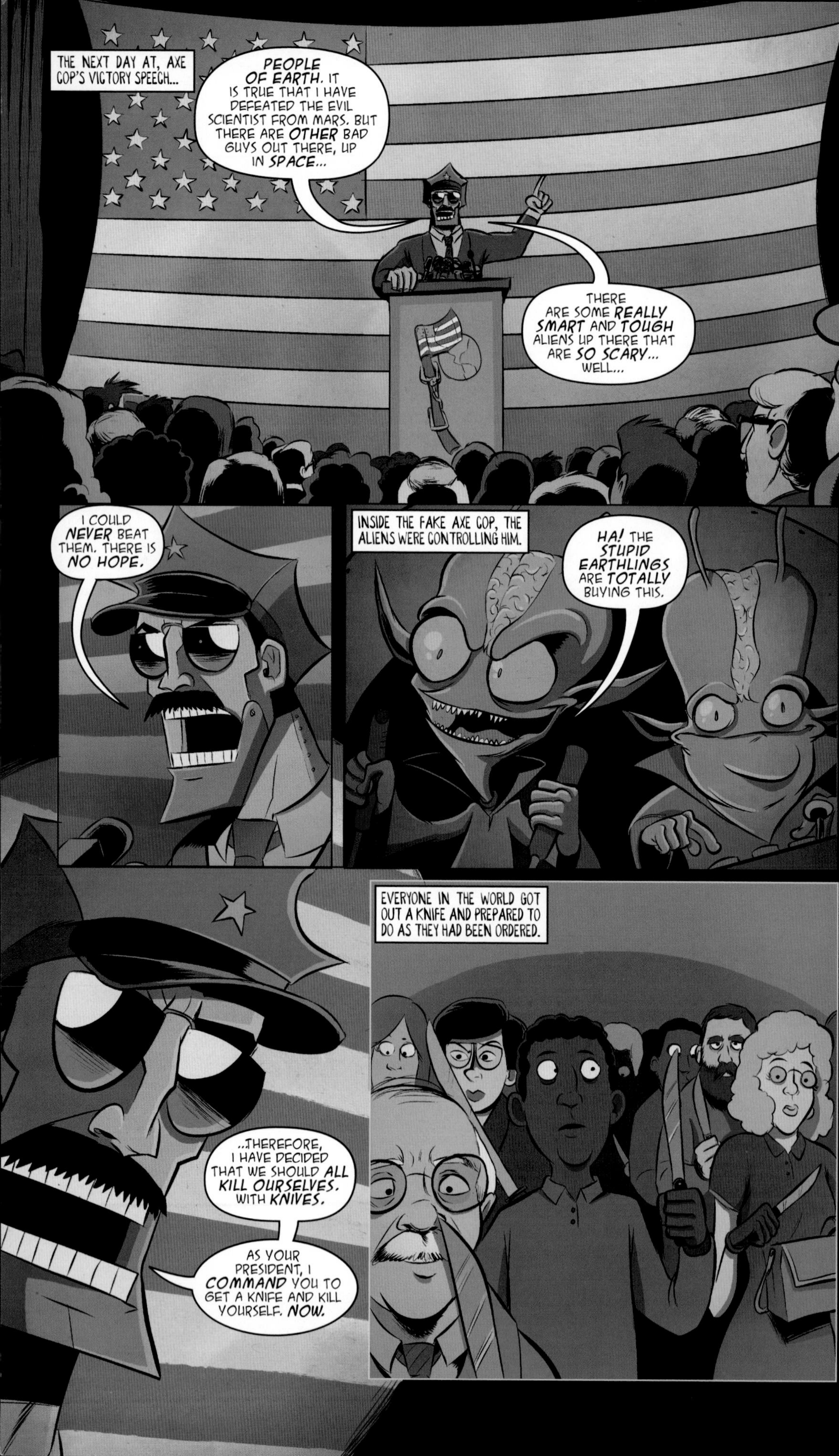

THE NEXT DAY AT, AXE COP'S VICTORY SPEECH...
PEOPLE OF EARTH. IT IS TRUE THAT I HAVE DEFEATED THE EVIL SCIENTIST FROM MARS. BUT THERE ARE OTHER BAD GUYS OUT THERE, UP IN SPACE...
THERE ARE SOME REALLY SMART AND TOUGH ALIENS UP THERE THAT ARE SO SCARY... WELL...
I COULD NEVER BEAT THEM. THERE IS NO HOPE.
INSIDE THE FAKE AXE COP, THE ALIENS WERE CONTROLLING HIM.
HA! THE STUPID EARTHLINGS ARE TOTALLY BUYING THIS.
EVERYONE IN THE WORLD GOT OUT A KNIFE AND PREPARED TO DO AS THEY HAD BEEN ORDERED.
...THEREFORE, I HAVE DECIDED THAT WE SHOULD ALL KILL OURSELVES. WITH KNIVES.
AS YOUR PRESIDENT, I COMMAND YOU TO GET A KNIFE AND KILL YOURSELF. NOW.

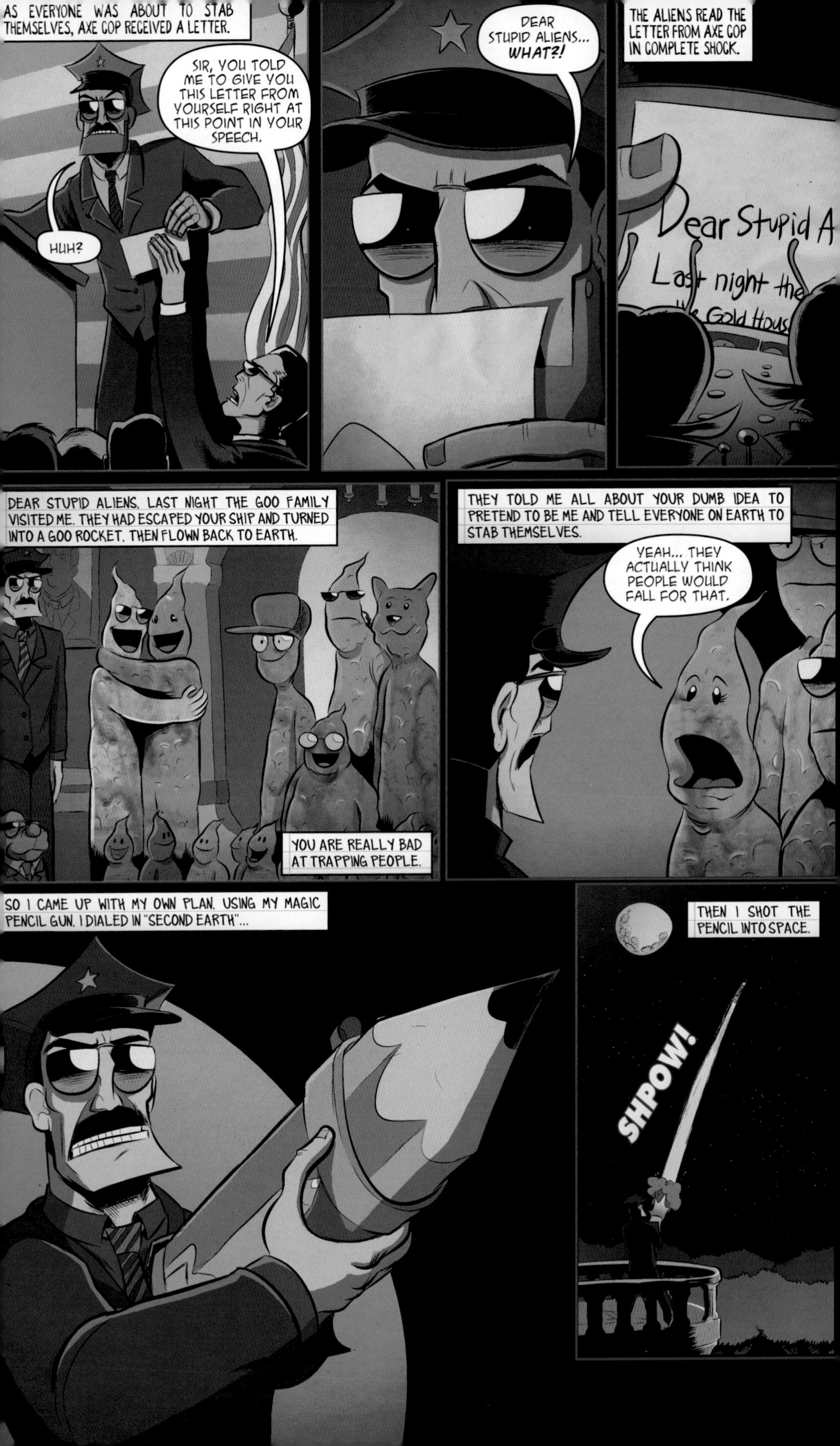
AS EVERYONE WAS ABOUT TO STAB THEMSELVES, AXE COP RECEIVED A LETTER.
SIR, YOU TOLD ME TO GIVE YOU THIS LETTER FROM YOURSELF RIGHT AT THIS POINT IN YOUR SPEECH.
HUH?
DEAR STUPID ALIENS... WHAT?!
THE ALIENS READ THE LETTER FROM AXE COP IN COMPLETE SHOCK.
Dear Stupid A
Last night the
Gold Hous
DEAR STUPID ALIENS. LAST NIGHT THE GOO FAMILY VISITED ME. THEY HAD ESCAPED YOUR SHIP AND TURNED INTO A GOO ROCKET, THEN FLOWN BACK TO EARTH.
YOU ARE REALLY BAD AT TRAPPING PEOPLE.
THEY TOLD ME ALL ABOUT YOUR DUMB IDEA TO PRETEND TO BE ME AND TELL EVERYONE ON EARTH TO STAB THEMSELVES.
YEAH... THEY ACTUALLY THINK PEOPLE WOULD FALL FOR THAT.
SO I CAME UP WITH MY OWN PLAN. USING MY MAGIC PENCIL GUN, I DIALED IN "SECOND EARTH"...
THEN I SHOT THE PENCIL INTO SPACE.
SHPOW!

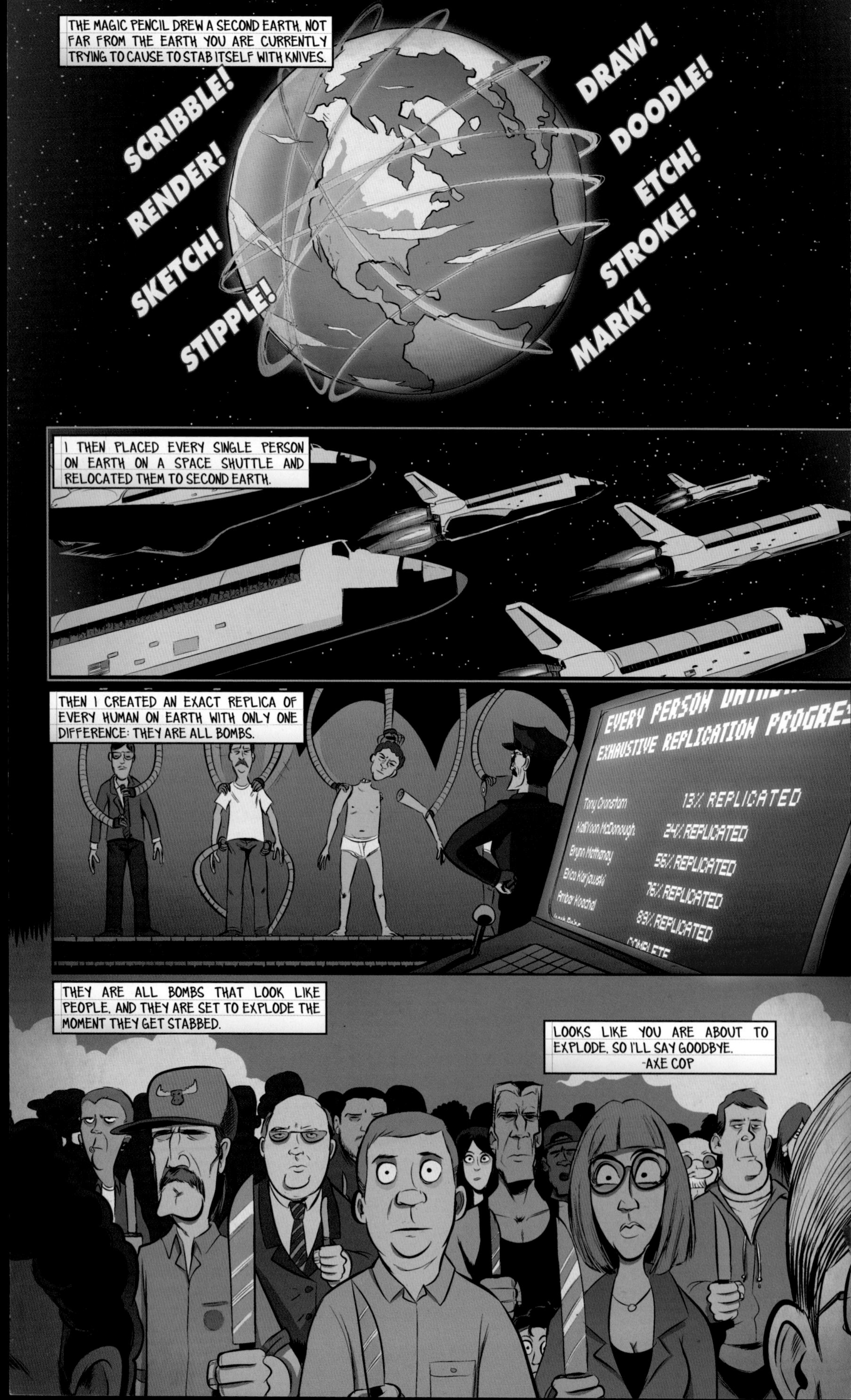
THE MAGIC PENCIL DREW A SECOND EARTH. NOT FAR FROM THE EARTH YOU ARE CURRENTLY TRYING TO CAUSE TO STAB ITSELF WITH KNIVES.
SCRIBBLE!
RENDER!
SKETCH!
STIPPLE!
DRAW!
DOODLE!
ETCH!
STROKE!
MARK!
I THEN PLACED EVERY SINGLE PERSON ON EARTH ON A SPACE SHUTTLE AND RELOCATED THEM TO SECOND EARTH.
THEN I CREATED AN EXACT REPLICA OF EVERY HUMAN ON EARTH WITH ONLY ONE DIFFERENCE: THEY ARE ALL BOMBS.
EVERY PERSON
EXHAUSTIVE REPLICATION PROGRES
Tony Cronstam 13% REPLICATED
KaliYoon McDonough. 24% REPLICATED
Brynn Mathaney 56% REPLICATED
Erica Karjewski 76% REPLICATED
Amber Koechel 89% REPLICATED
THEY ARE ALL BOMBS THAT LOOK LIKE PEOPLE. AND THEY ARE SET TO EXPLODE THE MOMENT THEY GET STABBED.
LOOKS LIKE YOU ARE ABOUT TO EXPLODE. SO I'LL SAY GOODBYE.
-AXE COP

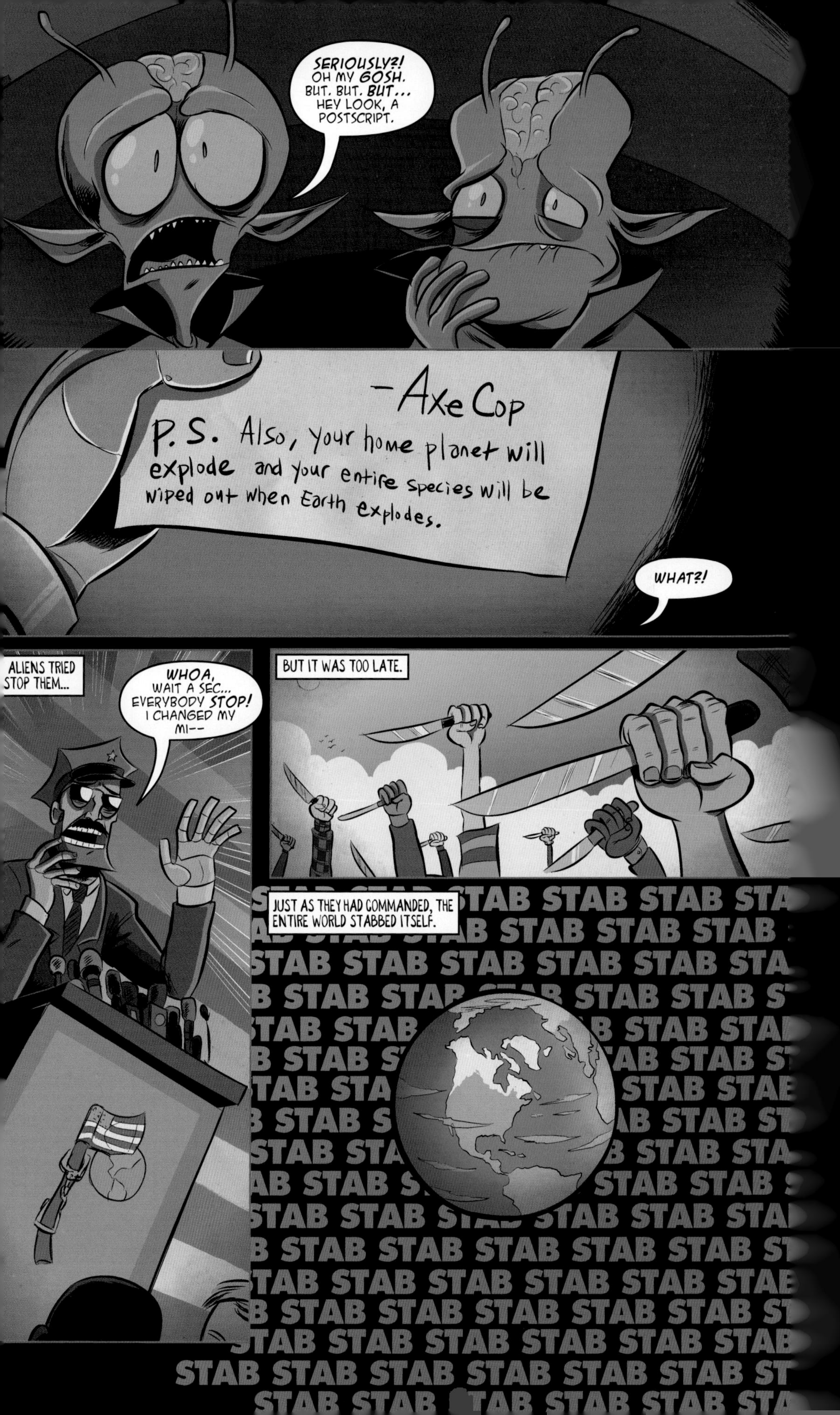
SERIOUSLY?! OH MY GOSH. BUT. BUT. BUT... HEY LOOK, A POSTSCRIPT.
-Axe Cop
P.S. Also, your home planet will explode and your entire species will be wiped out when Earth explodes.
WHAT?!
ALIENS TRIED STOP THEM...
WHOA, WAIT A SEC... EVERYBODY STOP! I CHANGED MY MI--
BUT IT WAS TOO LATE.
JUST AS THEY HAD COMMANDED, THE ENTIRE WORLD STABBED ITSELF.
STAB STAB STAB STAB STAB STAB STAB STAB STAB STAB STAB STAB STAB STAB STAB STAB STAB STAB STAB STAB

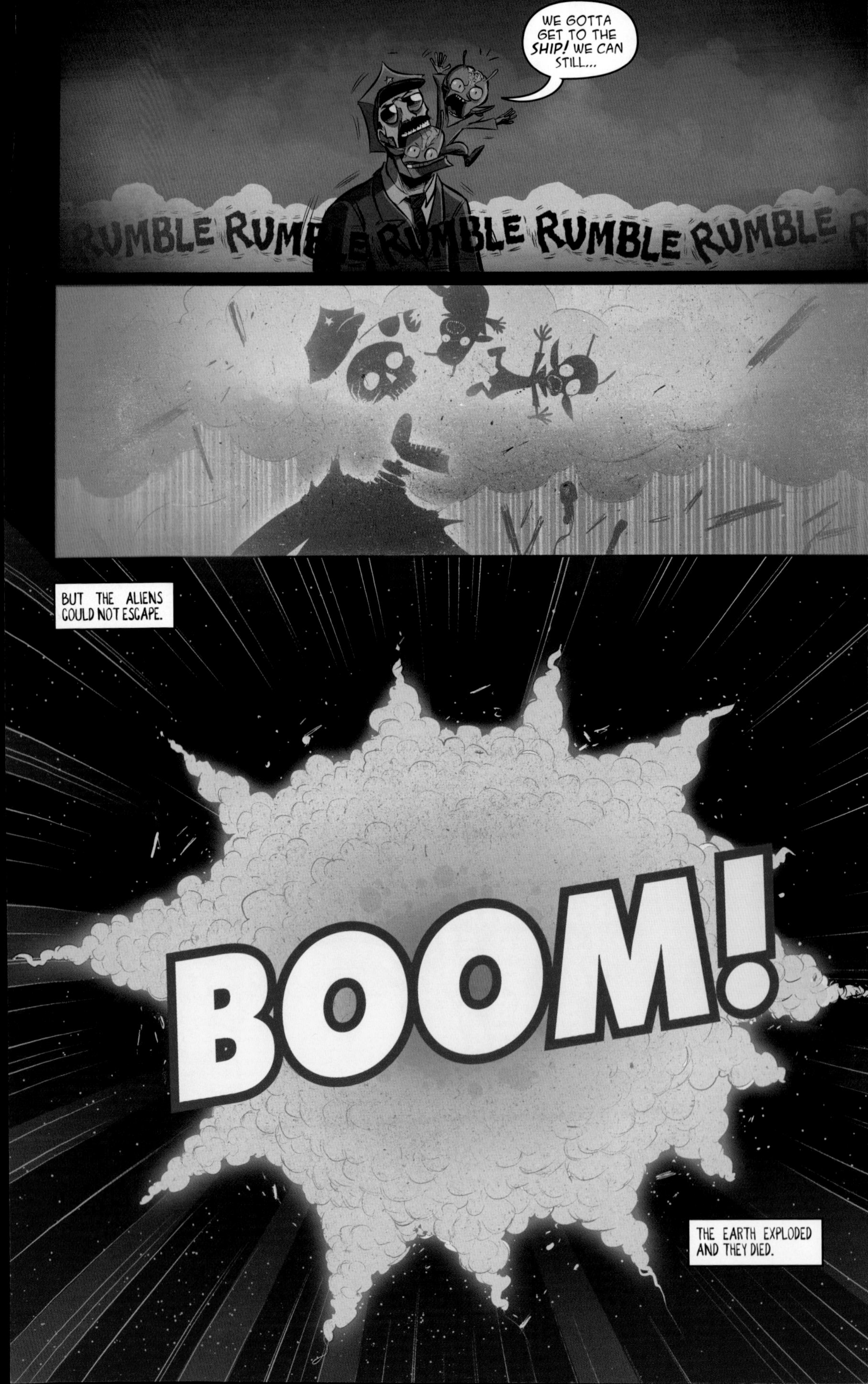
WE GOTTA GET TO THE SHIP! WE CAN STILL...
RUMBLE RUMBLE RUMBLE RUMBLE RUMBLE
BUT THE ALIENS COULD NOT ESCAPE.
BOOM!
THE EARTH EXPLODED AND THEY DIED.

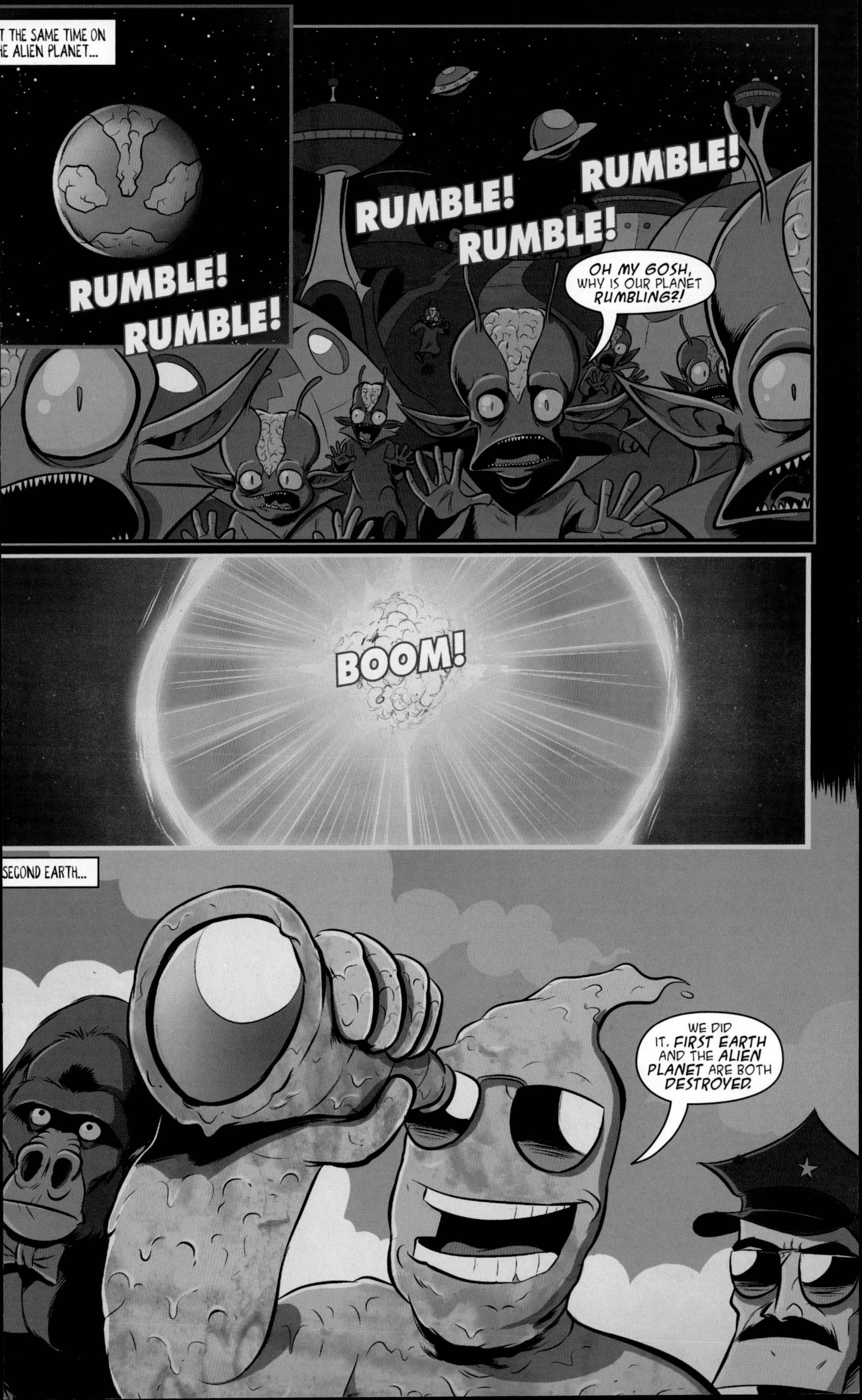
T THE SAME TIME ON
HE ALIEN PLANET...
RUMBLE!
RUMBLE!
RUMBLE!
RUMBLE!
RUMBLE!
OH MY GOSH, WHY IS OUR PLANET RUMBLING?!
BOOM!
SECOND EARTH...
WE DID IT. FIRST EARTH AND THE ALIEN PLANET ARE BOTH DESTROYED.

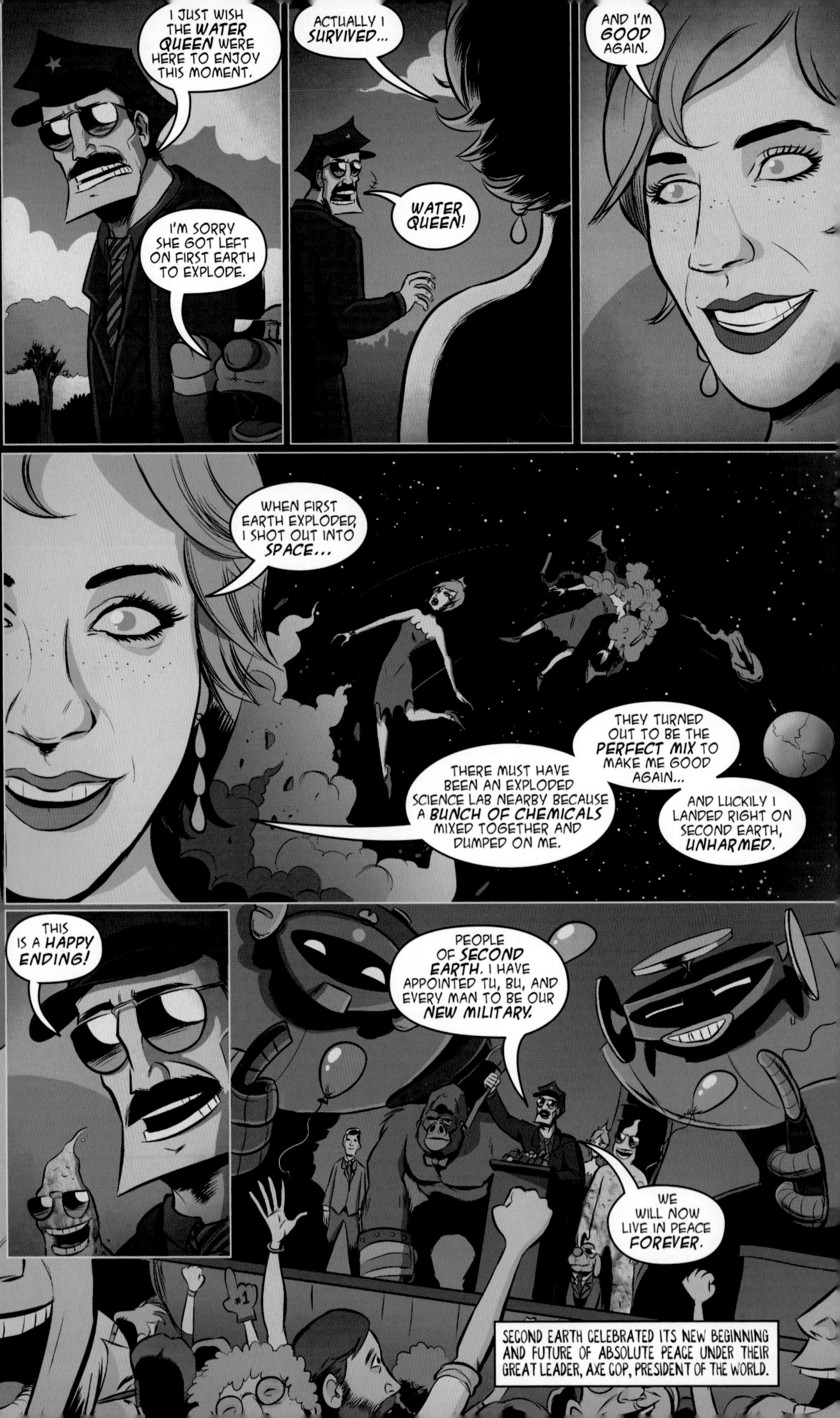
I JUST WISH THE WATER QUEEN WERE HERE TO ENJOY THIS MOMENT.
I'M SORRY SHE GOT LEFT ON FIRST EARTH TO EXPLODE.
ACTUALLY I SURVIVED...
WATER QUEEN!
AND I'M GOOD AGAIN.
WHEN FIRST EARTH EXPLODED, I SHOT OUT INTO SPACE...
THERE MUST HAVE BEEN AN EXPLODED SCIENCE LAB NEARBY BECAUSE A BUNCH OF CHEMICALS MIXED TOGETHER AND DUMPED ON ME.
THEY TURNED OUT TO BE THE PERFECT MIX TO MAKE ME GOOD AGAIN...
AND LUCKILY I LANDED RIGHT ON SECOND EARTH, UNHARMED.
THIS IS A HAPPY ENDING!
PEOPLE OF SECOND EARTH. I HAVE APPOINTED TU, BU, AND EVERY MAN TO BE OUR NEW MILITARY.
WE WILL NOW LIVE IN PEACE FOREVER.
#1
SECOND EARTH CELEBRATED ITS NEW BEGINNING AND FUTURE OF ABSOLUTE PEACE UNDER THEIR GREAT LEADER, AXE COP, PRESIDENT OF THE WORLD.

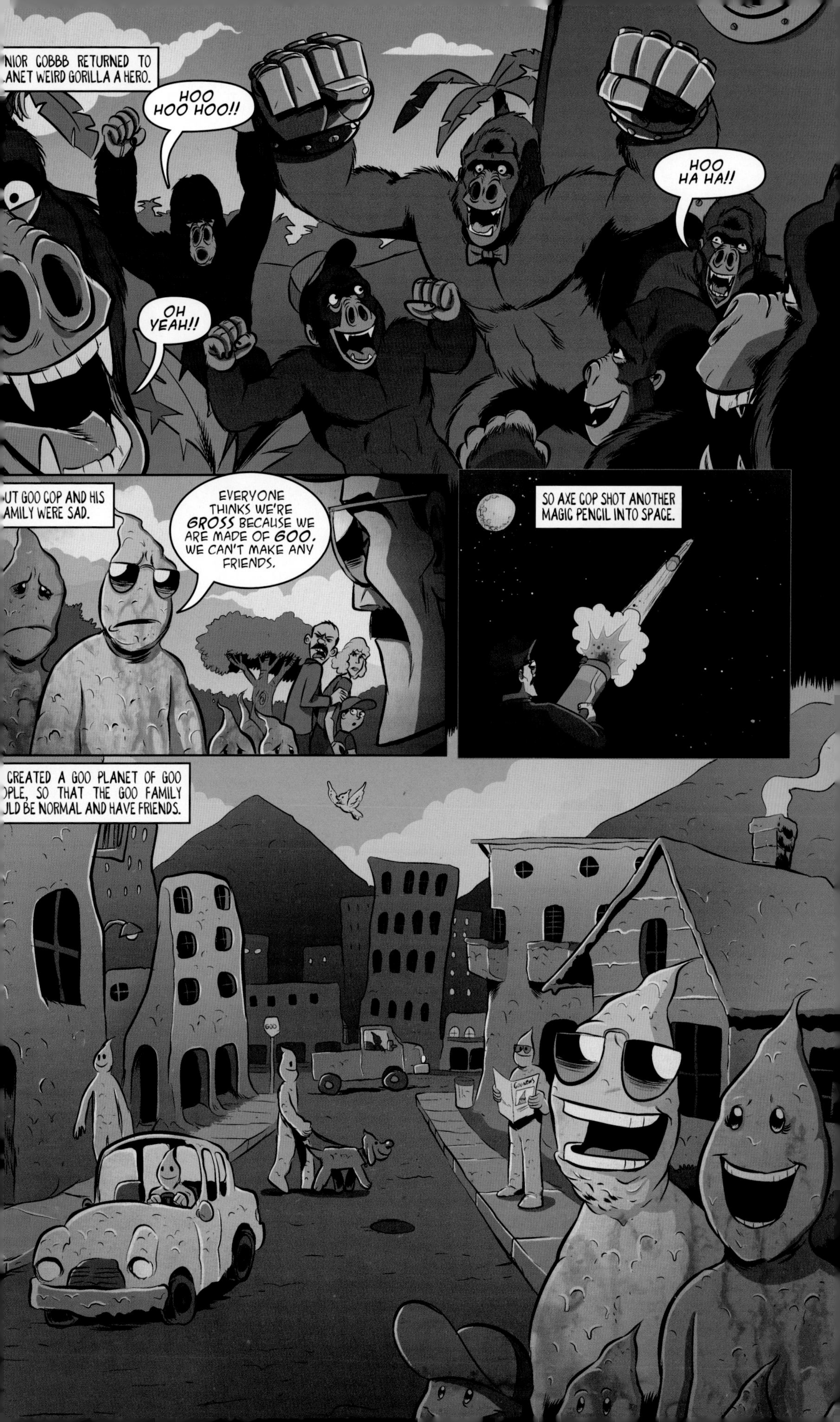
NIOR GOBBB RETURNED TO
ANET WEIRD GORILLA A HERO.
HOO HOO HOO!!
HOO HA HA!!
OH YEAH!!
UT GOO COP AND HIS
AMILY WERE SAD.
EVERYONE THINKS WE'RE GROSS BECAUSE WE ARE MADE OF GOO. WE CAN'T MAKE ANY FRIENDS.
SO AXE COP SHOT ANOTHER MAGIC PENCIL INTO SPACE.
CREATED A GOO PLANET OF GOO
PLE, SO THAT THE GOO FAMILY
LD BE NORMAL AND HAVE FRIENDS.
GOO

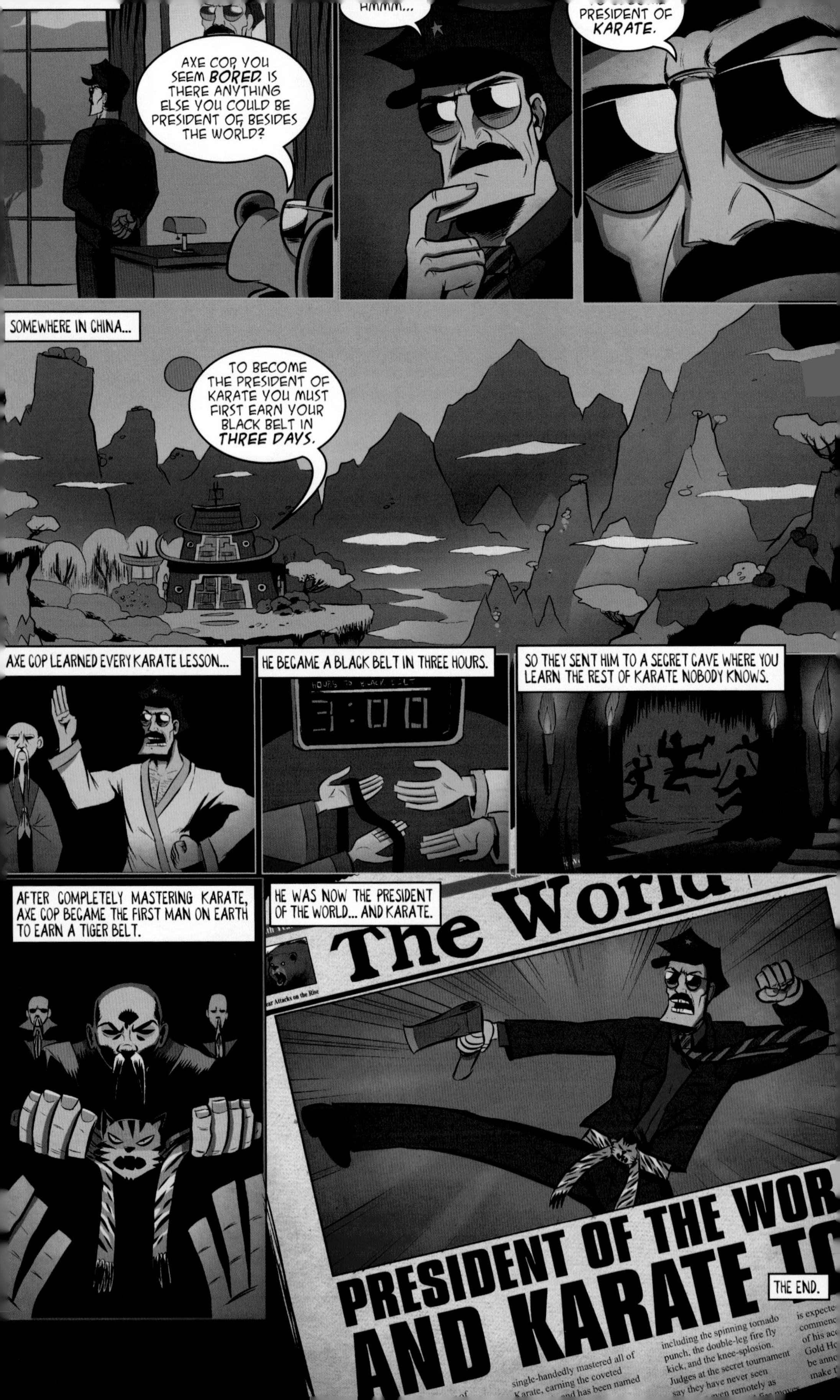
AXE COP, YOU SEEM BORED. IS THERE ANYTHING ELSE YOU COULD BE PRESIDENT OF BESIDES THE WORLD?
HMMM...
PRESIDENT OF KARATE.
SOMEWHERE IN CHINA...
TO BECOME THE PRESIDENT OF KARATE YOU MUST FIRST EARN YOUR BLACK BELT IN THREE DAYS.
AXE COP LEARNED EVERY KARATE LESSON...
HE BECAME A BLACK BELT IN THREE HOURS.
3:00
SO THEY SENT HIM TO A SECRET CAVE WHERE YOU LEARN THE REST OF KARATE NOBODY KNOWS.
AFTER COMPLETELY MASTERING KARATE, AXE COP BECAME THE FIRST MAN ON EARTH TO EARN A TIGER BELT.
HE WAS NOW THE PRESIDENT OF THE WORLD... AND KARATE.
The World
Bear Attacks on the Rise
PRESIDENT OF THE WOR
AND KARATE T
single-handedly mastered all of
Karate, earning the coveted
and has been named
including the spinning tornado
punch, the double-leg fire fly
kick, and the knee-splosion.
Judges at the secret tournament
say they have never seen
THE END.

THE MAKING OF PRESIDENT OF THE WORLD

ONE YEAR AFTER I SPENT A MONTH CREATING *BAD GUY EARTH* WITH MALACHAI, WE CAME TOGETHER TO SPEND ANOTHER MONTH CREATING THE "SEQUEL." I HAD ALWAYS ASSUMED THAT AXE COP BECOMING PRESIDENT OF THE WORLD WAS A LITTLE GAG AT THE END OF THE STORY THAT WOULD NOT CARRY INTO FUTURE AXE COP TALES. I WAS OF COURSE WRONG. THE NEXT STORY, IT WAS DECIDED, WOULD BE ABOUT AXE COP'S NEXT STEPS AFTER *BAD GUY EARTH* ENDS. WHAT HAPPENS TO EARTH? DO BAD GUYS RETURN? WHAT DOES EVERYBODY DO NOW THAT THE BAD GUYS HAVE ALL DIED?

WHEN WE CREATED *BAD GUY EARTH*, WE MANAGED TO STAY IN THE *BAD GUY EARTH* STORY LINE MOST OF THE TIME I WAS VISITING. BUT DURING THIS SECOND ATTEMPT WE CREATED A WHOLE BATCH OF STORIES. I KEPT TRYING TO GET BACK TO THE *PRESIDENT OF THE WORLD* ARC, BUT THEN WE WOULD WRITE OTHER STORIES, LIKE THE FUNNY EPISODE, THE DOGS, JACK AND JOHN, AND MANY OTHERS. IT WAS OUR MOST PRODUCTIVE VISIT EVER.

THE STORY THAT BECAME *PRESIDENT OF THE WORLD* STARTED AS TWO SEPARATE TALES. MALACHAI WAS TELLING A STORY ABOUT AXE COP TEAMING UP WITH JUNIOR COBBB, AND HE WAS ALSO TELLING A STORY ABOUT A TEAM UP WITH GOO COP. BUT THE BAD GUYS TU AND BU WERE IN BOTH STORIES, SO I KEPT ASKING QUESTIONS TO GET THE TWO STORIES TO MERGE INTO ONE.

PARTS OF THIS STORY WERE ACTUALLY CREATED IN FRONT OF LIVE AUDIENCES. JUNIOR COBBB WAS CREATED AT MELTDOWN COMICS IN LOS ANGELES AT AN EVENT CELEBRATING *AXE COP*'S FIRST YEAR. I DREW AS MALACHAI MADE UP A NEW CHARACTER IN FRONT OF THE AUDIENCE. HE LITERALLY SAID, "KING KONG," SO I CORRECTED HIM AND SAID THAT KING KONG HAD ALREADY BEEN MADE UP. SO HE SAID, "JUNIOR KONG." I TOLD HIM IT WAS PROBABLY THE KONG PART HE NEEDED TO CHANGE. SO THEN HE SAID, "JUNIOR COB." I ASKED IF THAT WAS COB WITH ONE B OR TWO, AND HE PAUSED, THEN SAID, "THREE." HE PROCEEDED TO DESCRIBE HIS TAIL, BOW TIE, AND GUN FISTS. JUNIOR COBBB WAS BORN. I, BEING A HUGE KING KONG FAN, WAS EXCITED TO DO THE AXE COP VERSION OF THE GIANT GORILLA CHARACTER.

ALSO, AT ANOTHER CONVENTION (I THINK DENVER COMIC CON) DURING A Q&A WITH MALACHAI ON THE PHONE, SOMEONE ASKED IF AXE COP IS THE PRESIDENT OF ANYTHING ELSE. MALACHAI ANSWERED, "UM, HE'S THE PRESIDENT OF KARATE" AND PROCEEDED TO EXPLAIN HOW ONE ACHIEVES SUCH AN OFFICE. I WAS ACTUALLY WORKING ON DRAWING THE FINAL PAGES OF THE STORY AROUND THE SAME TIME, SO I WAS ABLE TO USE IT.

WE ARE CURRENTLY GEARING UP TO WRITE THE THIRD FULL-LENGTH STORY AND FOLLOW-UP TO *PRESIDENT OF THE WORLD*. IT IS INSPIRED BY *THE AVENGERS*, A STORY WHERE AXE COP CREATES A TEAM OF AXE-WIELDING SUPERHEROES TO DEFEND THE EARTH. MALACHAI WILL HAVE TURNED NINE BY THE TIME THIS BOOK IS PUBLISHED, AND THE *AXE COP* ANIMATED SHOW IS DUE OUT IN JULY OF 2013. BEING THE BIG BROTHER IN ALL THIS HAS SURE BEEN A BLAST.

-ETHAN NICOLLE
FEB 5, 2013

ASK
AXE
COP
FIVE STAR
CHO
ABRAHAM LINCOLN:
EXPLOSION
GOD

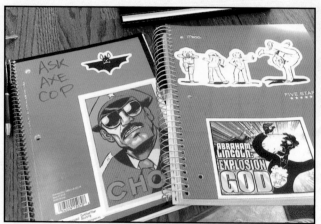

TAKING NOTES

WE HAD TWO NOTEBOOKS WE ADDED TO DAILY: ONE FOR STORIES AND ONE FOR "ASK AXE COP" QUESTIONS. I WENT THROUGH THE E-MAILS AND WROTE A QUESTION ON EVERY PAGE. EACH DAY WE TRIED TO ANSWER THREE. THE BOOK HAD DIVIDERS AND I TRIED TO KEEP THE STORIES ORGANIZED BUT IT GOT PRETTY MESSY.

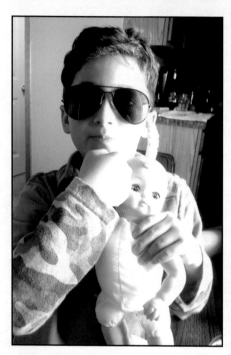

GETTING IN CHARACTER

WE ALWAYS HAD AVIATORS ON HAND AND VARIOUS PROPS. WE SPENT NEARLY $100 AT A DOLLAR STORE BUYING WEIRD TOYS THAT COULD COME IN AS TOOLS FOR STORY INSPIRATION. WE JAMMED A MAKESHIFT HORN INTO A DOLL BABY'S HEAD AND MADE A UNI-BABY TO CARRY WITH US TO CREATE THE STORY "AXE COP BABYSITS UNI-BABY."

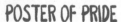

POSTER OF PRIDE

THIS POSTER HANGS ON MALACHAI'S DOOR. IT'S A PROJECT HE MADE AT SCHOOL SHOWING HIS FAVORITE THINGS, HIS FAMILY, HIS PETS, HIS FAVORITE ICE CREAM, AND HIS PUBLISHED COMIC BOOK.

Malachai
Nicolle
born: March 6, 2004
Malachai - messenger of God
My Crazy Family
Malachai
Accomplishments:
AXE COP
AXE COP
This is my comic book
Sports
Soccer
T-Ball
Favorite Foods
Pizza
apples
ice cream
I have a signed BEN 10 Poster from all the characters
I like to fish and play XBOX

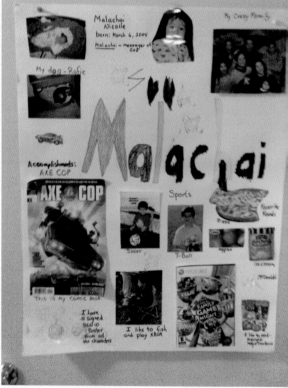

MAGIC PENCIL GUN

MALACHAI FOUND THIS GUN-SHAPED PIECE OF STYROFOAM IN THE PACKAGING OF A BARBECUE GRILL I WAS ASSEMBLING WITH MY DAD. WE DREW DIALS AND BUTTONS ON IT AND IT BECAME A FAVORITE PROP IN OUR STORY-CREATING ADVENTURES.

IN THE COMIC, AXE COP IS NOT VERY GOOD AT DRAWING. MALACHAI IS NOT REAL INTO DRAWING EITHER, SO HE GAVE AXE COP THE SAME HANDICAP. I GUESS WHEN YOUR BROTHER WILL DRAW WHATEVER YOU SAY YOU DON'T HAVE A LOT OF REASON TO LEARN TO DRAW.

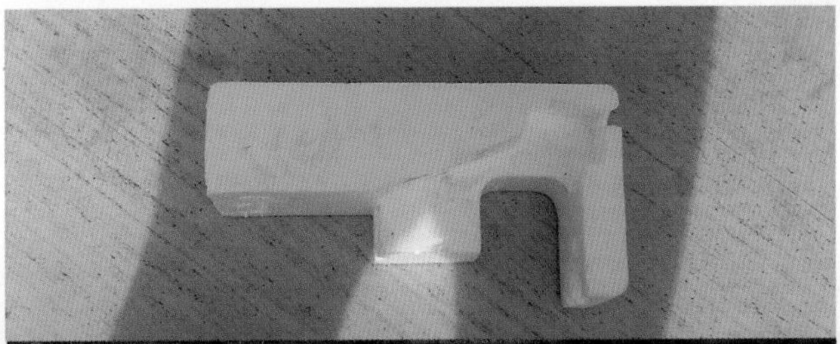

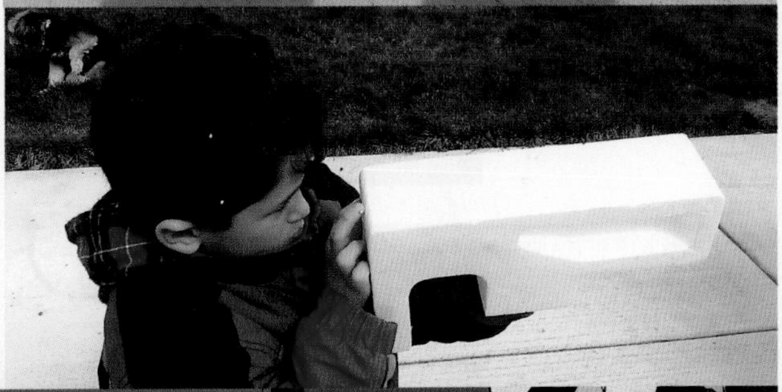

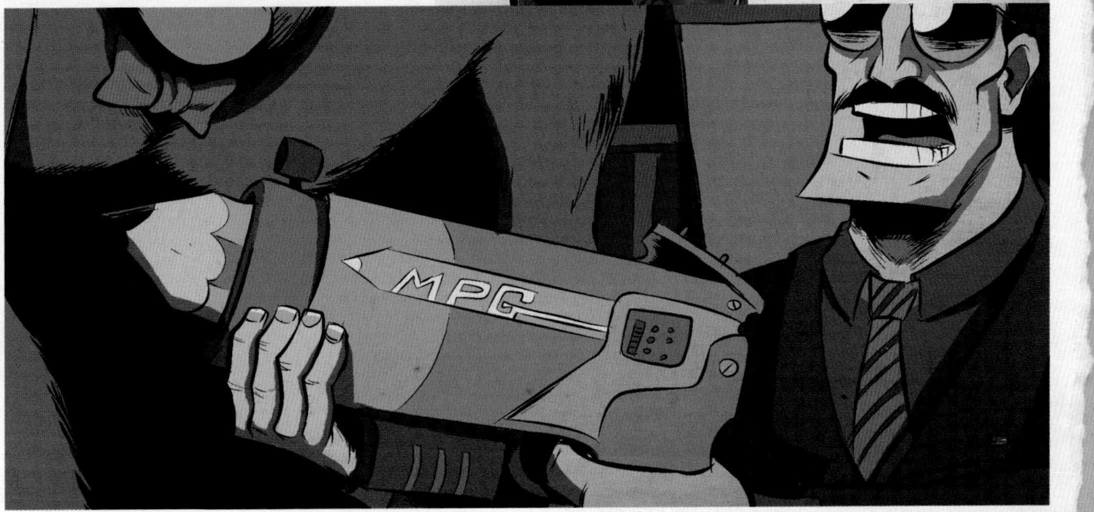
MPG

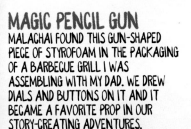

NOTE CARDS, MARKERS, AND AN IPAD

SOME OF MY MOST BASIC TOOLS. THE IPAD IS GOOD FOR TAKING NOTES AND BRIBING MALACHAI TO GET INTO CREATIVE MODE IN TRADE FOR GAME TIME AND NEW APP DOWNLOADS.

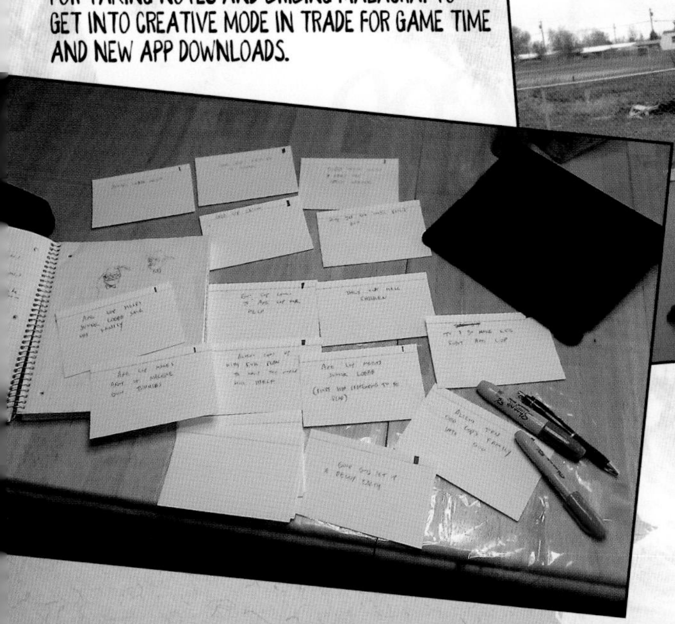

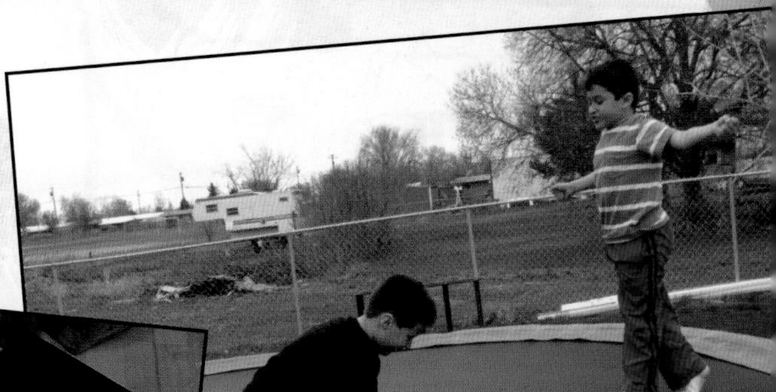

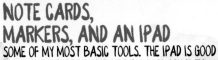

FRIENDS AND TRAMPOLINES

MALACHAI'S NEIGHBOR VISITS TO PLAY ALONG AS MALACHAI DIRECTS THE ACTION. THE BOUNCY WORLD BOUNCE-OFF IS INVENTED.

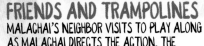

SKETCHES

I DIDN'T HAVE AS MUCH TIME TO SKETCH AS USUAL DURING THIS VISIT, BUT FOR THE RECURRING CHARACTERS I CAME UP WITH DESIGNS I LIKED BEFORE PUTTING THEM IN THE COMIC.

Poison Ice Cream Planet: A mysterious and hostile world that never made it into the final story.

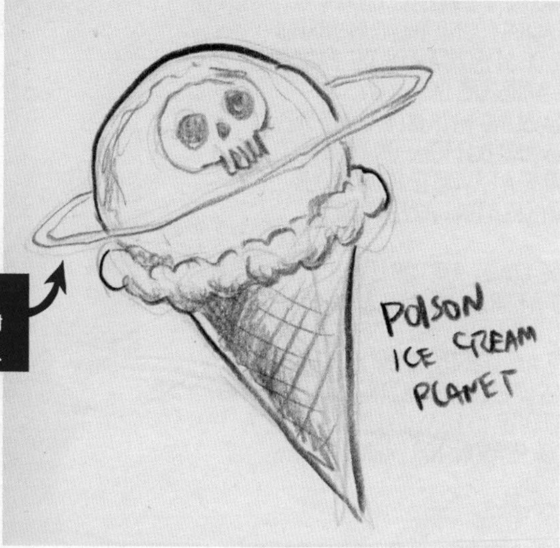

POISON
ICE CREAM
PLANET

Goo Cop: As Malachai described the new gooey character to me I took these notes. It was never mentioned in the comic that he eats earwigs.

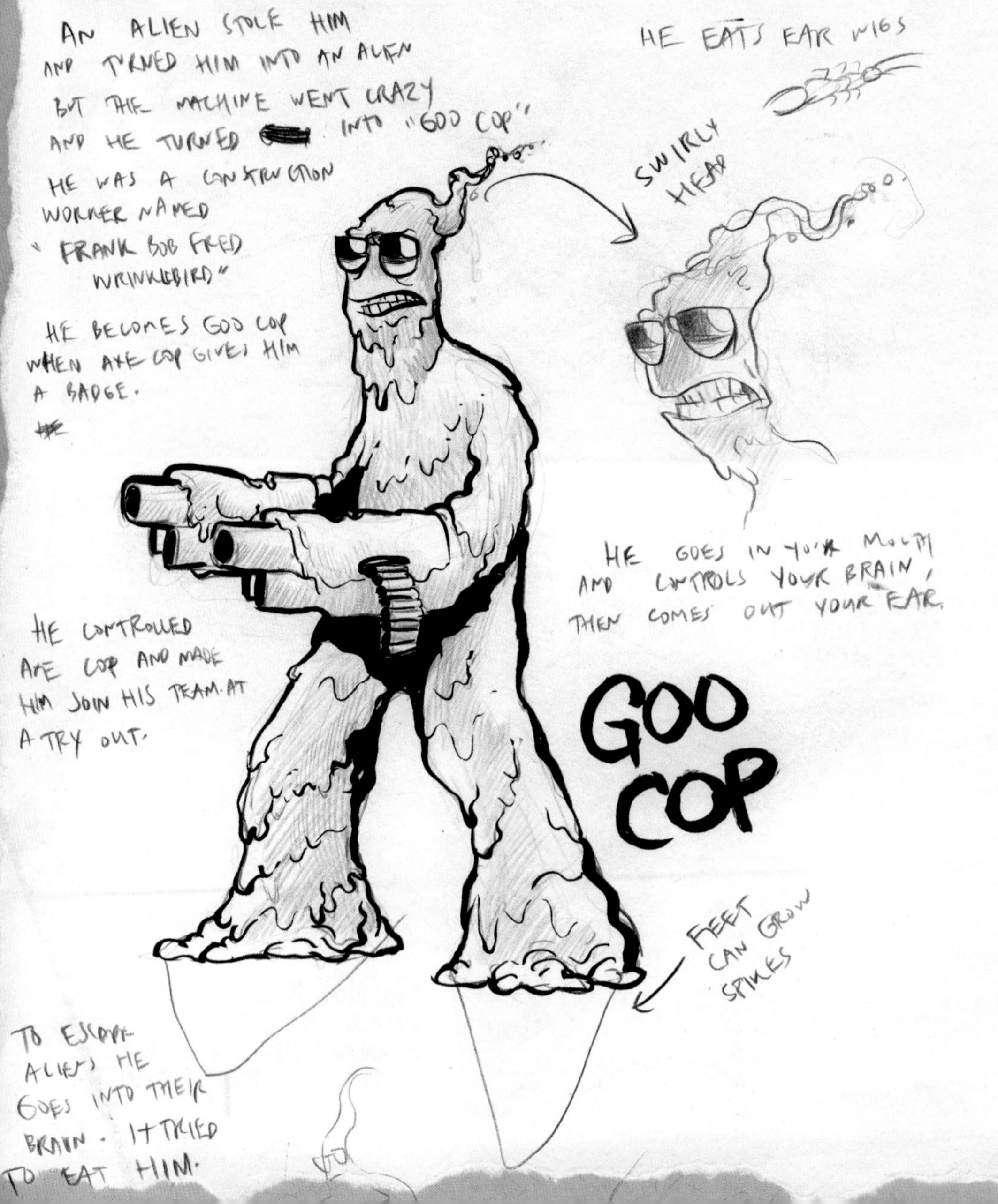

AN ALIEN STOLE HIM AND TURNED HIM INTO AN ALIEN BUT THE MACHINE WENT CRAZY AND HE TURNED INTO "GOO COP"
HE WAS A CONSTRUCTION WORKER NAMED "FRANK BOB FRED WRINKLEBIRD"
HE BECOMES GOO COP WHEN AXE COP GIVES HIM A BADGE.
HE EATS EAR WIGS
SWIRLY HEAD
HE GOES IN YOUR MOUTH AND CONTROLS YOUR BRAIN, THEN COMES OUT YOUR EAR.
HE CONTROLLED AXE COP AND MADE HIM JOIN HIS TEAM AT A TRY OUT.
GOO COP
FEET CAN GROW SPIKES
TO ESCAPE ALIENS HE GOES INTO THEIR BRAIN - IT TRIED TO EAT HIM.

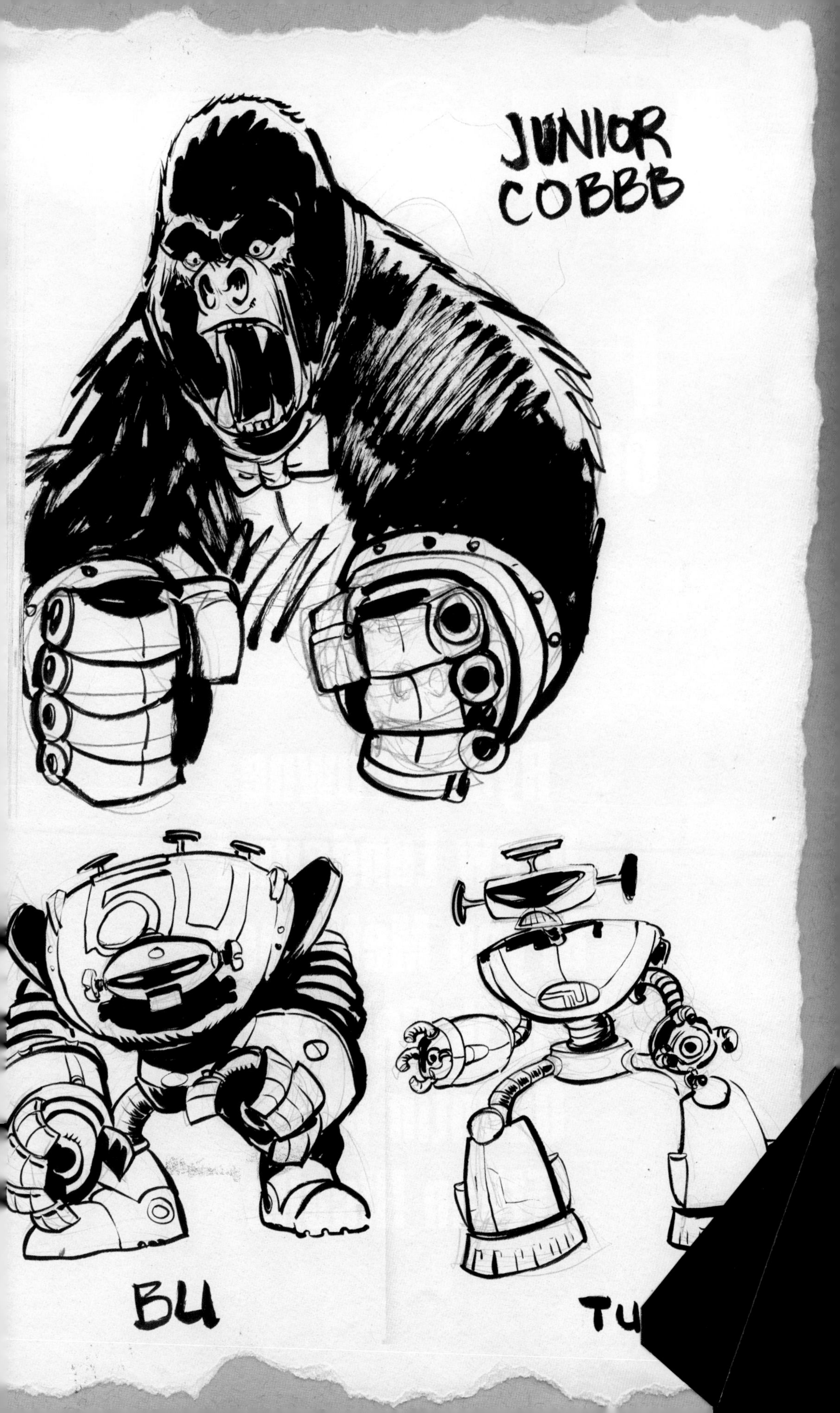
JUNIOR
COBBB
BU
TU

AXE COP

POLICE OFFICER · AXE · COP · EST. 2009

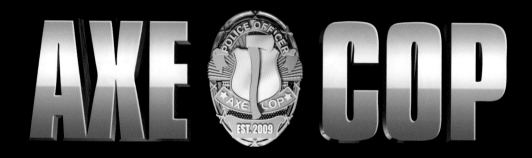

PRESIDENT OF THE WORLD

PINUP GALLERY

PINUPS BY

Ryan Browne
Drew Lundquist
Brynn Metheney
Henrik Sahlstrom
Quentin Bauer
Ethan Nicolle

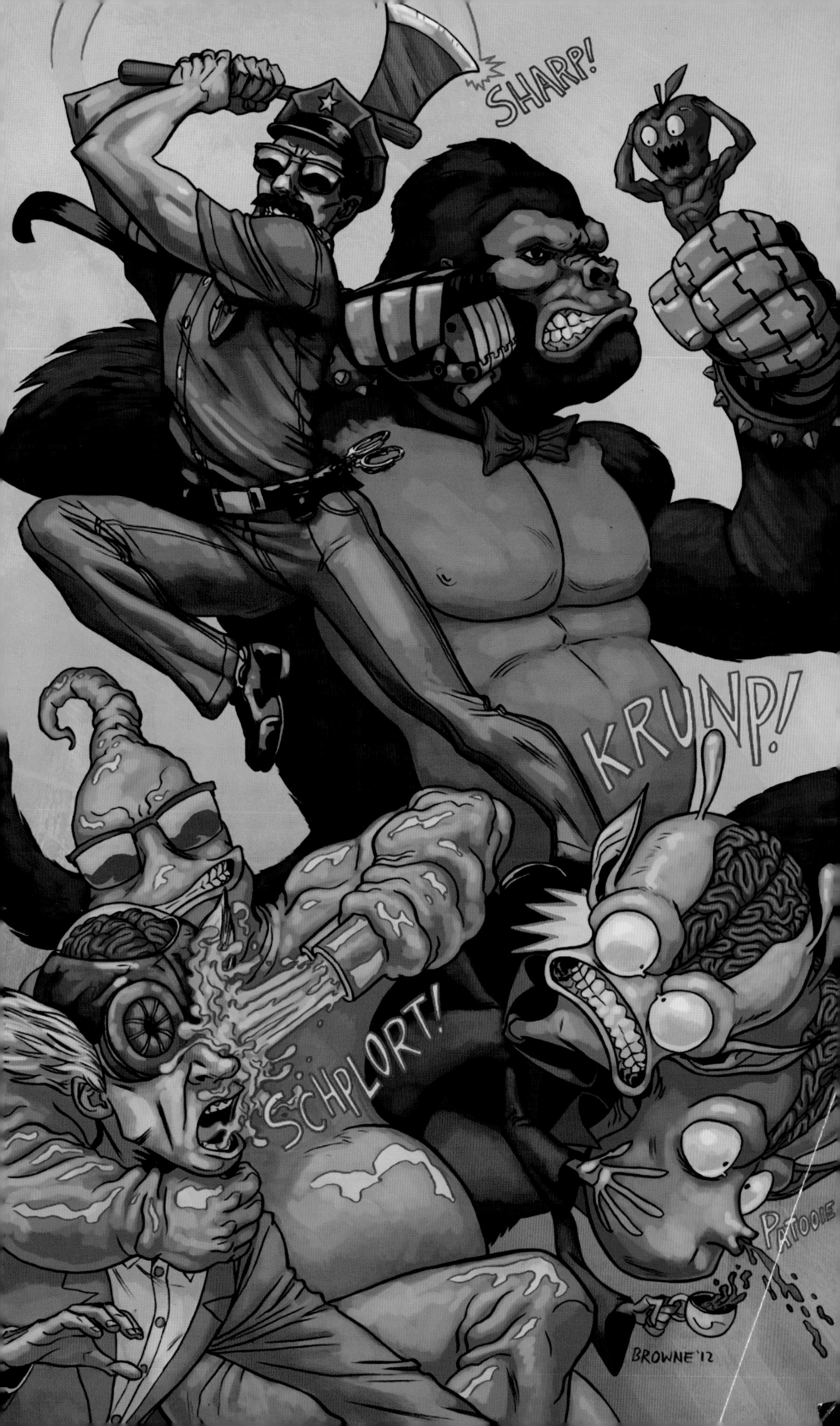
SHARP!
KRUNP!
SCHPLORT!
PATOOIE
BROWNE '12

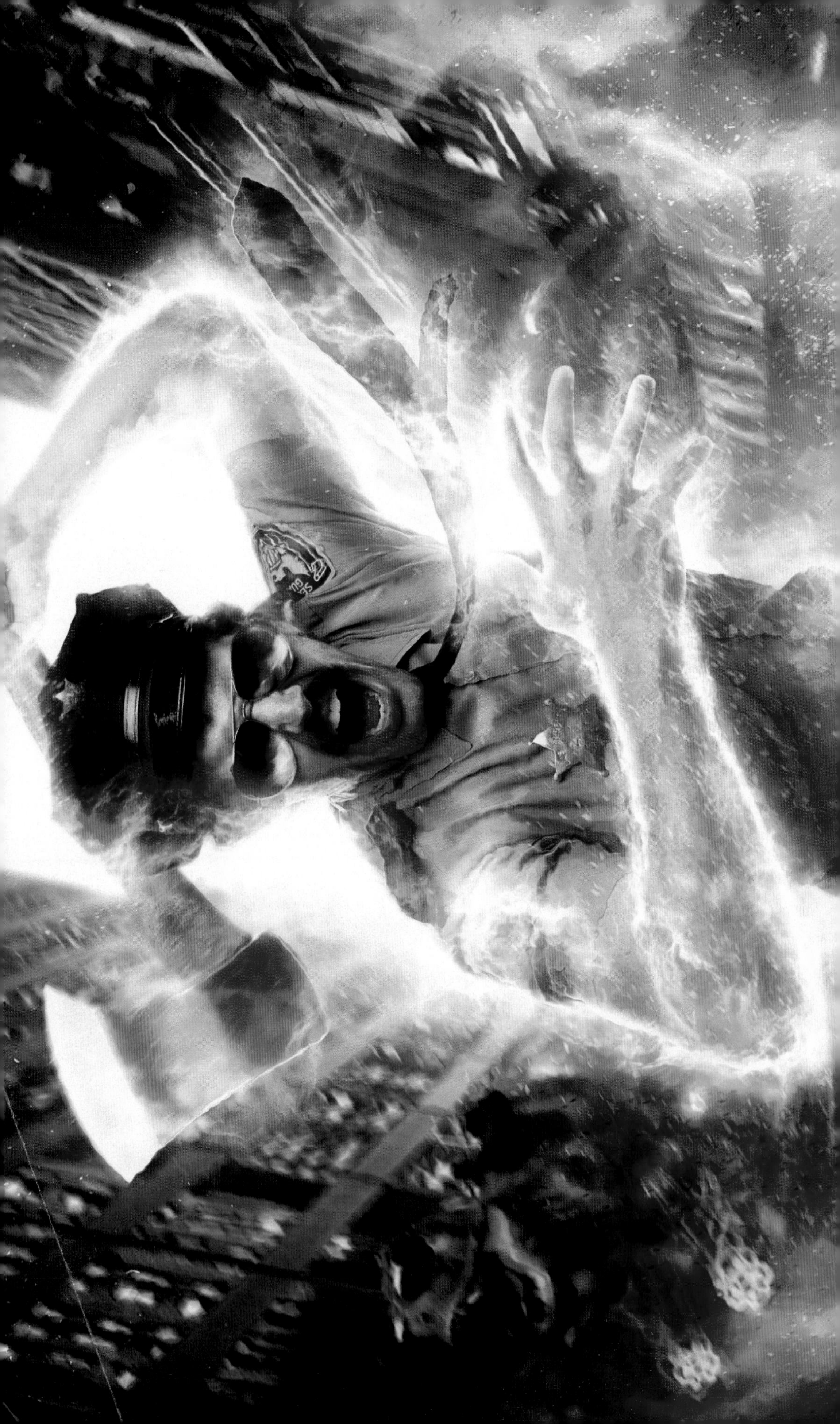

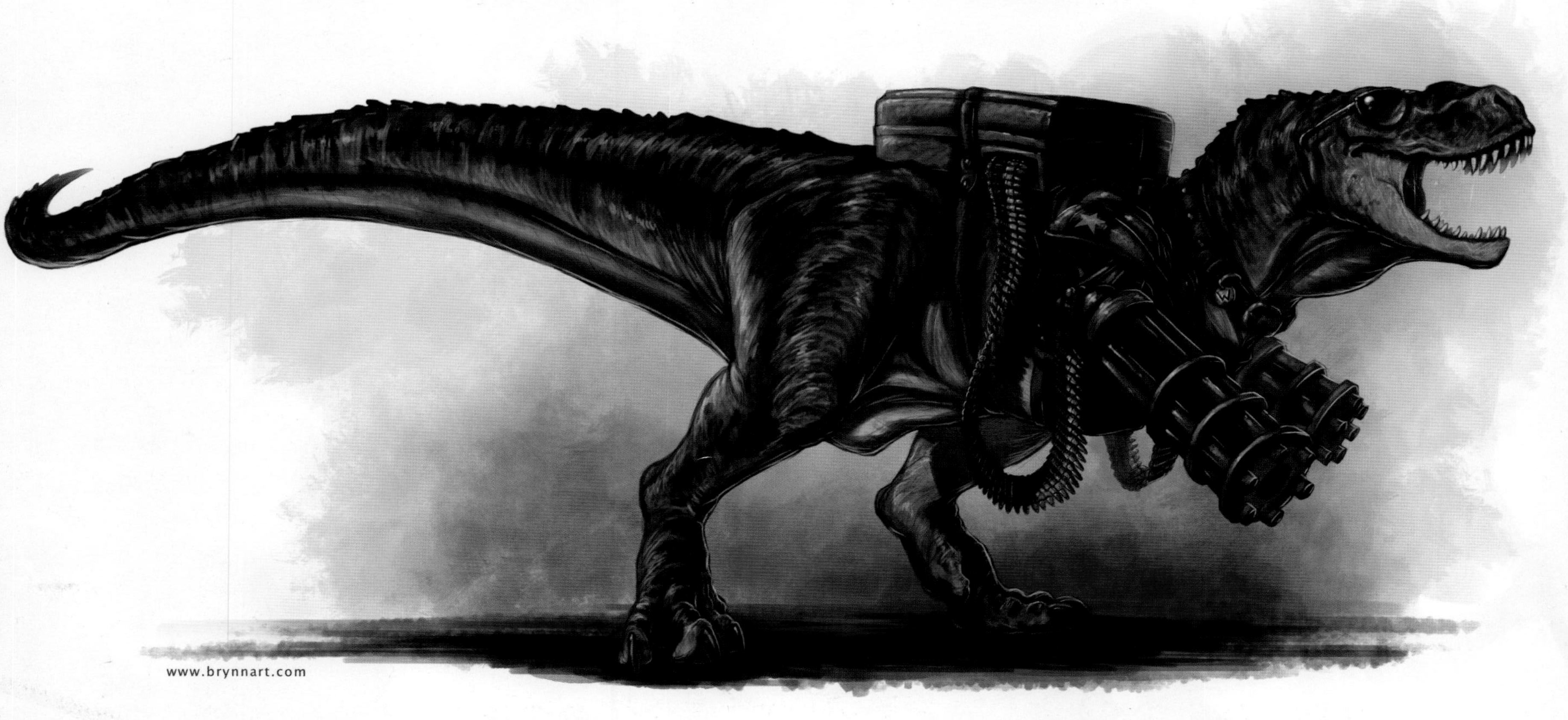
www.brynnart.com

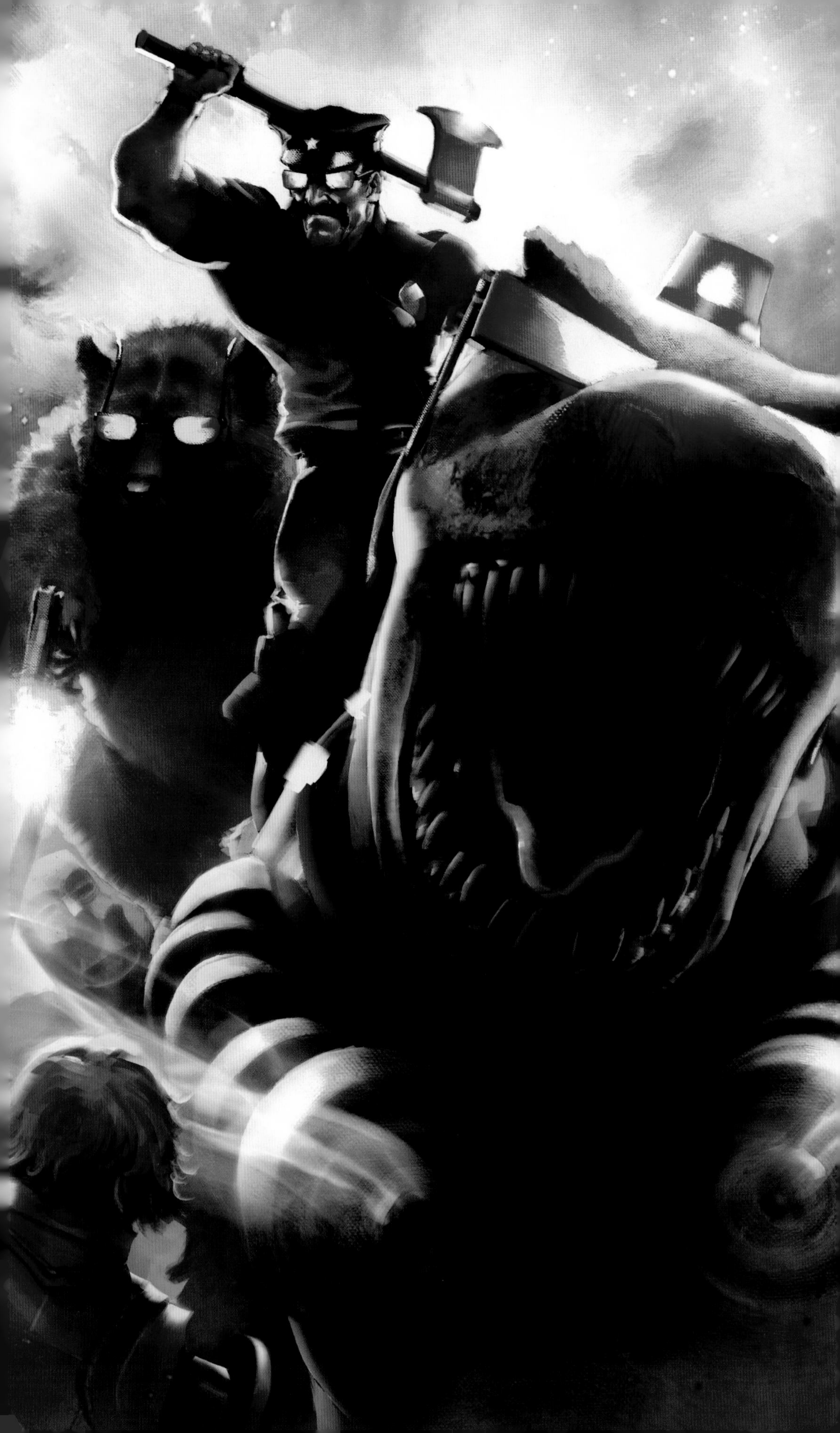

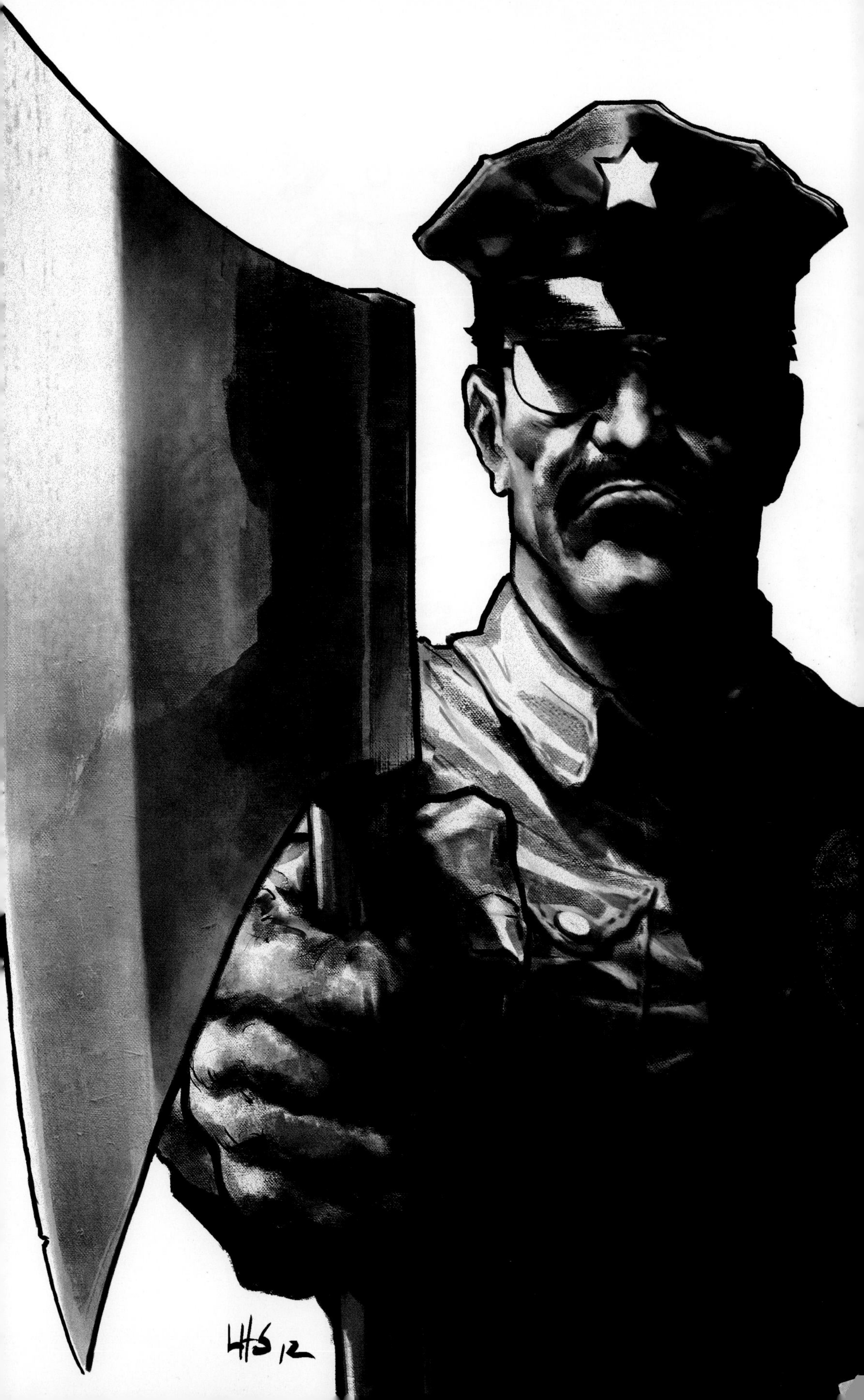

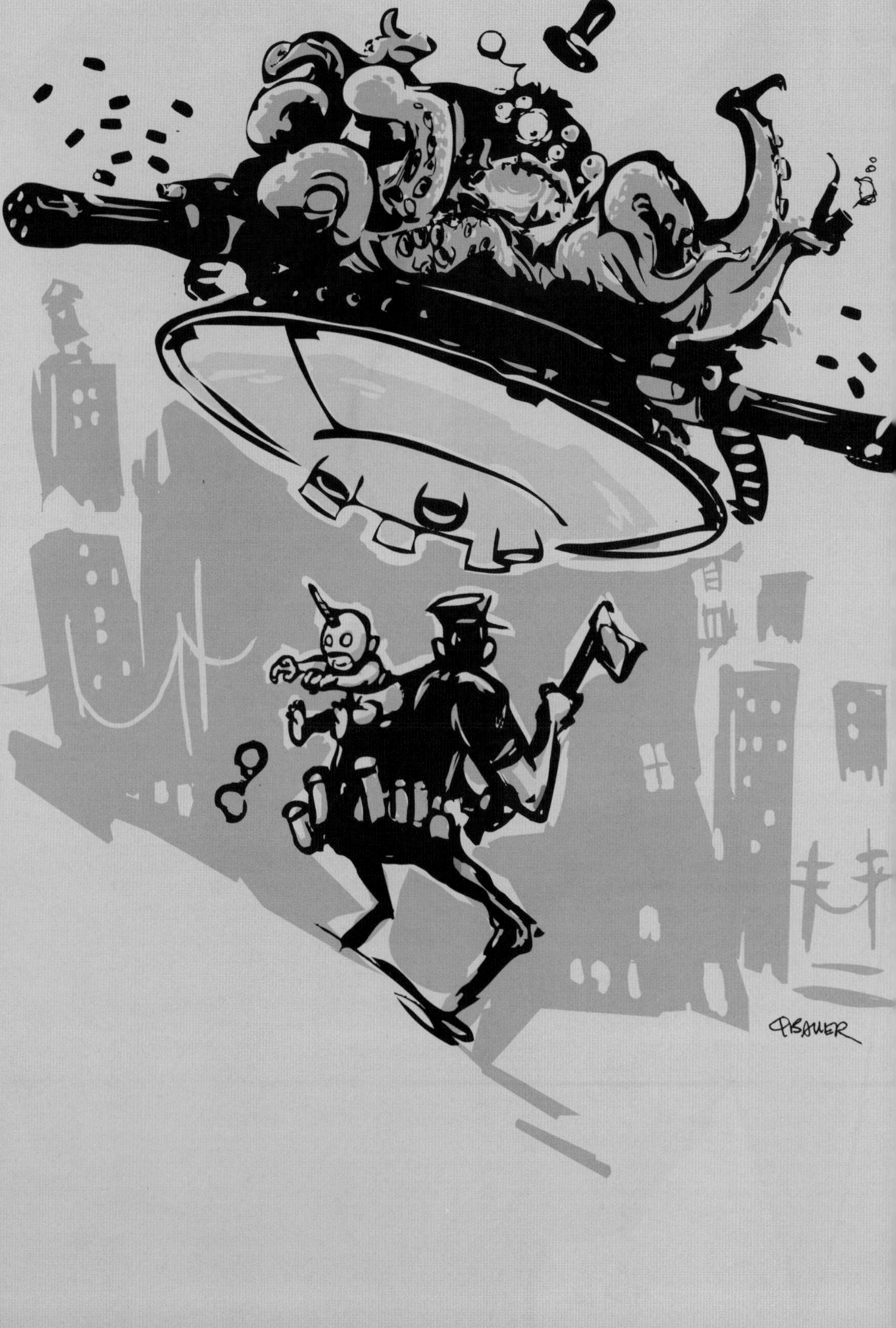

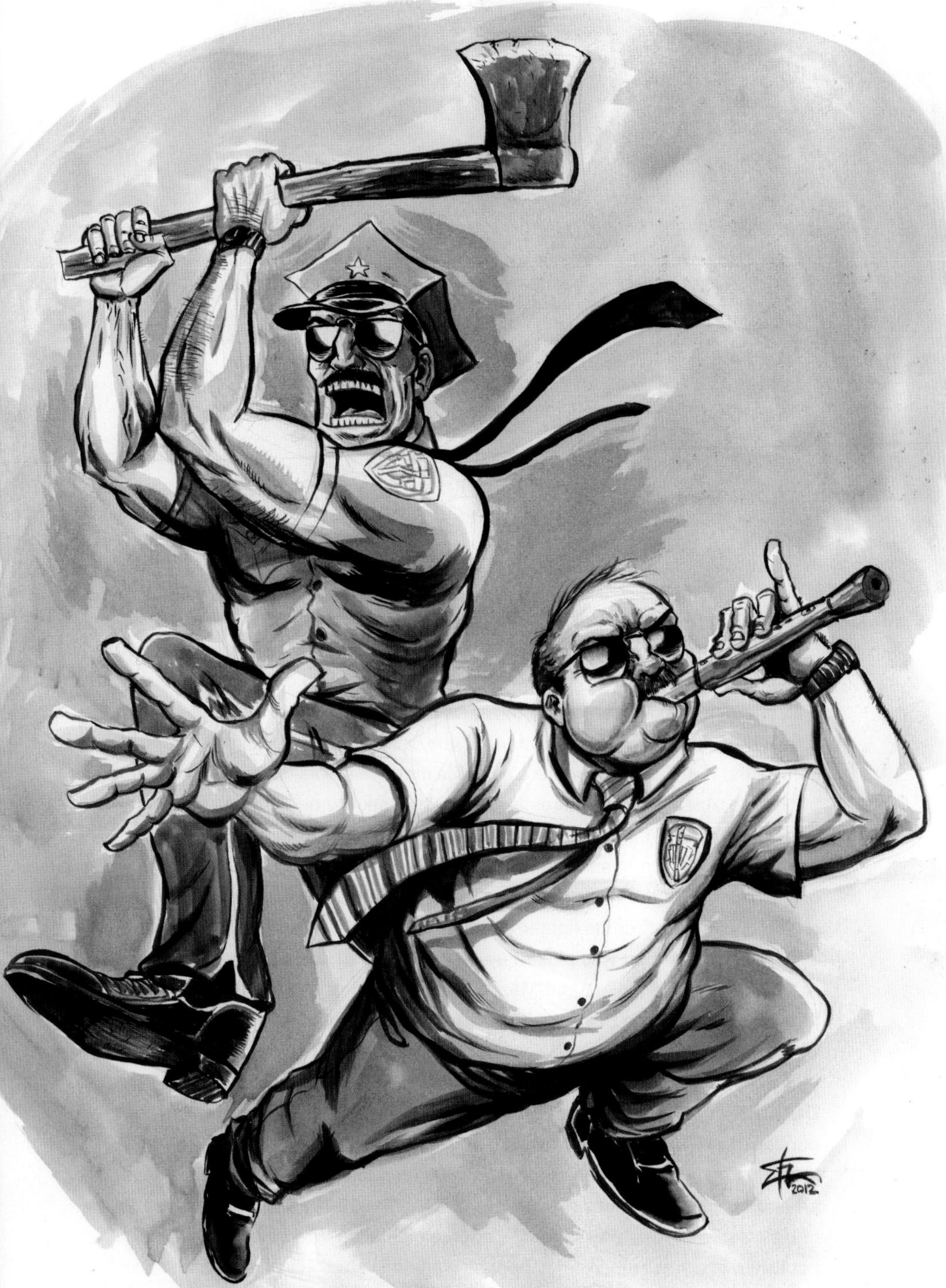

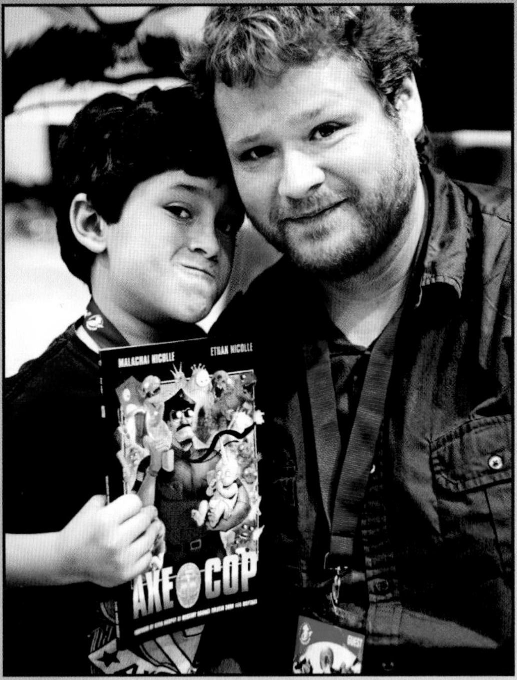
MALACHAI NICOLLE
ETHAN NICOLLE
AXE COP

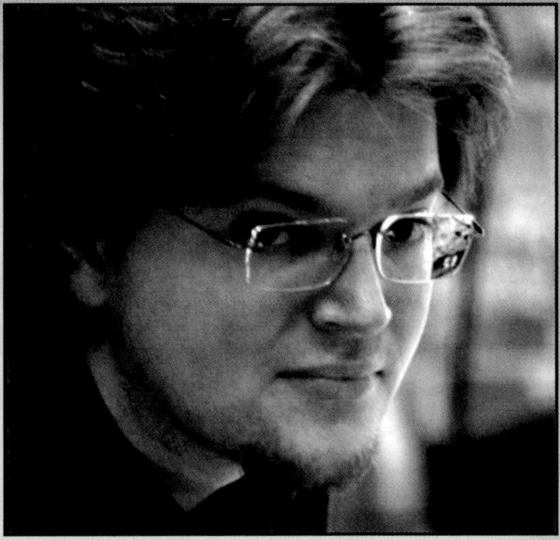

PHOTO BY MOLLY McISAAC

ETHAN and **MALACHAI NICOLLE** are brothers born twenty-four years apart. Ethan was twenty-nine and already an accomplished (and Eisner Award nominated!) humor artist when he started drawing comic strips based on then-five-year-old Malachai's newly invented character, a hard-nosed cop with a fireman's axe and a talent for dispatching bad guys. After the online debut of their collaborative comic strip *Axe Cop*, the brothers gained a massive media following and began publishing *Axe Cop* adventures in print with Dark Horse Comics. Now ages thirty-two and eight, respectively, Ethan and Malachai are currently at work on their third *Axe Cop* miniseries for Dark Horse, a third print collection of the online archives of the webcomic, and various games and other projects based on the mustachioed crime fighter and his insane exploits battling the forces of evil. In 2013 *Axe Cop* was picked up by Fox to be an animated series on their ADHD block of animation, and Mezco Toyz introduced a line of *Axe Cop* toys. Ethan currently lives in Los Angeles, while Malachai lives in eastern Washington with his family.

DIRK ERIK SCHULZ is from Berlin, Germany. With no training in art, he first published art and comics in school and later in local newspapers. In 2002, after earning his high-school diploma, he decided to start a career in the field of art and entered art school in 2004. He graduated in 2007 with the best results of his class. His thesis was a sixty-page comic called *The Mossgod*, which he published in a small run. After school he worked in studios including Hahn Film, Laika Films, and Stenarts as a character designer and colorist for animation and big comic projects. Since 2009 he has worked as a freelancer. Dirk's webcomic, *The SWEFS,* is successful on the Net and receives positive reviews. In 2010 he colored *Axe Cop: Bad Guy Earth*. In 2012 he did the artwork for the card game Hot Rod Creeps.

Bad guys, beware! Evil aliens, run for your lives! Axe Cop is here, and he's going to chop your head off! We live in a strange world, and our strange problems call for strange heroes.

Axe Cop Volume 1
ISBN 978-1-59582-681-7 | $14.99

Axe Cop Volume 2: Bad Guy Earth
ISBN 978-1-59582-825-5 | $14.99

Axe Cop Volume 3
ISBN 978-1-59582-911-5 | $14.99

Axe Cop Volume 4: President of the World
ISBN 978-1-61655-057-8 | $12.99

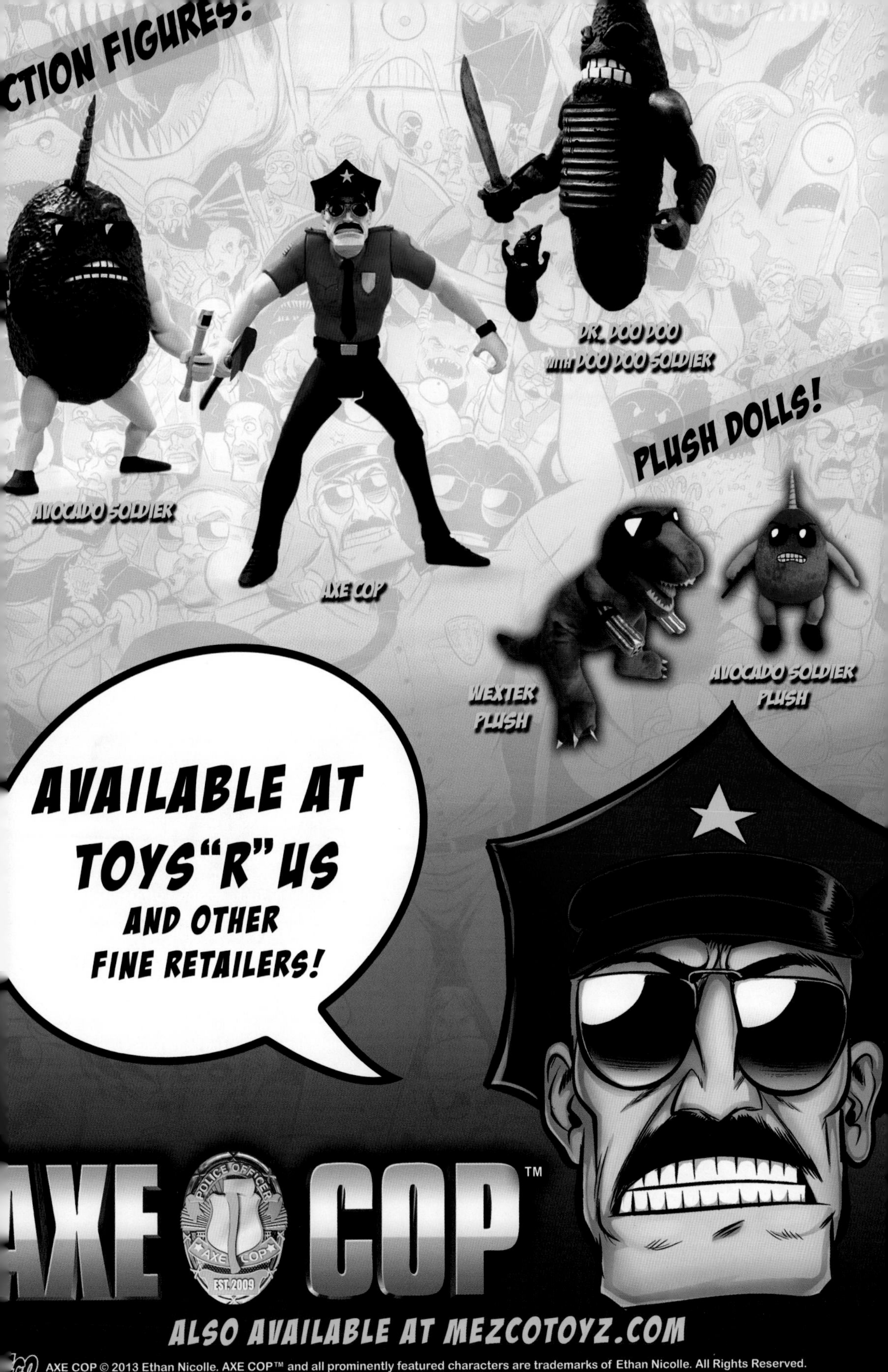
CTION FIGURES!
AVOCADO SOLDIER
AXE COP
DR. DOO DOO
WITH DOO DOO SOLDIER
PLUSH DOLLS!
WEXTER
PLUSH
AVOCADO SOLDIER
PLUSH
AVAILABLE AT
TOYS"R"US
AND OTHER
FINE RETAILERS!
AXE COP™
POLICE OFFICER
AXE COP
EST. 2009
ALSO AVAILABLE AT MEZCOTOYZ.COM

...RINGS YOU THE BEST IN WEBCOMIC...

...popular cartoon gems were once only available online, but now can be found through Dark Horse Books with loads of awesome extras!

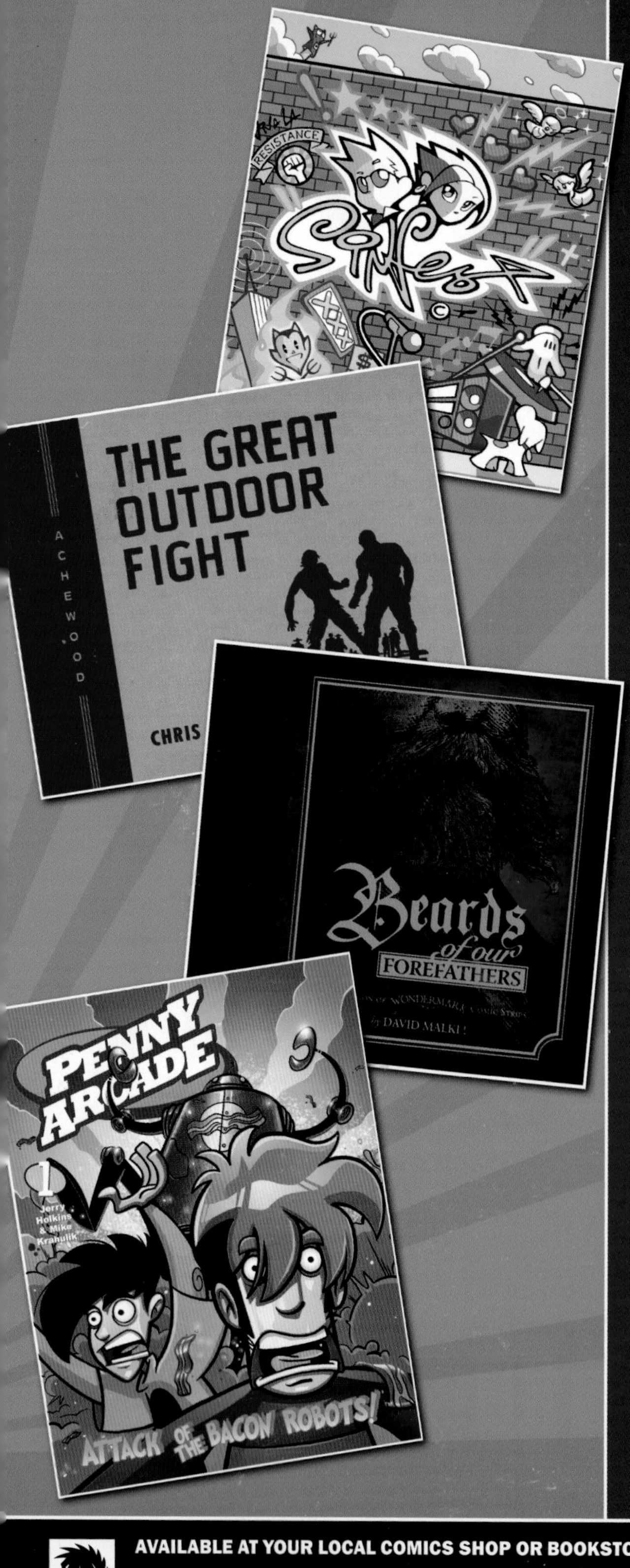
RESISTANCE
Sinfest
THE GREAT OUTDOOR FIGHT
ACHEWOOD
CHRIS
Beards of our FOREFATHERS
by DAVID MALKI!
PENNY ARCADE
1
Jerry Holkins & Mike Krahulik
ATTACK OF THE BACON ROBOTS!

SINFEST

By Tatsuya Ishida

Sinfest is one of the most-read and longest-running webco
out there, and explores religion, advertising, sex, and politi
a way fleen.com calls "both brutally funny and devastati
on-target." What other series has had the chutzpah to m
characters out of God, the Devil, Jesus, Buddha, Barack Oba
Sarah Palin, and corrupt Wall Street CEOs? If your comic-
craving hasn't been satisfied since the nineties, deliveran
finally at hand.

Volume 1 TPB
ISBN 978-1-59582-319-9 | $14.95
Volume 2: Viva La Resistance TPB
ISBN 978-1-59582-424-0 | $14.99

ACHEWOOD

By Chris Onstad

Since 2001, cult comic favorite *Achewood* has built a six-fi
international following. Intelligent, hilarious, and adult bu
filthy, it's the strip you'll wish you'd discovered as an unde
preciated fifteen-year-old. "I'm addicted to *Achewood*. C
Onstad is a dark, hilarious genius." –Dave Barry

Volume 1: The Great Outdoor Fight HC
ISBN 978-1-59307-997-0 | $14.99
Volume 2: Worst Song, Played on Ugliest Guitar HC
ISBN 978-1-59582-239-0 | $15.99
Volume 3: A Home for Scared People HC
ISBN 978-1-59582-450-9 | $16.99

WONDERMARK

By David Malki!

Dark Horse Comics is proud to present these handsome h
bound collections of David Malki's Ignatz-nominated comic
Wondermark. Malki repurposes illustrations and engravings
19th-century books into hilarious, collage-style comic st
More than just webcomic collections, the *Wondermark* bo
have been praised for their magnificent design and load
extra content for casual readers and superfans alike.

Volume 1: Beards of Our Forefathers HC
ISBN 978-1-59307-984-0 | $14.99
Volume 2: Clever Tricks to Stave Off Death HC
ISBN 978-1-59582-329-8 | $14.99
Volume 3: Dapper Caps & Pedal-Copters HC
ISBN 978-1-59582-449-3 | $16.99

PENNY ARCADE

By Jerry Holkins and Mike Krahulik

Penny Arcade, the comic strip for gamers, by gamers is
available in comic shops and bookstores everywhere. Experie
the joy of being a hardcore gamer as expressed in hilario
witty vignettes of random vulgarity and mindless violence!

Volume 1: Attack of the Bacon Robots! TPB
ISBN 978-1-59307-444-9 | $12.99
Volume 2: Epic Legends of the Magic Sword Kings! TPB
ISBN 978-1-59307-541-5 | $12.99
Volume 3: The Warsun Prophecies TPB
ISBN 978-1-59307-635-1 | $12.99
Volume 4: Birds are Weird TPB
ISBN 978-1-59307-773-0 | $12.99
Volume 5: The Case of the Mummy's Gold TPB
ISBN 978-1-59307-814-0 | $12.99

AVAILABLE AT YOUR LOCAL COMICS SHOP OR BOOKSTORE | To find a comics shop in your area, call 1-888-266-4...

For more information or to order direct: •On the web: DarkHorse.com •E-mail: mailorder@DarkHorse.com
•Phone: 1-800-862-0052 Mon.–Fri. 9AM to 5PM Pacific Time.